KT-225-651

Eleven Lines to Somewhere

Alyson Rudd

HQ

ONE PLACE. MANY STORIES

This novel is entirely a work of fiction. The names, characters and incidents portrayed in it are the work of the author's imagination. Any resemblance to actual persons, living or dead, events or localities is entirely coincidental.

HQ
An imprint of HarperCollins*Publishers* Ltd
1 London Bridge Street
London SE1 9GF

This edition 2020

1
First published in Great Britain by
HQ, an imprint of HarperCollins*Publishers* Ltd 2020

Copyright © Alyson Rudd

Alyson Rudd asserts the moral right to be
identified as the author of this work.
A catalogue record for this book is
available from the British Library.

ISBN HB: 978-0-00-827858-8
TPB: 978-0-00-827832-8

MIX
Paper from
responsible sources
FSC™ C007454

This book is produced from independently certified FSC™ paper
to ensure responsible forest management.

For more information visit: www.harpercollins.co.uk/green

This book is set in 11.7/15.5 pt. Caslon

Printed and bound in Great Britain by
CPI Group (UK) Ltd, Croydon, CR0 4YY

All rights reserved. No part of this publication may be reproduced, stored in a retrieval system, or transmitted, in any form or by any means, electronic, mechanical, photocopying, recording or otherwise, without the prior permission of the publishers.

This book is sold subject to the condition that it shall not, by way of trade or otherwise, be lent, re-sold, hired out or otherwise circulated without the publisher's prior consent in any form of binding or cover other than that in which it is published and without a similar condition including this condition being imposed on the subsequent purchaser.

Eleven Lines to Somewhere

Alyson Rudd was born in Liverpool, raised in West Lancashire and educated at the London School of Economics. She is an award-winning sports journalist at *The Times* and lives in South West London. She has written two works of non-fiction and *The First Time Lauren Pailing Died* was her debut novel.

Dedicated to the memory of Bob Dylan Willis

Prologue

In profile he is mesmeric, carved from white oak, a long and slender marionette. More than one model scout had approached him only to withdraw as they noted his eyes, full of mistrust and confusion. Isak watched as a woman, only last week, strode towards him purposefully, her lips glossy, her smile wide, her handbag bigger than her torso.

'Not me,' he mumbled, and let his head drop. They must have sent her. He had just spent £95 at Harvey Nichols. It was cash, he had made sure it was cash, but there are cameras everywhere. It was becoming impossible for him to pay for anything surreptitiously. The woman's smile waned as she half opened her mouth to address him and then closed it to turn on her heel. He exhaled. There must have been a glitch but even so he needed to be more careful. He sighed. He had six days to wait until he could swim again and most of those would be filled with pointless conversations about his feelings. They were, in the main, trick questions but when Isak told them he knew they were tricking him, they reminded him that he was there with his mother's blessing and that of Andrew. That gave him plenty to mull over, which usually prompted them to tell him how much progress he was making.

That pleased him. Progress was, for Isak, a march through dense forests, a dagger in his belt, the beating wings of a dragon overhead. Progress was another cloud-covered mountain climbed, another black river crossed so that he could fall onto a bearskin blanket next to an open fire and be hailed a hero.

He looked up and scoured the street. He had reached Gloucester Road Underground station. He would hide in the tunnels for now, the tunnels that could take him anywhere he pleased. He would peer into the mouths of them as the wind slapped his face and made the litter scurry away in fear. He sometimes wondered if he was meant to walk through the tunnels but no one else ever did so he was nervous about trying it.

Ducking under his arm, for Isak is very tall, and preparing to leave at South Kensington station, is the relatively diminutive and punctual Ryan, his cheeks a warm red for he has just touched a girl's shoulder. She had swung around with a startling degree of indignation and glared at Ryan, who had, naturally, been embarrassed but also a little indignant himself that the girl had been wearing just a cable-knit jumper and no coat on a chilly morning. Ellen had never worn a coat and he had assumed she was the only girl in the country who avoided them. He had, therefore, concluded that the commuter must be Ellen even though it could not possibly be her.

Ignoring this tableau is a woman in a dove-grey trench coat whose bag is placed on her lap and who has closed her eyes in the manner of one who sees more when not looking.

A schoolboy weighed down with a rucksack and a violin case is lost in the music piped through his too-big earphones but he notices the woman and wonders why it is that her hair makes him wish he had a bag of sweets in his pocket. He turns towards Isak and wonders how he fits into the carriage at all. He does not notice Ryan, who slips through the doors, determined not to dwell on the girl he had, for a moment, thought was someone else. His day will hold no empty minutes in which to consider the reasons he was so stupid to have tapped the shoulder of this stranger in a cable-knit jumper. His will be a day of mildly interesting routine for he has yet to set eyes on the woman in the dove-grey trench coat.

Later, when Isak's mother asks him how his day has been, ignoring the bag which so clearly contains yet another pair of swimming trunks, he tells her he has just travelled on nine of the eleven lines, and she nods, but Andrew beams. 'Nine!' he exclaims. 'We'll have to go exploring in Egypt or the bush,' he says. Isak does not understand but likes how Andrew is impressed and retreats to his room, contented. He runs his finger over the remote control for his stylish and large TV screen. Fantasy beckons. He will be lost in Middle-earth until the early hours and when he wakes it will be with annoyance that someone might have watched him sleeping.

Chapter 1

The Piccadilly line train swept into North Ealing station with a degree of impatient majesty. So many commuters and so little time. The bodies pushed and squeezed and held screens to their noses, then disgorged, sweating sometimes, sometimes panting, or with grace and familiarity. Among those stepping aboard was Ryan Kennedy, a man in his early thirties, slightly on the short side, with thick black curls and the demeanour of being with a companion even when alone.

He scanned the front carriage from habit, searching for the peculiar passenger or an intriguing one. Today, the main attraction was the chap sat with a Labrador at his feet. The dog had its head on the man's left foot and the man, wearing sunglasses, was rubbing a patch in front of the animal's left ear. It was hypnotic. Most passengers were watching. The dog was not in need of reassurance in the crowd. It was relaxed, almost playing dead. The man was, Ryan decided, using the journey to repay the guide dog for the hours of duty that lay ahead as he traversed the Underground and then the busy streets above.

Ryan half turned as if to whisper to a friend that he felt

the urge to bend down and pat the Labrador himself but he said nothing. Only if you looked closely would you notice that his face possessed an added note of amusement as if he had indeed just confided in someone and they had smiled or nodded or whispered back, 'Why no guide cats?'

He returned his gaze to the man and his best friend. Next to them was a wiry teenager in Lycra and startling indigo trainers and next to him was a young woman whose hair, he realized, was a colour he did not know. He wondered what he would tell the police if forced to describe her and settled on 'nearly red'. He would be dismissed as pretentious if he said it was the blended colour of a summer sky's orange and pink sunset clouds. Her hair was the colour of dark candyfloss or wild strawberries – but not quite. He was quite bewitched until he alighted at South Kensington, leaving the woman, and the dog, behind.

A week later he wondered why he felt on high alert as he noted that the front carriage was almost airy and without a whiff of last night's garlic. That was often the advantage of the front carriage at this time in the morning, that and the fact that it was the only carriage in which he had seen her. Three times he had seen her and he understood, now, that he would keep on using the front carriage just to see her again. And he did, on and off, and it brightened his day, giving him a false sense of being proactive when in fact he did nothing but catch the Tube to work just as he usually did.

She always had a seat, so Ryan guessed that she started her journey towards the top of the line, at Uxbridge, or perhaps she began her commute at Rayners Lane, the station he used when visiting his mother. He assumed the girl with the nearly red hair favoured, as he did, the front carriage. Always the front carriage – although this was, he admitted, false logic as he did not see her every day and on those occasions when he did not see her, she might very well be in a middle or end carriage. Still, he felt it to be true, that they had this in common at least, which was not a connection to be scoffed at given they had not exchanged a single word in the three months and thirteen days since he first saw her. Ryan was not even sure they had exchanged a smile. So keen was he not to appear creepy that he suspected his expression when they did make eye contact was one of a man badly needing to scratch the inside of his thigh, which was not ideal, not when she was his only, if marginal, love interest.

He had an idea that his hand had brushed the side of her dress before he had seen her face, that he had sat next to her and felt only her warmth, detected her scent without knowing it but the knowing of it, well, that amounted to the whole of spring. He wondered how Ellen would describe his fixation. This had not been how *their* relationship had begun. Theirs had been instantaneous, a deep-sea dive, a jump from a plane, revving engines and abrupt acceleration. He caught sight of her through the carriage's window and half lifted his hand before dropping it, his brow furrowing. He always fell for it; he always caught his breath when he glimpsed Ellen before understanding he could not have seen her, not really.

Catching the right train became part of his routine. He would leave the house at 7.55 a.m. instead of 8 a.m. and peer inside the front carriage of the first train to arrive. If the candyfloss girl was not there, he would wait for the next and then, if necessary, the next. Once he let five trains pass him by. More than five attempts felt pathetic and on a more practical level meant he was late for work. Once he was unable to retreat, the sheer weight of commuters forcing him to climb onto a train he did not want to catch.

He wondered if it was a sort of addiction or a spell that could be broken the instant he heard her speak or saw her kiss another man. And then, on a damp May midweek morning when they had pulled into Hammersmith, a breathless mini-skirted student wearing a rucksack asked the carriage in a general way in poor English and in some panic if this was the right train for Victoria.

She had looked up and smiled and told the student to cross the platform. The student froze and so she stood up and took her arm and walked her the four steps to the adjacent platform just as the District line train pulled in. She guided her on and then calmly re-entered the same carriage she had momentarily left. Ryan had watched this unfold with an intensity most people reserve for footage of cheetahs tearing at the neck of a pretty impala. The doors shut immediately and her seat had been taken but she was too far away for him to offer her his. Instead he offered it to a stout woman with a small bald patch and moved slowly towards the candyfloss girl as they approached Barons Court.

He had no plan in mind and knew he would not speak to her but the variation on a theme was welcome; to be standing together, rather than sitting nearby. He was maybe two inches taller than her and he was close enough to see pale freckles across the bridge of her nose. She did not grimace at having to stand and instead held the pole with a curious sense of serenity. As always, Ryan left the train with her still on board.

As he filed onto the escalator his shoulders suddenly drooped in exasperation. He could have smiled and told her he had seen her help the student, told her that her timing, to have managed to get back on the train, was impeccable; and if he had said that then tomorrow he could have said: 'Hello again.' And then the day after they could have smiled at each other and then the day after that… who knew how it could have unfolded if he had spoken. If.

The girl with the nearly red hair stood as far as Green Park and left the train surprised at how much the journey had begun to jolt and jangle at her. She rarely stood for quite so long and wondered if she had to stand every day whether it would, in the end, make her ill. It was quite a relief to walk on firm concrete and then sit down on the Jubilee line. She looked at the time on her phone. She had nine hours of work ahead of her but she felt she had already achieved one tiny thing by being helpful to the young student who had been a in small panic of disorientation. She looked at the map on the wall, trying to see it from a novice's perspective. The Underground could be mystifying to anyone if new to the capital. It could also be quite distressing.

Ryan's nine hours were punctuated with grimaces of self-hatred, ruing his missed opportunity. That had been his chance. He had blown it, he thought, as he walked home after what some might regard as a dull, sedentary day. Ryan, though, liked the steady rhythm of his hours and his duties. They were his glue; they had been his glue since leaving university, since embarking on life in the real world without Ellen.

*

Ryan lived in the sort of house that made people pause before entering.

It is so very vertical, Ryan thought when he bought Number 4, and he never stopped thinking it.

It even had stilts, which framed what was supposed to be a carport but Ryan did not own a car so that was where he kept his bike and the washing-machine he hoped someone would steal as it no longer worked other than for its front display to flash angrily if asked to spin or even wash some sheets.

Number 4 was part of a short row of modern townhouses that had narrow back gardens and their kitchens on the first floor. His neighbours all had different uses for the room behind the carport but Ryan used his to house a lodger whose rent helped to cover the mortgage.

Naomi was also very vertical and studying for a Masters in biodiversity, which meant, as Ryan saw it, that she was much smarter than him as well as being taller. As he worked as a laboratory manager at the same university, sometimes they travelled in together on the Tube, but that was often an accidental journey and one that made him feel slightly self-conscious as Naomi, who liked two-inch heels, was five feet eleven barefoot and he was five feet eight in his trainers.

On one side of Number 4 lived Theo and Jenny, who were in their fifties, Ryan assumed, and who always beamed genially whenever their paths crossed. On the other side lived a younger couple who had arrived from Warsaw in their late teens and who were now fully aspirational with two young and immaculately dressed children. They were as uptight as Theo and Jenny were sunny and carefree, always frowning, always harassed, always washing the windows or tidying the carport. They were polite towards Ryan, though, relieved he had bought Number 4 to live in rather than to rent out to people who would allow the carport to fill with so much rubbish that it would spill out onto the paved driveway and undermine the whole of Cotton Lane's townhouse appeal. They all made assumptions as to how it was that Ryan could afford to own such a home. Theo and Jenny decided he had an inheritance; Naomi believed he must have charmed his mortgage lender; and the Mizwa family assumed that he was a very important, well-remunerated figure at his university.

Ryan would have preferred any of those routes to home ownership to the one that had propelled him up the housing ladder. He had simply saved. He had saved somewhat slavishly because he had little else to do with his average salary. His carefree days had ended abruptly before he had even graduated. Ryan and Ellen's would have been a profligate partnership had it lasted but it did not last long at all. Ryan without Ellen was, it transpired, a thrifty state of affairs. Ryan without Ellen was quiet and rather inexpensive; he simply had no desire to spend his income on anything much at all.

Sometimes Ryan would arrive home, pause, and wonder at how suburban his supposedly urban life had become and how, when Grace, his mother, had clubbed together with his sister to buy him a small lawnmower, he had been touched and grateful rather than appalled.

Ryan's mother struggled to understand Naomi. Initially she failed to comprehend how a man and a woman could share a house without there being some romance attached to the arrangement.

'Was it love at first sight, eh, Ryan?' she had said, her eyes gleaming.

'No one else was interested,' Ryan replied.

'But what luck that it was a girl, eh, Ryan?'

And then, once she had, briefly, met Naomi, Ryan's mother was baffled by her height, her composure, her evident complete lack of adoration for her son.

'Really, Ryan,' his mother said, 'she could just as well be a man.'

Ryan smiled. His mother had not wanted to hear about girls when he was a teenager, had been mistrustful of them when he was in his twenties and now that he was about to hit thirty-three she was in a form of permanent mild panic that he would remain single forever.

'Do you watch TV together, then?' Grace asked, staring about the square living room.

Ryan opened up his arms to indicate the space where a TV might be found if there was one.

'Oh,' his mother said, deflated, and he laughed.

'We'll have a beer and a chat and her mates are fun so it's all fine, Mam, it's all fine.'

Grace had travelled home in a cheery mood. Naomi had friends and not all of them would be so tall and self-contained. One of them would be smitten with Ryan. It was just a matter of time. This was something upon which she and Naomi were agreed. Her shorter friends all liked him but, so far, he had been either slow to recognize the signals or deliberately overly avuncular. It seemed to Naomi that Ryan behaved like a man who was already in love, the only flaw to her theory being there was no woman in his life.

Not even online. Not even secretly. Not even the hint of an affair. But who was she to speculate, she who had joined the university bridge club just to be in the same room as Cappi, a towering, serious introvert from Milan with a stupidly happy-go-lucky name?

This, then, was the sum total, almost, of what could be construed as romance within Number 4 Cotton Lane, a modest and slender house built in 1976, just a five-minute walk from North Ealing Underground station, which was eight stops from South Kensington, where both Ryan and Naomi would alight to go to the university. Just eight stops. Ryan was tempted to make it nine, to make it twenty, to have longer in which to look at her, the almost-always-there girl with wavy, nearly red hair.

He found himself looking for her one Sunday in June. The chances of her being on the way home at noon on a non-commute day were so slim that he vowed he would speak to her if he did spot her. It would be rude not to, he smiled weakly to himself.

London was quiet. It was bathed in a claustrophobic heat. It was hot enough for the city to smell differently, to emit the stench of Naples or Lisbon. He changed from the Piccadilly line at Rayners Lane onto the Metropolitan. It was hot enough for him to reject out of hand walking to his mother's house from Wembley Park and so he changed lines again and trundled the two stops to Dollis Hill on the Jubilee line.

He had a key but always knocked. He knocked. Hana opened

the door, squeaked as if it was a surprise to find him there, and gave him a quick squeeze of a hug.

'Happy birthday, little bro',' she said and wondered, just as she had the previous June, if she would always feel protective of Ryan. Would she call him little bro' when he was fifty-three? Seventy-three? They were warm, sweet and deeply sad affairs, these meals at his mother's house. Only on Ryan's birthday would his mother refer to Tom's age.

'He'd have been thirty-seven this year. My word, thirty-seven. To think of having a thirty-seven-year-old,' she said.

'Mam, I'm thirty-nine,' Hana said, half hurt, half amused.

Her mother grasped her hand and sniffed stoically.

'But you don't look anywhere near it,' she said. 'Does she, Ryan?'

'Hmm,' said Ryan, which delighted his mother and caused Hana to growl comically and point to the sideboard where, on an intricate cake stand, stood the birthday cake she had helped bake for her brother. All three of them knew that once the cake had been cut into, Grandpa would open his eyes, accept a plate of it, then, still propped up in his spongy leather armchair, nod off again. At around three o'clock he would weep in his sleep. It was a routine that had begun several years earlier. Grandpa would eat only biscuits or tarts or cakes for lunch and weep in the afternoons.

As she stood to clear the table, Ryan's mother tapped her nose and his heart sank a little for the gesture signified she was about to hand him his gift. He unwrapped it gently, aware she was scrutinizing his face.

'Oh, that's very nice,' he said brightly as he gazed upon a white porcelain gravy boat. His mother had taken to giving him love-nest crockery ever since he had moved to Cotton Lane. He felt she was buying all the items, one by one, from an imaginary wedding list at John Lewis. 'I don't believe in marriage,' Ellen had said. He held the gravy boat as if it was a cruel joke of a prop.

'You must cook your own Sunday roasts sometimes,' Grace said, uncertainly.

'Yes, indeed we do,' he lied, and his sister glanced at him with something approaching sympathy.

As Grandpa's tears trickled down his cheeks, Ryan stood and stretched.

'I'm meeting a few mates for birthday drinks,' he said, checking his phone.

Pub with garden being found. Come home first

read the message from Naomi. He smiled because even now it was strange to be in the house where he grew up and for another building to be referred to as his home. Was home necessarily one place only? he wondered. Could he not be a home bigamist? Grace and Hana hugged him tightly as they always did on special occasions and each time he felt the obligation to live and keep on living if only for their sakes. He loved them very much, these women who were both simultaneously fragile and possessed the strength of ten men.

Grandpa was still asleep, a golden crumb of birthday cake lodged in the creases around the corner of his mouth, and Ryan shook his head fondly.

'Tell him I said goodbye,' he said, trying to stifle the fear he felt of late that each time he saw his grandfather might be the last time; that the old man's tears were a presentiment of his imminent demise. He was, still, a comforting presence for Ryan, someone he had always known, someone who had never left, who had never mentioned the word 'love' and yet was, in his gruff way, consistently loving.

As he climbed aboard the Piccadilly line train, he scanned the carriage just in case. It was full of men in flip-flops and women in sundresses, none of which had nearly red waves, although he was struck by the white hair of a tall, slender, ethereal lad whose fingers curled and uncurled with a startling rapidity.

Across the city, the boy, Isak, was agitated by the humid weather. Andrew and his mother had said, given *the weather*, they should all swim in the rooftop pool of the club Andrew rarely used these days. Isak could think of little worse than swapping his basement pool for one high in the sky exposed to satellites, to cameras, to nearby windows. It would be busy, his mother had admitted as much, and although he liked very much the thought of the three of them together in swimwear, he would prefer it to be in a quieter, darker place. 'I'll need some new trunks,' he had said, and Andrew had not blinked. His mother had not sighed. Of course, he would like swimwear that suited *the weather*, they said, and so he had travelled into town to buy some, vaguely aware that his new shorts should be brightly coloured and most definitely not brown or navy or black. He was meeting them at the club. His name would be at the door but it was daunting, all this jolly behaviour prompted by *the weather*, and so he was taking a circuitous route on the Underground to delay his arrival, to delay the moment he walked out onto a sun-drenched terrace exposed for all the world to see.

Ryan could see Beth and Tamsin as soon as he turned the corner into Cotton Lane. They were sat on green striped deck chairs on his tiny square of delicately mowed front garden, each holding a glass of rosé and sporting Hollywood sunglasses. Beth was wearing a polka-dot halter-neck sundress and Tamsin was in shorts and a glinting, metallic bikini top.

'Happy birthday, Ryan,' they said in unison.

He reached for his phone and took their photograph. It was such a dazzling, lurid scene that it was oddly beautiful. It was a scene that told him there was no trip to the pub, that Naomi had gathered his and her friends together at Number 4 to celebrate his birthday. The only route to the garden, if you discounted the narrow, ivy-strewn back alleyway, was via the sliding doors from Naomi's bedroom, and Ryan knew this would have meant she had had to tidy her room and accept that it would become one giant depository for bags and jackets and empty cans.

As he walked past her bed, he could smell sausages just before he found Theo standing over a barbecue he had wheeled around the back. The two men shook hands as if they were old buddies with amnesia. They knew nothing about each other whatsoever.

'I wouldn't have, but this weather demanded it,' Naomi said with the air of someone having an out-of-body experience.

'And Theo has that posh barbecue thing he was going to fire up anyway. So.'

'And where is the paddling pool?' he laughed.

Naomi glanced towards the fence where the Mizwa family lived.

'The children were splashing earlier and saw the balloons and wanted to know whose birthday it was, so… They are popping round too. Before it gets too rowdy.'

Ryan shrugged. The heat had made everyone slightly barmy so he glugged down a cold lager as Stu's latest girlfriend applied thick sun cream to Ryan's nose.

Stu, a carefree, sometimes there, sometimes not, friend, sidled up to him.

'There is no better way to get to know a gang of people you've never clapped eyes on before than to slap Factor 50 on their faces,' Stu said. 'I thought she would cling to me but she's more popular than Florence Nightingale.'

Chapter 2

And now Ryan was thirty-three and it was hot in his small, narrow garden and Stu had a new girlfriend and Ryan found himself making small talk to a seven-year-old who wanted to know when the other children were arriving.

'Will there be a magician?' he asked.

'Not that I am aware of but have another sausage,' Ryan said as he moved to the safety of Naomi, who was sat on one of the canvas chairs lent by Theo and fiddling with the knot at the back of her halter-neck dress. Her bare shoulders, he thought, made her look Amazonian, although he had a hunch she was attempting to look more softly feminine.

'I know it's your birthday but I invited Cappi, but he won't come and, actually, he seemed a bit confused that I thought he might even *think* of coming. And you know why that is, don't you?'

She paused and gently punched Ryan's arm.

'No?' he said.

'Because I don't know him. I speak to him in my head most of the time. I was practically a stranger giving him, another stranger, instructions on where I live and how much I'd like him to be here.'

Ryan smiled at the thought that Naomi could be someone who might go unnoticed.

'He was probably delighted to be asked and is just shy or something,' he said. 'But hey, you took the plunge. It's good that you invited him. If nothing else you can now ask him if he got lost or hates parties or only mixes with Italians.'

The sun left the garden and Theo started to pack up his barbecue accessories while the two Mizwa children bounced up and down on Naomi's bed, causing the empty beer cans to clank and clink in a merry birthday tune.

'I'm not sure their parents actually came round,' she said. 'But they seem to be having fun.'

The heatwave stretched into Monday and Ryan involuntarily pictured his woman from the Underground in a white summer dress as if stepping straight out of *Picnic at Hanging Rock* – a film defined entirely by heat and pretty, unworldly girls in white dresses. But she was not there today. He let two trains pass and then gave up and sat in a reflective mood, his nose a healthy, steady colour thanks to Stu's girlfriend, while all around him were bright pink noses and sunburnt forearms, the faint odour of summer hangovers, perspiration and an overwhelming sensation of mass dehydration.

He felt sorry for his students. They had practical exams to take in his laboratory and would have had to prepare for them in the stifling heat while their friends had fried in the sun. Only once had a student complained about the exam conditions of his lab, that there had been a contamination of his aqueous solutions that spoiled his extraction of glycolic acid. The complaint was not proven but it had made Ryan extra meticulous on exam days and the rows of equipment gleamed with uniform brightness in the light that filtered through the long, drawn blinds. After it was over and the invigilator had collected in all the notes, the students filed out and just one shook Ryan's hand.

'Thank you,' he said and Ryan noted that the young man had the air of one under pressure to succeed in a realm that might be beyond him. That the standard of chemistry students was on the decline was a common refrain in the staff rooms.

He wondered if the young man was even studying what he wanted to study. There were always students who caved in to parental pressure to study science when they felt empathy with the arts. Ryan's own childhood had been one of watchful freedom but he had never lost the sense of duty to his family and a sense of gratitude that the loss of Tom, his older brother, had not left a sediment of resentment or discomfort. The photographs that lined the narrow hall of his mother's house revealed a curly-haired Tom who looked just like Ryan. He was a reminder then, and still, of what she had lost but if that hurt her she hid it well. Ryan was well aware that he could easily have grown up in a home lacking smiles and sunshine, that every stick-man painting he brought home from school, every cardboard rocket, every spelling-test score, could have been greeted with sad, regretful eyes, but instead either Grace or Hana would utter warm words of encouragement and heap praise upon all his little achievements.

As he walked home the sky darkened and there was a low grumbling of distant thunder just as he bumped into Theo, who, fully aware of the cliché he was uttering, said: 'That's our summer over, then.'

Number 4 was quiet. No Naomi. He hoped she was having dinner with her Italian but doubted it. All the same, the thought of it meant he suddenly craved a pizza, which he ate with one of the beers still in the fridge from the party, and then felt bored. He was too old for this kind of existence. The student who had the decency to shake his hand was more grown up than he was. Maybe he did not own a porcelain gravy boat but he possessed a seriousness that implied a willpower stronger than the impact word association had on Ryan's diet. Ryan patted his stomach. He was not tall enough to carry any blubber. He had always been on the wiry side but there were signs of some flab these days. He threw the last slice of his American Hot in the bin, resisted a second beer and pulled the ironing board away from the wall. He could be proactive instead of beery. 'I'll never iron a shirt for you,' Ellen had said, and he had smiled because he had known, just like 10cc had lied while crooning 'I'm Not in Love', she had meant she probably would. One day.

The next morning, he wore a freshly ironed shirt to go with his close shave. Naomi pretended not to notice.

'Ready? I'm off now if you are,' she said.

Ryan did not want company on the Tube so he said he had to find some paperwork. She shrugged and left.

Five minutes later he took the same route as his lodger. He peered inside the usual carriage and there she was, sat right next to the driver's door, a book on her lap, her bag at her feet. There was just one seat available and it was directly opposite her. No one else had noticed it because it was obscured by an obese man who had an old-fashioned briefcase perched on his knees. Ryan had spotted it though, he had become rather adept at finding a seat near… her. He wondered what her name was and then realized he had been thinking of her as Millie because it rhymed with Piccadilly. He didn't particularly like the name Millie, but it was stuck now in his head.

She did not look up; she did not catch his eye. He coughed. Still she did not look at him. He imagined her standing just as the train braked sharply, causing her to fall into him. She would have to look at him then. But she never, bar the one-off seamless movement at Barons Court, stood up before he did. He always left first and he had no idea where she alighted. If he fell into her lap she would curse him as an oaf. He was stuck. Unless. He looked at his watch. He had time, just, to stay on until Knightsbridge, to find out if that was her stop. It was, after all, why, he now realized, he had ironed a shirt. He was having a proactive sort of day. He remained seated and looked for a sign that she was readying to leave but instead she turned the page of her novel.

Ryan sighed and left the train but noted the name of her book. *East Lynne.* It meant nothing to him so he repeated the words as he dashed along the Brompton Road for a longer than usual walk to the university while Millie continued reading as far as Green Park, although she was tempted, really tempted, to keep trundling on and on, reading, glancing up maybe from time to time, and reading some more all the way to Cockfosters. It was preferable to recalling that day. The day when everything changed.

*

Three months earlier…

Sylvie had put the phone down with a shiver. She had never been called into Jane Jessop's office before. As far as she could recall such a message was rarely a good thing to happen to an employee of the consultancy.

'Ah, Sylvie, please take a seat,' she said.

Sylvie could feel inverted goosebumps jabbing at her internal organs. She smiled weakly.

'Never the most pleasant side of my role here,' Jane Jessop said, 'but I am afraid we have to let you go and, in line with our policy, that will be with immediate effect.' She paused and smiled. It was a sickly, half-hearted smile and Jessop's eyes remained cloudy.

'However, the severance terms are exceptionally generous. You will receive a full year's salary upon signature… right here.'

Sylvie had expected something unpleasant but not quite this. She was good at her job. It made no sense to axe her.

Jane Jessop, who hoped that behind her back she was known as JJ, shuffled some papers and cleared her throat.

'Look, I can see you are surprised but this is business, purely business, and while you might want to, er, challenge the decision you would not get a better deal than a year's full pay anyway. I do not represent you, I represent the company, but I'll level with you: it would be counter-productive in every way not to sign. You've been with us two years, that's all. This is extremely generous and it comes with a top-notch reference explaining that we restructured and would have preferred to have kept you. Which we can't.'

'Restructured?' Sylvie said slowly.

'Yes, sadly, restructuring. It happens.'

Indignation rumbled in Sylvie's belly but did not erupt. She was mostly numb but knew that her pay-off was too good to ignore for the sake of fighting for a job that was not one she loved anyway, not since Gerry, her boss, had begun to sulk.

She read the document as slowly as she dared and then provided her signature.

'Excellent,' Jane Jessop said. 'Jason will escort you from the premises. Don't be alarmed. It's standard procedure as I'm sure you know.'

Jason had appeared stealthily and handed Sylvie a box, which she peered in to as if it might contain a pair of kittens or a bowl of expensive fruit.

'For you to clear your desk,' Jane Jessop said, but she was already punching a speed-dial number and thinking of other employees. Sylvie was a small problem sorted.

Jason stood deferentially to one side as Sylvie cleared her desk of the cashmere scarf she kept for emergencies, her spare make-up bag and the plump echeveria cactus that had sat dutifully by her phone for the full two years. The box, she felt, was barely necessary. The thought of entering the lift holding it made her almost retch. She placed it slowly, as if it were a bomb, on her desk. She wrapped the scarf around her neck, placed the make-up into her handbag, lifted the cactus off the desk and spun around to give it to Cheryl who had been housed at the adjacent desk for under a month and who seemed pleasant enough.

'A parting gift,' Sylvie said and Cheryl blushed, not in delight but in embarrassment at being seen to be favoured by the sacked one. Jason frowned but said nothing. He wondered what the magic words might be to ensure that by the time he and Sylvie were on the street, they had arranged to meet for a coffee.

They took the lift in silence, Sylvie inwardly smarting at the injustice of how easy it had been for Jane Jessop and Gerry and the rest of them to erase her.

They reached the pavement.

'Splendidly escorted,' Sylvie said in soft sarcasm and walked towards the Tube station.

Jason, knowing no magic words, simply stared at her as she walked away.

She realized she was sat on a westbound Piccadilly train without having made a conscious decision to be there. The idea of engaging in her normal commute six hours earlier than usual filled her with dread. She would dawdle, maybe go to a gallery. She was not ready to walk in through her front door, place her keys on the table, fill the kettle and face life as someone unemployed. The train had other ideas. It was perky, this train, she noted. It was not rush hour so it could open its doors, collect its passengers, slam the doors shut quickly and then speed off as if late for a doctor's appointment. She understood for the first time the attraction of the *Thomas the Tank Engine* stories. Trains could be humanized, have personalities, quirks of character.

They had already left Hyde Park Corner behind. She tried to concentrate. There was culture galore if she got off at South Kensington but she recalled big crowds and long queues and she was more in the mood for a gentler perusal of art or at least a calmer sort of dodging of reality. She was fairly sure the Tate was near Pimlico so she changed onto the Circle line at South Kensington and then changed again at Victoria but when she emerged at Pimlico there was a swirling wind whipping up the rain and she decided that to wander the marbled corridors of the Tate with dripping hair and wet feet was not quite the diversion she had envisaged.

Her mind empty of an alternative, Sylvie boarded a north-bound train hoping for inspiration. She looked at the map. What she really wanted was to stroll across Regent's Park but she was prepared to accept that was only the case because the weather made it impossible. The train whistled into Oxford Circus and still she had not formulated a plan – but there was no point staying on the Victoria line so she hopped off, stood on the platform helplessly and then hopped straight back on. Her rather dull proposal, formulated in desperation, was to go to King's Cross St Pancras station. She had never seen that station, it was supposed to be architecturally impressive and she was hungry. She could eat lunch there without the need to brave the weather and then, once fed, she could assess if she felt ready to go home with her cashmere scarf and abundance of make-up.

The station was enormous, like a mini-city from a sci-fi film. There were glossy shops with sparkling-clean glass doors and windows, and cafés and restaurants. The trains were hidden and she was intrigued enough to cease feeling the gnawing self-pity and decided to explore. Some trains were upstairs and some were behind barriers away from the eateries. She bought a feta cheese Greek salad and sat at the sort of scrubbed chunky wooden table usually found in a farmhouse kitchen. She took out her phone and laid it beside her carton of lunch. She was unemployed and had no idea what kind of emails and messages an unemployed woman might receive.

The answer, she discovered, as she crunched a piece of

cucumber, was very few. She was off the mailing list. There was a message, though, from Catherine, a PA to a man very like Gerry, only chubbier.

You must be livid, sweetie. Fancy a drink one night next week to vent?

It was a curious sort of note, Sylvie thought, both thoughtful and brusque. Am I livid? she wondered. She decided she was not. She was hurt. As she took her last bite of the last olive, she winced. How had it taken her three hours to realize what had actually happened?

She jabbed the plastic fork into the back of her hand. A tiny drizzle of olive oil trickled towards her wrist. She licked it and noticed a man sat opposite, leering. She sneered at him by curling her lip and narrowing her eyes. He did not blush, he simply kept staring. She rose slowly. She was ready to go home now.

Sylvie did not rush, though. She wandered into a clothes store that was half full of cardigans for spring and half full of expensive new-range dresses for a summer that was still three months away. She fingered the knitwear. She was rich, or rather in a mirage of wealth. She could afford to be impulsive but nothing took her fancy. A young man in a faded frock coat was playing at a white piano as she walked towards the Underground. She paused, noting how he was too immersed to flirt, to notice how many women stopped to listen, and she shivered as she recalled Gerry's dry, gingery breath on her neck as he leaned too closely.

Chapter 3

Over a tuna mayonnaise sandwich, four hours later, Ryan searched for *East Lynne* on the computer in his small office. The plot summary was impenetrable. He was not at all sure he could bluff that he had read it – so he ordered it instead and then asked his boss if he could come in a little later the next morning as there were no exams for him to oversee. Ryan smiled to himself. He was definitely being proactive, albeit subtly so; so subtly that nothing he was doing could really match the dictionary definition of the word but he felt relatively empowered rather than his usual floatingly useless self and that made a nice change.

It was a risk, using up a favour from his boss when he could not be sure Millie would even be on his train the next day. He arrived at North Ealing station five minutes earlier than his usual five minutes early and surveyed the first carriage of the first train to pull in. He drew back and looked at the departure strip. Three minutes until the next eastbound train to Cockfosters. He felt good about that train and he scanned the carriage with narrowed, focused eyes. She was there. If he was sprightly he could grab a seat on the opposite row and two places apart. He made it. She did not notice the fact. Her novel, with its image of a woman in white, slumped in despair at a small desk, was held in front of her face but not for long. She sighed as if she had reached the end of a dissatisfying chapter, closed the book and then closed her eyes.

Ryan frowned. Millie appeared for all the world like someone who was settled in for a long ride. He had imagined her destination to be, if not Knightsbridge, then Green Park or, at worst, Covent Garden. He fidgeted and looked at his watch. The doors opened at Green Park and then closed again and still Millie's eyes were shut. They pulled into Piccadilly Circus. Nothing. No movement. The train trundled slowly towards Leicester Square and her eyes flashed open. She put her book in her bag and stood.

Ryan held his breath. He had not thought beyond this moment. Was it even useful for him to know this was her stop? He sat, in paralysis, for a few seconds and then darted through the doors. 'I appear to be following her,' he said to himself, as if the narrator of his own story. He was half amused and half embarrassed. And then he became irritated. Millie was following the signs for the Northern line. Her journey was much longer than he had assumed. He had to abandon this lunacy. He would be pushing his luck back at work.

As he climbed back onto the Piccadilly line he wondered at his disappointment, at the lack of any logic to it. He thought they had the Piccadilly line in common but she had wandered off to the Northern and for all he knew she would change again, onto the Bakerloo or Jubilee. He gazed at the Tube map on the wall and imagined her at Waterloo station, maybe taking a mainline train to… He racked his brains for towns served by Waterloo. Bournemouth. She could be on her way to the coast by now.

By the time he reached the university he believed he knew less than he knew before and he had much preferred his assumption that she worked only a few stops away from him. Now he realized she could be anywhere in London or anywhere outside of London. On the days he did not see her she could be in Poole or Southampton with her boyfriend or lover. He deliberately stubbed his toe against the wall and whispered that he was an idiot, not because he did not know her route or her real name but because he was jealous of whoever was waiting for her by the sea and he briefly forgot about the inventory he was supposed to be compiling and daydreamed, involuntarily, of her stood in front of a huge rock in Australia, a distant ocean breeze taking hold of her long white dress as pan pipes played from above.

He felt a bit grubby for a few hours and then, just a smidgen, triumphant. He had trailed a stranger and that was highly peculiar but it was not just because of her pretty, candyfloss hair. If he had been asked to find the words to describe why he was drawn to her he would have been nervous of trying but he believed there had been something that connected them the day she had helped the helpless student. There had been a familiarity, a thread of something almost comforting, a premonition of knowing her, a need to know more about her when he had assumed he would never be intrigued by a woman ever again.

He shook his head, exasperated by his inability to pin down his feelings, as he wandered aimlessly down the aisle of his nearest supermarket. Ellen had hated food shopping and had flitted at speed, collecting the bare essentials and appearing at the till while he was still comparing the prices of packs of mince. She would sit cross-legged, sucking dramatically at the strings of spaghetti he had cooked for them, she would make fun of him in a way that lifted his spirits and expanded his ego. That was quite a skill, he realized now for the first time. She had not cared he was not Tom. She had not considered that life is fragile, that to take off her jumper in her mother's too-stuffy car could have consequences, that it could be devastating.

Chapter 4

'You're in a bad mood,' Naomi said. 'Everything OK?'

She was making pasta for them both and usually, if she did that, Ryan would perch on a kitchen bar stool and chat. Instead he sat on the sofa staring blankly at the screen of his laptop.

He made a strange tutting sound so she carried on chopping mushrooms in silence and soon took him a plate piled high with penne tossed in her creamy mushroom sauce. She brought her own plate to the sofa and curled into the corner to make sure there was as much distance between them as possible.

'Maybe I can help,' she said in a voice that she hoped sounded sisterly and not the least nosy. She had grown much fonder of Ryan than she assumed most lodgers to be of their landlords.

He swallowed a forkful of pasta, a tiny splash of cream landing, as usual, on his chin, then tapped his plate.

'Good as always,' he said and they sat without speaking for a few minutes.

'Shall I distract you with Tamsin's latest drama?'

'Go on, then,' he said. 'Actually, why I don't distract you with how pathetic I was today.'

She smiled. 'I bet it's not as pathetic as you think.'

He took a breath. This was almost interesting. He had no real idea how odd his behaviour had been. He was usually so predictable, he knew that, but maybe his small adventure was part of an average day for most other men his age. He wondered how to precis who Millie was and how she had become an obsession. He wondered whether if he formulated the words for it all, the spell would be broken: Naomi would giggle, he would guffaw, and by the weekend he would have forgotten all about her and be found clubbing with Beth, Tamsin, Naomi, Stu and Florence Nightingale.

'There's a girl on the Tube,' he said as if relating the plot of a box set. 'I see her most days, not every day, and she's, well, she has *got* to me. I've no idea why. We've never spoken. Never smiled at each other even. I asked if I could go in late today so I could find out where she gets off. And she gets off at Leicester Square so I do too and then she goes to the Northern line and so—'

Here Ryan raised his hands. 'And so I turn around and get back on the train so I won't be too late and she seems more of a stranger than she did the day before. As I promised; pathetic.'

'Well, not really,' Naomi said.

'Oh, I forgot to mention I spent the whole day obsessing about her visiting her boyfriend who probably lives in a big villa overlooking the sea.'

'He probably doesn't,' Naomi said and Ryan smiled.

'Yeah, I just needed to get that off my chest. Now I know how ridiculous it sounds, I'll stop stalking her.'

'Hmm,' Naomi said.

Hana had booked a walking holiday in Devon. It was customary for Ryan to stay at his mother's when Hana was away. It was tough for Grace if left on her own day and night with Grandpa. Not one of them had ever suggested he should go into care. There was nothing wrong with him. He was, simply, sad, sometimes grumpy, and lost in a world of clockwork tears and cake.

Ryan arrived on the Saturday morning as Hana was holding Grandpa's hand and saying she would be back in a week's time.

'I bought you this for the journey,' Ryan said as he handed her the novel he had ordered online.

'Thank you,' Hana said, puzzled as she looked at the slouched woman on its cover.

'Is it a Mills and Boom thingy?' Grandpa said, somewhat sharply.

'Boon,' Hana said with a half-smile. '*Boon*. And I do hope not.'

'A colleague recommended it,' Ryan explained. 'And as you watched that Dickens thing, I thought—'

'OK,' she said. 'Thanks. The bedding's all changed for you and there's loads of space in the wardrobe.'

'I've cooked a chicken for us,' Grace said, trying not to appear too excited to have Ryan back home, all to herself. 'We'll have it cold with salad, shall we?'

It was, Ryan knew, good for him to spend the occasional week at home. It underlined just how saintly his sister was for living with Grace and Grandpa when she ought to be more selfish, more married or more of a mother. She had been married, once, to a man who had been devoted in a saccharine manner while they were engaged and a mean-spirited sloth once hitched. He had dragged Hana's self-esteem into the dirt and stamped on it as if extinguishing a lit cigarette; they never had any children, which was obviously a blessing, as his mother would say, and yet Hana had nothing now to compensate for the nasty years, the wasted years.

Grace, beaming at the prospect of the week ahead, had bought in copious amounts of bacon, sausages and eggs for the Sunday fry-up and the bacon sandwiches she would make for Ryan before he headed off to work.

'Now then, I haven't bought in the food for Monday's supper so you'll have to let me know what you fancy,' she said. 'You know what I'm good at anyway.'

Grandpa stirred at seven o'clock and fumbled for his handkerchief to wipe at his rheumy eyes. Grace went upstairs, returned with a warm face cloth, and proceeded to pad away at his tear-stained cheeks.

'Ryan's home,' she said and he looked over at his grandson with such wistfulness that Ryan was almost moved to tears himself.

'It's not Tom, is it?' Grandpa said.

'No, it's not Tom,' Grace said in a voice that told of a barrier erected many years ago in order to cope with Grandpa's questions.

'Where's my scarf?' he said. This was the cue for them to

walk him slowly to the local pub, one that would be quiet even on a Saturday evening. It showed no football nor served food but it was clean and the staff always made a fuss of Grandpa, found a cushion for his chair and brought him his whisky without being asked.

Once settled, Grandpa smiled and told them the history of the pub, something he did quite a lot, but neither Ryan nor Grace minded because it was gratifying to see him animated and content.

'Now then, marriage,' Grandpa said.

Ryan and his mother exchanged a surprised glance. This was a fresh departure.

'What about marriage, Grandpa?' Ryan said.

'Didn't suit your sister one little bit,' he said.

'No,' Ryan said and he suppressed a twitch of guilt that he had never helped Hana out, never talked to her properly about her life, that he had been happy to let her shelter him from the worst of it. There were only six years between them but Hana treated it like a gulf, like she was another mother to him. As the dust peculiar to pubs danced its way towards the polished tables, Ryan, not for the first time, inwardly scolded his lack of maturity as he sat alongside this pair of older, seen-it-all, seen-too-much relatives who had in their different ways shielded him from dramas about which he only knew an outline.

'But you mustn't let it put you off, son,' Grandpa continued. 'Me and your grandmother had a wonderful fifty years together. A real team we were. You can't get through life on your own. I've never had to sew a button, never washed a shirt, not even my filthiest underpants.'

Grace rolled her eyes.

'Like magic, isn't it?' she said and Ryan laughed out loud, wondering how at eighty-five his grandfather could get away with saying anything.

The next day it rained and all three of them watched *The Quiet Man*, with, as Grace put it, 'the most beautiful Maureen O'Hara in my favourite film of all time'.

Grandpa, rather than doze, as Ryan expected, was transfixed.

'Have we seen this before?' he asked.

'Never,' Grace said as she winked at her son.

They ate lemon sponge cake at three o clock and had roast beef at seven. Then it was time to haul Grandpa to bed. He always insisted he spend the night in his armchair but Grace was convinced that would be the beginning of the end for him and was strict about his routine. Afterwards, Ryan began wondering about his journey into work. It made sense for him to take the Jubilee line from Dollis Hill to Green Park and then change onto the Piccadilly line from there but that would ensure no sighting of Millie. He knew it was stupid to choose the long route via Rayners Lane but there was the tantalizing prospect that he might be on the train before her and would find out where she began her journey each morning. Such knowledge would surely compensate for the anti-climax on the Northern line. There was a problem though. He needed to calculate what time he should board his train. After much scribbling on a pad of paper, he decided he would vary the timings unless he got lucky and made a plan to arrive at Rayners Lane at 7.35 the first day and then three minutes later for each following day.

Grace called upstairs to ask if he wanted his bacon sandwich toasted or fluffy. She had always called untoasted bread fluffy and as he passed the photographs of Tom he thought, for the first time, that maybe it had something to do with his big brother.

'You don't usually leave the house this early, do you?' his mother asked and he said it was a particularly busy week.

'Shall I be washing the clothes on your floor?' she said as if to do so would be as big a treat as being handed a bottle of expensive perfume wrapped in thick cream paper and tied with a velvet bow. It had been so hard not having any need to wash Tom's clothes that she had sometimes in the distant past washed Ryan's shorts twice in a day. Usually Ryan would refuse the offer, not wanting to be a burden, not understanding that it was something his mother needed, still, to do. He would have said no but he felt an urge to be freshly laundered so he kissed her cheek and said yes, if she wouldn't mind, thank you.

'It's all magic anyway,' she smiled.

'Of course,' he said and left the house. As he closed the door he heard his grandpa shout out as to why it was he could smell bacon on a Monday and had Grace forgotten to do the washing-up.

As Ryan reached the platform at Rayners Lane he scanned the crowd for almost red hair. There was some, but it belonged to men. He sat in the front carriage feeling proprietorial, expectant, nervous. He rubbed his nose and sat up straight as the train approached South Harrow. No sighting. Sudbury Hill. No sighting. Sudbury Town. No sighting. Alperton. No sighting. Park Royal. No sighting. At North Ealing he got off. 'No one can doubt my commitment,' he said to himself but the next train was not fruitful either so he stepped in and stood the rest of the way as an act of penance.

In the canteen, as he ate a sun-blushed tomato and mozzarella salad, Naomi sat opposite him.

'I miss you,' she said sarcastically.

'Will you last the week?' he said.

'What's with the rabbit food?'

'Rabbits don't eat mozzarella,' he said. 'My mother is fattening me up. I don't see how I can eat anything else given I've already had a massive bacon sarnie today.'

'I was thinking,' Naomi said. 'We could try to solve each other's problem. It's easier when it's not your own heart or lust or sad loserdom or whatever.'

Ryan had no interest in psychoanalysing the morose giant that was Cappi. Actually, he thought, I have no desire to even stand next to a guy that tall. On the other hand, he liked the sound of Naomi offering help. Now he had confessed his obsession, there seemed little downside. It intrigued him that having bared his soul he felt no differently. He had not been shamed into giving up on the whole notion of ever speaking to Millie. If anything, saying the words out loud had added a sheen of reality to what was, in essence, an immature crush. It was now a real thing. Millie was a real person who might, one day, meet Naomi. Who might one day sit at this very table and lean over and stick her fork into a tiny ball of mozzarella, pop it into her mouth and then pretend to choke while wondering if she was eating a piece of plastic. 'I hate cheese,' Ellen had said, sprinkling Parmesan on top of her spaghetti bolognese.

The mozzarella date was, though, only a possibility if he continued to be proactive and bold. I can be bold, he thought.

'OK,' he said. 'Me first?'

'Concurrently,' she said sternly.

'Deal,' he said. 'These tomatoes are shite.'

'You should have asked me about them first,' she said.

Two hours later, Ryan headed to the street, to stretch his legs, and saw Cappi sat on a bench in the foyer scrolling on his phone. Ryan paused. This was, he had to admit, excellent timing, and sat down he could cope with his own lack of height. Ryan plonked himself down too, cleared his throat and offered his hand.

'Hi, I'm Ryan, the guy whose party you were invited to in Ealing.'

Cappi shook his hand but looked puzzled.

'My friend Naomi, she's my lodger; she told me she thought you were coming.'

'I am sorry but I don't know this.'

'You are Cappi?'

'Yes.'

'Right. OK.'

Without registering it and in his eagerness to be helpful to Naomi, Ryan had shuffled so close to Cappi that he said these last words into the man's nostrils. Ryan felt himself blushing and once he realized he was reddening he knew it might seem as if he was hitting on the Italian. He wanted to dash off but that might make it worse. He needed to backtrack, to explain, but instead Cappi slowly stood and walked away, muttering a 'Ciao' without looking back.

Ryan remained seated, numb with embarrassment. The numbness gave way to an inner groan at his stupidity. He had not even had a plan of action. He had ruined Naomi's life with a guileless act of spontaneity. He was glad to be staying at his mother's that evening.

He set off the next day after a fluffy bacon buttie three minutes later than the day before but the outcome was the same. Wednesday and Thursday were equally frustrating but on Friday she was sat, without a book, without a paper, just sat there, in the front carriage looking at her nails. There had been too big a gap in the service and there was nowhere for him to sit but he felt a smidgen of triumph that he now knew she lived beyond Rayners Lane – but as he looked at the map on the carriage wall that fact made little sense. If she needed to change at Leicester Square then it was much faster to take the Metropolitan line, which served all the same stations as those on the Piccadilly line before Rayners Lane.

Ryan frowned and stole a glance at her. She was reading now, the same *East Lynne* novel by the looks of it. He thought about his brief exchange with Cappi. It was a warning that to try to engage with Millie would be disastrous without planning. Still, he now had two topics of conversation. The novel and her route.

Grace and Ryan were playing Scrabble when Hana arrived home. Her cheeks were as sun-blushed as Ryan's sun-dried tomatoes and her arms were a rosy pink and she seemed happy.

She looked at the board.

'"Yowza" isn't a word,' she said.

'Oh, but it is,' Ryan said.

'He's got an app thing that checks,' their mother said, as if she was playing a board game with a scientist from a different galaxy, 'but we'll stop now for tea.'

Grace had made a beautiful sponge cake filled with fresh whipped cream and English strawberries and there was a moment when all four of them were silent as they savoured its magnificence.

'I'll never leave home,' Hana said as she took a second slice.

'Not sure about the fruit,' Grandpa said as Grace took his plate, and soon he was dozing as a solitary tear trickled slowly down his face.

'So, Hana; food, weather, scenery. All acceptable?' Ryan said.

She nodded.

'I had a full cream tea every day but walked it off come rain or shine and there was plenty of both. We stuck to the coast most of the time and…'

Grace and Ryan blinked to fill the pause. Grace felt her heartbeat quicken.

'And I met a guy who said he would phone me, which he already did when I was on the train.'

Hana had not been on a date since leaving the sloth. She had been timid, a home bird, uninterested in any man who glanced at her in a way suggestive of flirtation. Ryan could tell this was an important moment for his sister and he wanted to both encourage and discourage her. She did not deserve to be hurt again.

'Is he living in Devon?' Grace asked, having decided this was the most neutral, least interfering question she could pose.

'East London. Could be better but he's nice. I like him. He suggested afternoon tea in town next weekend. I think that's a sign he's nice.'

Grace exhaled and Ryan was struck by how much store

Hana placed upon the man's niceness; as if most men were callous and she had stumbled upon a rare example of empathy.

'Oh, I think that sounds lovely,' Grace said.

'It certainly implies he knows a theme when he sees it,' Ryan said. 'We'll bring Grandpa, he likes scones,' he added and Hana tweaked his ear.

Chapter 5

'I thought about welcome-home bunting but instead I've stocked the fridge with booze,' Naomi said that evening.

'Very thoughtful,' Ryan said as he disparagingly surveyed the two bottles of rosé.

'There's beer too,' she said. 'At the back. Beth's coming here at eight before we're off out so there's time to do some problem-solving.'

They sat at opposite ends of the sofa, drink in hand.

'Any more info?' she asked.

He filled her in and was pleased that Naomi agreed that Millie's route was indeed a mystery.

'Well, I've been giving it some thought. Don't you have to take two weeks off at the end of July?'

'Yes.'

'Will you be here in London?'

'I haven't booked anything yet.'

'In that case, leave a day at least where you can just stand on the platform until you see her and then follow her so that you know where she works and then you can take it from there.'

'From where exactly?'

'Lots of places. Like seeing her at a coffee shop near her office and striking up a conversation that you think you see her most days on your commute. It depends on the office she works in. Maybe she works in a shop and you can buy something from her and ask if she has time for lunch or a walk or a drink. That has to be better than speaking to her on the train, which is a bit weird. No one does that. What do you reckon? Genius or what?'

'It's, well, it's proactive I guess, and my word of the month is "proactive". It's also a bit creepy. She'll think I'm a stalker. Actually, wouldn't I technically *be* a stalker?'

'It's that or nothing, I reckon. We're all stalkers if you think about it. Why do I play bridge? Because I'm a stalker. I know where he will be and so that is where I make sure I will be. We are living our lives accidentally on purpose in the hope we will summon some courage – and speaking of which, had any thoughts about my Italian job?'

'Still thinking, still thinking,' he said, looking at the floor.

Beth arrived wearing four-inch heels to try to compete with Naomi.

'You should come with us,' Beth said, smiling at Ryan with an enforced steadiness, lest she appear needy.

'I'm meeting some mates,' he said, even though he was doing no such thing, 'but thank you, Beth, you are very inclusive. And tall today.'

'I feel sort of insignificant when walking with Names. Everyone looks at her and it's like being her poodle on a lead. But not really. Obviously. Because she's not like that and she'd probably say she feels too much like a tourist attraction sometimes.'

‘She’s not *that* different, is she?’ Ryan said, although he had noticed the way people stared as if offended that Naomi walked with confidence rather than stooped shoulders.

Alone, because he had no plans at all, he mulled over Naomi’s scheme. He did not mind sitting quietly in his house but had found it simpler, many years ago, to swerve nights out by claiming prior engagements; not that many people had ever asked. Friends sometimes felt the need to drag him along, assuming he would be grateful and drunkenly embrace them, but the longer he drifted away from his time with Ellen the less he wanted to do fun things without her. He was not in more pain – he doubted he ever felt much real pain anyway – it was a matter of respect. He could do anything. Ellen could do nothing. It was not fair.

In any case he needed to sit and absorb Naomi’s plan. It had sounded fun, wacky, harmless when she had described it but he knew it was flawed. Normal people did not follow strangers. Men who wanted to stalk pretty women were weirdos. He was thankful for his flatmate’s help but it was no real help. He would not stoop to it, but the interesting part to him was that he wanted a plan at all – even if the likelihood of him ever properly meeting Millie stood at zero.

The next day, however, his boss asked him if he would attend a mid-morning meeting at the University of East London the following Monday. It meant he could have indulged in a lie-in, but he took the same train as usual and was rewarded by sharing a carriage with Millie. He glanced at the map above her head. There was no good reason for him to change at Leicester Square. Unless. Anyone might take a circuitous route if they were too early for a meeting. He breathed in deeply. He might well change to the Northern line, just to waste time.

The train whistled away from Piccadilly Circus and almost immediately slowed down again, so short was the gap between stations. Ryan straightened as he glanced at her. She did not move. He relaxed. He would change at Holborn as required. As he stood, so did Millie, and he wondered at the irony that she was behind him as they alighted. He paused before a wall map so she could pass by him. He needed the Central line. She was heading to the Central line. And so it came to pass they were both in the same carriage heading east. It had been several years since he had last been on the Central line and he was not used to its trains. He had assumed the first one was out of commission because the windows were seemingly blacked out but as it came to a stand-still he could see it was almost full. For some reason they had designed the trains on this line differently.

He stood at Stratford. She remained seated and he wondered what her job might be that she needed the Northern line one day and the far reaches of the Central on another. He wondered how it was that she had not smiled at him, not even quizzically. He wondered, briefly, if she was real. He wondered, for a while longer, why it was he sat back down. He had time to kill, he told himself. Never a good idea to be too early for a meeting.

They travelled together but not really together to Epping. He did not, now, have time to follow her out on to the street so he stared at his feet glumly. He had knowledge about her that amounted to knowing nothing at all. This might be the only time in her life she would ever visit Epping so it was of no help to him whatsoever. He needed her to have a place of work, just as he had a place of work, so he could find a frame of reference, a Caffè Nero, a flower stall, a park bench.

He sighed, then stepped out onto the platform to check how to return to Stratford. It was the end of the line and he had to cross the white grilled footbridge for the next departure or wait for seven minutes. As he turned to climb down the steps he heard the doors of the train open and he skipped so as not to miss it. As he placed his right foot into the carriage he turned his face towards the platform and its departure board and saw a flick of candyfloss hair entering a carriage four ahead of his. He shook his head. He was so wrapped up in Millie that he was becoming hyper-sensitive to possible sightings of her. At least this time he did not need to move carriages to be near her. She would be in an Epping office or at an Epping friend's house. By the time he reached Stratford, he was running late and arrived breathless and apologetic with no time to consider if the reason for his tardiness was utterly ridiculous or, simply, a waste of time.

The lab closed completely in mid-July and Ryan's tentative plans to holiday with Stu had evaporated thanks to Florence Nightingale, with whom Stu was becoming increasingly besotted.

'She says you should come too,' Stu said, 'she says you have a fine nose,' and Ryan sneered at what was becoming the refrain of his bachelorhood.

But there was always Paul. Thoughts of Paul always caused Ryan to sigh contentedly. They had met at university but while life had happened to Ryan, Paul had made life happen to him and he used his specialism in molecular genetics to travel the world, lecturing at colleges who usually begged for his expertise and offered translators when needed and accommodation too. Ryan had met up with him in London and Manchester over the past six years when he was briefly back in the UK, as well as Geneva, Turin and Toronto, a touch of glamour in his life made affordable by cheap tickets and Paul providing a bed. Not once had Paul said he was too busy with a girlfriend or included a girlfriend in their adventures. He was currently posted in Seville, probably preparing to explore Spain before the start of the new academic year. Ryan decided a week of Iberian backpacking would be good for him and he hoped good for Paul too. He could probably extend his break and spend longer with his oldest friend. He felt the warmth of a plan well made and fired off an email to him. By the end of the day they had agreed to meet in Barcelona and so pleased was Ryan that he could be heard humming as he ran another interminable stock check the following morning.

His whole body felt energized and he smiled at how easily pleased he was – memories of Grace telling neighbours that he was such a sunny child came flooding back. His brain felt massaged and optimistic and as he reached for the Sudoku at lunch he paused. He had had a brainwave. He had solved Naomi's problem.

Chapter 6

Hana had been taken to afternoon tea at The Ritz. This, as far as Grace was concerned, meant there would soon be an engagement. She phoned Ryan, desperate to share the news. Fortunately, Ryan was still in an overly benign mood and was patient with his mother.

'It sounds great but, Mam, don't mention weddings, she's still, understandably, cautious and she should be cautious. She married that idiot too soon and look how that worked out.'

Grace sniffed that she knew perfectly well her daughter needed to be careful but that she had a *feeling*.

'I've never seen her so happy, Ryan,' she said.

'Oh, Mam, you've not even met him yet,' Ryan said, trying very hard not to sound impatient.

'I've told Hana he's very welcome to join us for a Sunday lunch and she's going to ask him.' There was a note of triumph in his mother's voice. 'And when he does, you have to be there too of course.'

'Of course,' Ryan said, making a mental note to take Millie to his mother's only after he had been seeing her for at least three years.

It was a thought that punctured his buoyant mood and reminded him that he was a deluded obsessive who had seriously considered stalking a woman who might be in a very happy long-term relationship with a handsome lawyer or surgeon. A tall lawyer. A well-built and athletic surgeon who owned a cleverly designed glasshouse that overlooked the sea from its position in front of a giant rock where there were hidden music chimes and ledges for picnics for Millie to share with her lace-clad friends.

Grace filled the pause.

'And so that leaves my lovely Ryan,' she said. 'Anything romantic in the air?'

'You'll be the first to know, Mam,' he lied.

Naomi was late home that evening. Ryan heard her trying to be quiet in the way all people who have had one drink too many try to be quiet. There were a few stifled hiccups and then the piercing clink of a dropped tumbler. He decided not to leave his room. He did not want to find himself offering to sweep up the shards of glass but mostly he wanted to deliver his smart route to Cappi while she was fully attentive and therefore fully appreciative.

He booked his flight to Barcelona at his desk, having travelled in earlier that morning without a sighting of Millie. His boss had given him a strange look when he had asked to extend his two weeks.

'Amazed you didn't ask sooner,' he said. 'I'm off for a month but as long as Abi can cover, we're OK.'

His life was back on track. The optimism returned and it

was as if Millie, her hair clipped back but strands falling over her cheeks, had turned to smile at him. He could picture her face clearly and although he had seen her smile properly just the once, when helping the panicked student, he felt as if he had known her smile for years.

Ellen had a beautiful smile too. They had met in the student bar, played cards together, gone for long walks, had sex in the sea off Santorini, wandered around art galleries hand in hand, speculated on what they would call the puppy they would own when they had a home of their own, had been inseparable for the next fourteen months until her mother killed her.

Ryan bit his lip. Ellen always returned when he was at his happiest. She had liked Paul and he had liked her so the three of them often sat up late with a cheap bottle of wine or some cider and discussed the things that students thought mattered. He could feel the warmth of her smile whenever he thought about Paul. It made sense. No one else he knew now had ever known her. Grace had met her but only for an afternoon, and Hana too, but only for an hour or so.

He drummed his fingers on the desk. It might look like guilt but it was not guilt. There had never been any guilt. He knew what guilt was, he had seen his mother very definitively guilt-ridden for years, and nor was it pain. It was not even grief. He was too young to grieve properly. Ellen's death bore no meaning. Young, healthy people did not die. One second she was there and the next she was not and it felt like a break-up. He had seen break-ups, counselled friends through break-ups. One second there were couples, there was Dom and Lois, Callum and Suzanna, and then the boys were single again. He still went drinking with Dom and Callum but, once it was over, he never spoke to Lois or Suzanna. Perhaps he never even set eyes on them again. It was like that with Ellen. He saw her the night before it happened but had not seen her, not properly, since. He might have cried, he was pretty sure he had cried, but more in disbelief than sorrow. He was just another student with a gone girl.

He scowled at the fridge as if his agitation would be enough to summon something edible.

'The cupboard is bare, Ryan,' Naomi said, 'but all is not lost. I really want to sit at an outside table at that new café with the papers and pretend I am in Paris. I'd rather go with you than alone. So?'

He smiled. This was the perfect way to unveil his grand plan. They hovered close to a couple who had drunk their lattes and paid their bill but were still deep in conversation. There were only five outside tables and all of them were taken.

A waitress came up to them and asked if they were there for drinks or having brunch.

'We'd like to eat,' Naomi said loudly and the engrossed couple's body language indicated they knew they should leave.

'I'm sure a table will be free soon,' the waitress said, not quite as loudly but loud enough.

Finally, they were sat in front of plates of eggs Benedict and Ryan waited.

'So, where are we with our plans?' she said, adopting an air of joviality. Ryan was not fooled.

'I think you're sorted,' he said.

'Oh, am I now?'

'Cappi thinks I am gay and that I have tried to, you know, *flirt* with him. And he seemed pretty pissed off about it. This gives you the exceptionally good reason to apologize for my behaviour, tell him I was trying to do you a favour because, in fact, the person trying to flirt with him is you. Lovely, that is. Could be a scene from a Richard Curtis film. In fact, it ought to be. And it's also genius because if he shrugs then at least you know he isn't interested and you can abort the mission.'

'Clever, I'll help you with the screenplay. But why does he think you're gay in the first place?'

'It just sort of went a bit awry after I shook his hand,' Ryan said.

Naomi nodded, picturing the slightly too friendly, slightly too sensitive, arguably attractive Ryan touching Cappi's hand instead of grasping it, then grinned.

'I'll do it,' she said. 'Now, over to you.'

'Sort of in progress but definitely proactive, which is clearly my word of the summer. I have three weeks off, not two, and the third of them will be, well, it will have something to do with Millie. Look, I can't follow her but I promise to smile at her, speak to her. Something. I promise.' He did not tell her that he had accidentally on purpose followed her a second time.

Naomi pouted.

'I've been thinking it through, though,' she said. 'I decided you should wear a baseball cap or something, just in case she half recognizes you. You shouldn't be Commuter Ryan, you should be Sherlock Ryan.'

Ryan shook his head while trying to calculate how he could be a detective without being a stalker. Would wearing a deerstalker hat take the edge off how sinister it all felt? The thought of it made him smile at least. You could argue, he thought, that I have already done quite enough following as it is.

The rest of the brunch was spent in a jovial climate. All things were possible, after all. They could be geniuses. Just as people put off folding the laundry or filling in a tax return, they can also put off the more pleasant chores because they suspect the anticipation might be as good as it gets. Ryan and Naomi were on the same adventure trail but had reached a fork in the road which meant they had to find their prize on their own from now on. This moment was the best, when they could be self-deprecating but optimistic, each prodding the other to have faith. They were each creating a bubble for the other, one in which they could be daring, close to heroic, prepared to give fate a shove in the back, and because both of them were – right now – dreamers, their chatter lacked cynicism. Naomi believed if Ryan could pull it off then so could she. Ryan believed if he could guide Naomi into the arms of the shy and surly Cappi then surely he could one day share eggs Benedict with his Piccadilly girl.

There was one more formal bridge class before the summer break. Numbers had steadily dwindled since the end of May and there were just four of them and eight packs of cards. Naomi disliked the game but liked how when sat opposite Cappi he was forced to look at her and she would try to inject some sexual tension into a bid of 'three clubs'. It never worked. Ryan's plan was a good one but she felt it was high risk and tried to make herself believe that if he did indeed shrug off her declaration of attraction she would be half grateful that she could dump the bridge club.

Gordon, the avuncular professor who ran the club, had brought along some prosecco to mark the end of the semester. He did not ask if anyone wanted a glass, he just poured and firmly handed all four of them plastic picnic flutes that were an odd shade of cloudy orange. If unbreakable glassware could go stale then this is what it would look like, thought Naomi. On the other hand, Gordon could not have performed better had I bribed him, she decided.

They all made small talk, about their summer plans, their courses, their papers, the weather. It was too intimate a gathering to pull Cappi to one side. She walked over to the window to break up the quartet and, a few moments later, there was a tender tap to her elbow. She half turned, she half smelled an Italian aftershave, but there stood Gordon.

'I wonder if I might interest you in accompanying me to the National Portrait Gallery next week,' he said and she realized, almost immediately, that he had been summoning the courage to speak to her alone for a long time and that the prosecco was not to toast the wonders of bridge but for her. Be kind, she thought to herself. Don't flinch.

'That's a nice thought,' she said. 'I'm always thinking I don't do art or museums enough.'

She held his arm and leaned in. 'I'm being presumptuous but, just in case you are asking in the going-on-a-date sense of asking, I'm already dating.'

Gordon gulped, smelling more now like a man who was wearing too much English deodorant. 'Of course, of course,' he said. 'Nice prosecco, isn't it?' And he moved back to the table.

Naomi remained rooted by the window as she heard Gordon tell the group: 'It's tough being single actually these days. I expect you're both in relationships, I know Naomi is.'

Bemused by the bitterly personal detour in the small talk, Cappi and the sweet undergraduate called Sami, stood to leave. Love, actually, thought Naomi, is a nightmare.

Chapter 7

He sat on one of the smooth grey Gatwick departure-lounge chairs. Boarding information was a full forty minutes away. He looked around at his fellow passengers and could almost hear Ellen's voice. 'They are on honeymoon,' she would have said. 'That pair, they have just met.' She would be warming up, flexing her powers of observation. 'And those two, by the vending machine, they broke up last week but neither wanted to be the one to give up on the holiday.' Ryan looked closely at the vending-machine couple. Maybe Ellen was right. There was a stiff politeness to their demeanour, laced with intimacy. 'Let's pretend we are brother and sister,' she once said, hoping to induce a few gasps of horror when they kissed. 'Hey sis,' he spluttered, 'Hey bro,' she said, straight-faced. 'What shall we buy Mum for her birthday?'

Ellen had been the energetic one, she had pulled him into bed and then out of bed in order to explore, to be alive. She could have written a book on how to have fun on the cheap. She saw beauty in almost everything, prodded him to acknowledge it and then whisked him off in the opposite direction. Someone had said, afterwards, that she had lived life to the full, as if that made her loss easier. But it made it worse. All that vibrancy and optimism gone to waste, and without her he had slowed right down again, reduced to daydreams about a woman with nearly red hair who was so still, so serene and so not like Ellen.

'Cheers. Great to see you, buddy,' Paul said.

They were sat in a square full of bars. There was a flautist nearby and an atmosphere of indulgence. They were but two minutes' walk from the apartment Paul had rented. They were the same age, but Ryan felt younger, less experienced. Mostly, though, he felt completely at ease. He would never say it out loud but he loved this man like a brother and he wondered, fleetingly, if Tom were here, would he love *him* as much as this?

'Trouble is,' Paul said, 'you can't give the city just one night. I reckon we should stay three days before heading…' He shrugged. 'We have an end point, which is Seville, but we can get there however you fancy.'

'Or maybe we'll just stay put,' Ryan said as he sipped at his Estrella.

Four beers later they reluctantly stood up.

'This might be the worst bar we visit, we need to explore, man,' Paul said and so they glided through the city heading towards the beach, slowly becoming as drunk as every other English tourist in Barcelona that day. They bought some bottles of water and sat on the sand in silence, comfortable in each other's company and with enough shared memories to bridge the fact they rarely met up these days. In front of them a group of students, all of them attractive, played volleyball. They both hoped to be asked to join in. They both slowly realized they were too old to be noticed.

'Odd to say this now, in front of so many young women frolicking in the sun, but I need to get a job in England soon,' Paul said. 'I don't know why, really, but I think it's because I was dating this girl,' – he waved his hand dismissively – 'in Italy, in Turin, and she was something. Everything? But nothing because… Because she didn't get it.'

'Get what?'

'The joke. There's this humour thing, this humour gap I've found. You can't have a proper laugh unless it's with someone from home.'

'So you broke it off because she didn't laugh at Mr Bean?'

'Exactly and oppositely. She did like Mr Bean. It was impossible.'

They both chuckled and Ryan realized his heart was thumping at the prospect of his best mate working in London, maybe at the same university.

'Yeah, well, do what you have to do but don't move to Glasgow or Aberystwyth. I want a pal based someplace I'd like to visit.'

'I was thinking London,' Paul said. 'Your turn to be the host, mate.'

'You can join me in my latest hobby.'

'Yeah? You a free runner now, flying up the side of Tower Bridge?'

'Sometimes, but mostly I follow women on the Tube.'

There was a silence. Paul did not want to be flippant. He knew his friend would expand.

Ryan sighed.

'I'm telling you to cure myself before it gets too weird and hard core. Basically, I see this girl on the way into work and she's got to me, so I stayed on the Tube longer than I needed to and when she got off I got off too. She went towards the Northern line and I had to get back to work, so I did, but… you know, pathetic stuff.'

'OK,' Paul said patiently, keeping his voice neutral.

'I just thought, and Naomi thinks it too, if I knew where she works, I could try to buy her a coffee more easily…' he trailed off. If there had a been a plan, it now escaped him. 'Anyway, I had to go to Stratford and so I was half thinking of following her on the Northern line first for a bit, but she went to Stratford too and I was early so I stayed on until the end of the line because that's what she did.'

Paul snorted.

'And?'

'I had to go back again immediately. I had become the guy who's late because he was too early.'

'Shame,' Paul said. 'Maybe she's a double-glazing saleswoman.'

'No she isn't.'

'She's a Jehovah's Witness.'

'No. She isn't.'

'Then find out.'

'Naomi thinks I should spend a day stalking her but I'm *not* stalking someone.'

'Again.'

'Whatever. I didn't feel great about it.'

There was a silence between them as summer sounds

buzzed and sand, kicked up by the volleyball players, flitted past their outstretched toes.

At last Paul spoke.

'It's not technically stalking any more. You'd be solving a mystery. You could call it research.'

'Research for what?'

'Your soul, my curiosity. Hell, what have you got to lose? You can't keep spotting her on the train and mooching about it. Have fun with it. I would. If you can't say hi to her on the train then you have to find a way to speak to her in the street. Simple, really.'

Ryan wondered why he did not own a baseball cap and then remembered that whenever he had worn one his curly hair had sprung from the sides, making him look like a clown or a five-year-old. Any other form of hat would be inappropriate given it was July. He would have to risk recognition. He was taking another risk too. She might easily be on holiday herself.

He arrived at the station fifteen minutes earlier than usual, ready for a long haul or a very brief interlude. He had made himself porridge for breakfast, a rare event, which was why he had nothing but raspberry jam to add to it, but he did not want to become sidetracked by hunger. He let thirty trains come and go and then walked back to Cotton Lane and watched the entire first two series of *Scrubs*, his favourite-ever sitcom. He set off twenty-five minutes earlier the next day and was just as unsuccessful. She's in California, he thought, or Mallorca or Tenerife or she has simply decamped to her lover's palace on the seafront.

On Wednesday he spotted her on the tenth train. He boarded as nonchalantly as possible, sat down and pretended to read the morning's free newspaper. He was fairly relaxed. There were thirteen more stops until they reached Leicester Square, fifteen until Holborn, although he was surprised to see her put her book in her bag – a different title, it seemed – as they pulled away from Barons Court. But then she stood up. He looked to see who she was giving her seat to, but there was no one obvious and she tiptoed her way to the double doors. As they opened at Earls Court, he stood abruptly. He was confused. He had always left her seated when he alighted at South Kensington and he suffered a small surge of panic that she was testing him. Nonetheless, Ryan left the train as well and calmed himself down. People have to go to all sorts of different locations all the time, he thought. She might have a meeting in a different building, that's all. There was bound to be a simple explanation.

He kept his distance, expecting her to pause to look at signs or maps, but she walked unhesitatingly until he found himself ten feet away from her as she boarded an eastbound District line train that was headed to Edgware Road. It was a train seemingly without carriages, one of the long, snake-like trains you could walk the full length of if you so desired, so he kept his distance, stealing glances only as it slowed before each station. She stood as it pulled into its final destination and he followed her onto a Circle line train that extended their journey to busy Baker Street, where she alighted and headed along the crowded platform, turning towards an exit that brought together a mass of tunnels and steps and people. He looked up at the myriad signs and then looked ahead and she had vanished. He would have to guess, hope he would strike lucky, and he followed signs for the Bakerloo line but he could not see her anywhere. He had lost her in the crowds.

A boy, tall and slender and rather beautiful with silken ivory hair, pushed past him and Ryan frowned in brief, mild recognition before a woman touched his elbow.

The boy was Isak and he, like Ryan, had a week off. To have a week off was always a test, he thought, and he assumed he was supposed to spend as little money as possible if he was to pass the test but sometimes that was hard and so he had devised a plan. If he could shop somewhere miles across town then he would spend so long getting there that he would have little time left in which to spend his cash. Always cash. You couldn't trust cards. Cleverer yet, he would sometimes get lost on purpose to delay his arrival at the store. Today's store was one that had opened just a month earlier and although it was painfully trendy, it was expensive and therefore quiet and the staff had not seemed to mind that he carefully felt the texture of all its swimming trunks. He knew perfectly well the store was closest to Covent Garden station but Isak let the train take him in the opposite direction, to kill time. At home, his mother, Ulla, slid open the huge wardrobe in Isak's room and wondered where all the swimming trunks her son bought ended up. There were only ten pairs that she could see.

Ryan had stood stock-still as Isak sped past, looking so hopeless that a short, round and rosy, kindly woman touched his elbow and asked if he needed help with directions.

'Oh, no, but thanks,' he said. He was lost but not in the

way the woman imagined. Why on earth would Millie take such a circuitous route to Baker Street? And was he a very bad tracker or deliberately losing her?

He was now seven stops from Dollis Hill and his mother's house. He decided to surprise her and even bought a small bouquet of flowers en route.

Grace was so delighted he wondered why he was not more generous with his time for her.

'Oh my, this is nice,' she said several times.

He told her about his trip to Spain.

'You've always kept in touch with that Paul,' she said. 'I'm assuming, if you were to wed, he's to be your best man.'

'I hadn't given it any thought, but probably,' Ryan said.

'Putting it another way,' Grace said, her Dublin accent to the fore, 'if he got wed and he didn't choose you, would you be getting upset about it?'

'Nope. It's not a big deal, Mam, it's women who fuss over wedding dramas.'

Grace sighed good-naturedly.

'Well, maybe you'll find out for sure one day,' she said. 'And anyway what is it with my children and their travelling? Hana is staying in a castle somewhere in Kent this weekend with her new man, not that I've met him yet.'

Chapter 8

That night Ryan dreamed he was running through dark, clammy tunnels without end towards a woman he thought was Millie but who, the closer he got, gradually turned into Ellen.

He woke, his heart racing, his feet twitching from all the phantom running. The closest to this feeling he had had before was the day of her funeral. He had never been to a funeral and he had not wanted to go to this one. Paul had taken him, made him put on a suit, but they had got lost and as soon as it seemed likely they would miss the service, Ryan panicked that he had to be there and when he did arrive he was sick in the car park. He remembered how everyone was so kind to Ellen's mother. He avoided her. She had been driving and driving carelessly, stupidly. Fat, murdering cow, he thought then and had no reason to soften his view of her now.

And then it was over. They had been so in love they would stop to kiss in the street in the way that only the truly in love know the moment to kiss can happen to couples at any time and in any place. And then she was not there any more. He was yet another student suffering a break-up, only his was a properly clean break. No changing of minds, no playing of games, no flirting with strangers in front of one another. It was over forever. He didn't hate her for dying but he hated her mother for killing her. Fat, murdering cow.

He did not bother with porridge on the Thursday. He ate some toast smothered in butter that was gritty from previous toast smotherings and took up his position. Six trains trundled by and then he saw her in the seventh. She made her move at Leicester Square. He was feeling alert now after his trembling awakening. He decided the dream was a sign he should continue with his quest. He had nothing to lose except his dignity. Losing her at Baker Street had, in any case, riled his pride. That was no kind of story to tell to Paul or Naomi. He was determined not to let her vanish again.

Her steps were serene, always serene, he noted. This was not a woman who succumbed to panic. She was neither rushing nor dawdling. As she walked onto the platform the wind signified a northbound train was imminent and she paused, so he paused, and then she walked a few steps to a thinning of the crowd and entered the carriage. In order not to lose sight he was almost directly behind her, buffeted by two cheap-suited men wearing lanyards. He was forced to almost hide behind them because there were no seats and he could not be sure which direction she would look to next. They were on the train for just the one stop. She jumped delicately onto the platform at Tottenham Court Road. Ryan looked at the map as if trying to work out his route and made a fake last-second dash to leave the carriage. This, he was sure, was where she would leave the Underground altogether, but he found himself following her towards the Central line.

They were heading east and Millie looked settled. She took

out her new book. He tried not to stare. He tried to fathom why the windows were tinted as if to protect from the glare of a Saharan sun. He decided he did not much like the vibe of the Central line. It was gloomy and it was miserable. There was no Saharan sun. They travelled through Holborn and Bank and as Liverpool Street approached the vast majority of people in their carriage shuffled to their feet; she did not even look up. At last she put away her novel as they neared Stratford. She was having another bad day, the sort of day without hope. Nothing had happened on the Central line, just as she knew it wouldn't, and yet this huge weight had kept her there. It was like being in prison and whenever she felt this way Sylvie became claustrophobic. She needed the Underground version of the exercise yard. She was shy but she needed, she assumed, someone to see her, someone to tap her arm, someone to have need of her, and so she had to be patient until they did.

*

Ryan had begun to wonder why he had not brought a bottle of water with him. The Tube in summer could be dehydrating but Millie was still calm and composed. Stratford was as baffling as the last time he had been there. The concourse was almost overwhelming. There were staircases everywhere with people scurrying on different levels, bumping into each other. He had no idea what came next but she turned towards the sunlight and the Docklands Light Railway. He missed the fact that she lifted her face to the light and exhaled. Perhaps it was because he was embarrassed that he was so thirsty, so obviously in need of mothering, of the need to be reminded to take a drink on a long trip, that he felt he had been sucked into a children's TV show. The DLR was like a toy-town train and, more worryingly, not moving. He scuttled quietly further from view not at all sure in which direction they would be heading. It bothered him that he had not expected Millie to stay on past Stratford, that she had become utterly unpredictable.

The LED display told Ryan Pudding Mill Lane was the next station, which only confirmed that he was in some alternate reality, that some puppets would soon appear and speak to him in gibberish. They travelled past All Saints and West India Quay and then Millie rolled her shoulders. They would be changing at Canary Wharf. Or leaving. God, I hope this is where it ends, he thought. It was not. Millie headed for the Jubilee line. He followed. She took a train earmarked for Wembley Park. He followed. She stepped off at Waterloo and as the escalators took them higher and higher he breathed a sigh of relief.

They were leaving the Underground.

As he tapped his Visa card on the exit pad he thought how much value he had taken from the system and whether it mattered to the economy of Transport for London that he had spent almost three hours going nowhere in particular for the price of one single fare, unless the system was tracking him and charging him extra for breathing in all that subterranean air.

Millie's body language changed as she walked out onto the station concourse. He was not sure what it meant but she looked less sure of herself, hesitant. He hung back, she turned left. He followed. She turned again, and he saw that she was entering the Ladies toilets. This represented an opportunity for him to buy some water but he needed to buy it while keeping an eye out for her return to the concourse. He looked to his left and to his right. He needed a shop opposite the Ladies but there wasn't one. A Starbucks was situated next door but if he went inside he might miss her exit. He decided to risk it but there was a queue. He found a £2 coin and darted to the till.

'Sorry, emergency,' he said and handed over the coin while holding the water in front of his face. He darted back out again and leaned against the wall, glugging back the water, too thirsty to feel foolish, too tired to care that he might look as if he was trying to re-enact the sniper scene set at Waterloo station at the start of *The Bourne Ultimatum*.

Three minutes later, she emerged and turned left. She did not glance in his direction and he believed himself to still be completely unnoticed. She took the escalator that led up to a sort of mezzanine level. He followed. She sat at a banquette that overlooked the departure boards and she picked up the menu. He took a seat two rows behind her. She must be meeting someone for an early lunch or a drink, he thought. No one else came. She spoke to the waitress, who, a few minutes later came to him. He ordered a croque monsieur and an orange juice. He had already finished the bottle of water. Millie opened her book. Ryan ate without appetite. He was at a loss to explain what was happening. He watched her pay her bill, having already asked for his. She stood up sooner than he expected which meant he had to leave a larger tip than was necessary.

She walked towards him so he turned his head away as if seeking out the time of his train to Poole or Teddington and then saw her head dipping out of sight as she took the down escalator. He followed. She followed the signs to the Jubilee line and they travelled together, but not really together, to Green Park whereupon she stepped on to a northbound Victoria line train. This was the stuffiest line so far. He was hot and bothered and confused. At Warren Street, she alighted but sat down on a seat and took out her book.

This presented a problem. He could not loiter on the same platform even though she was not looking around her. He began to realize that her body language was that of someone waiting not searching. She was not even really travelling, this endless traveller, she was waiting, he thought, waiting for something that would make her stop moving.

He walked to the southbound platform and then strolled back again. She was still there, still reading. He worried that he was being watched on CCTV so on a whim caught a train to Oxford Circus – now beginning to feel he really was a sub-standard Jason Bourne – got off and headed back to Warren Street. She was still there so he quickly stepped back onto the train to the next stop, Euston, and repeated the trick. She was still there. He ran his hands through his hair, exasperated. He needed the bathroom. He left Warren Street station, used the Gents in the nearest pub, ordered a bottle of Becks, drank it quickly, reciting to himself the mantra that he was solving a mystery, and then returned to the Northbound platform. She was still there. Still serene. Still waiting.

He walked to the southbound platform and examined the Tube map. Camden was not far away. He had not been for a long while. He would wander around Camden for half an hour or so, return, and then make a decision if she had not made it for him by vanishing. He wandered, aimlessly, unimpressed by the diversions of overpriced urban fashion and returned to Warren Street. She was still there, not reading now, but gazing towards the far end of the platform. He began to feel twitchy and uneasy. 'I am solving a mystery,' he muttered, far from convinced he was close to any such thing. She reminded him of art students who sit on a bench in a gallery and stare too long at a single painting, as if the talent of the artist might snake its way into their soul. He took the next southbound train to Green Park, changed to the Piccadilly line, alighted at King's Cross and took the Victoria line back to Warren Street. It was, by now, 3.20 p.m.

She had gone.

There was a voicemail from Hana. Her voice was trembling. She was sorry to do this to him but she was going away with Ed the following weekend and could he stay with Mam, who had insisted she would be fine the previous time, but Hana could tell she was exhausted by it.

Ryan was gripped, momentarily, with panic. What if Hana left home altogether to live with this Ed in East London? Would he have to move back to Dollis Hill, take Grandpa to the toilet, eat bacon sandwiches, sometimes fluffy, sometimes toasted, to give his life variety, every day before work?

He texted her not to worry, that he could move in again for a few days and he thought, later, that to add the word 'again' was mean-spirited of him. Hana deserved some freedom, some fun. In fact, he was forced to concede, if he was being neutral, she really ought to leave home right now and let her brother take up the slack. It was his turn. She had spoiled him.

'Lovely tan,' Hana said breezily as she handed over the reins. Grace was quiet. She had expected Ed to pick up Hana from the house. She had expected to meet him at last but Hana had a few minutes earlier told her they were meeting at Euston station. Ryan squeezed his sister's arm in solidarity and then remembered he had given her a copy of the book he had seen Millie reading for a reason.

'How was that novel I gave you?' he said. 'Rubbish?'

'Oh, not too rubbish, all very melodramatic with a child, illegitimate of course, killed in a train accident and the mother mutilated and therefore unrecognizable when she lives with her husband and his new wife. Standard Victorian highly plausible plot.'

'Oh,' Ryan said. He was disappointed and also unsettled by the mention of train accident.

Hana, still bemused, if touched, that her little brother had bought the strange book in the first place, gave him a quick, strong hug before putting on her backpack. She had another hour before needing to leave but he could not blame her for dashing away. Neither could he blame Grace for feeling disappointed. After all, he too wanted to vet Ed, to check that his sister was not one of those people who repeated their mistakes, who had a weakness for the wrong relationship.

Grandpa was staring at the television. He held up his hand when Hana shouted her farewell as if absorbed by a complicated plotline that needed his full attention. Ryan glanced at the screen. Grandpa was watching a shopping channel.

'He seems to think he knows that one, Sandra Something,' Grace said as Sandra whizzed some fruit to make a smoothie, a drink Grandpa had never ordered, never tasted but appeared to be an expert on.

'Smashing girl,' Grandpa said as Ryan took his bag to his room where, as usual, everything was spick and span for him. Clean sheets, fresh duvet cover, space in the wardrobe. Photographs of his grandparents on their wedding day, of them holding Hana, holding him, holding Tom. Hard to tell really, he and Tom looked so alike. They might both look like their father but Ryan could not be sure. He had never met him, not properly, not that he could remember.

His brother had loved him, so he was told. As for the truth of Tom, he had no idea really. He had pieced together his death so meticulously it held the vibrancy of a pop video but the information was gleaned from so many different sources, from snippets spoken by his grandfather, his mother, his sister, the neighbours, the cousins they rarely visited. No one had ever sat him down and told him everything, beginning to end, the whole truth of it, and he had never asked. He had never wanted to make his mother cry.

What he thought he knew was that it started with him in a high chair screaming for a 'barna' and his father taking Tom to the shop to buy bananas and while they were there some milk and, with a nod and a wink, some cans for when the kiddies were in bed. It was April and the sun was shining on the fresh puddles and it was warm enough for Tom not to need his coat, which was excellent news for Tom hated wearing jumpers let alone extra layers with buttons or zips. And so off they bounced, Dad and Tom, while Ryan yelped for a 'barna' that never came.

*

His father's name was Joe. His brother's middle name was Joe. Grandpa's name is Joe. It is the twist in the tale for Ryan that Grandpa is his father's father, that Grace loves him like her own and Grandpa forgets sometimes that she is not a blood relation at all. It is the twist and it is the beauty in the ugliness of it all, the way her life was shattered. No more winks, no more cans when the kiddies had gone to bed.

Joe had walked on the pavement of the high street and let Tom run on an adjacent path, flanked by flower beds, and belonging to a long, low block of 1920s flats. It was safer that way. Tom saw it as his personal racetrack and he ran at speed, his face turned towards his father. 'Look at me run,' was the expression on his face. 'Look at me, running on my own. I'm faster than the bus, I'm faster than the cars, I'm running faster than you.' Joe smiled, sidestepped a woman with a buggy, a trio of teenagers, all the while his own head turned to watch the wind in the hair of his eldest son, one last time.

Joe did not, afterwards, have the answers she needed so Grace would not let him look after Hana and Ryan on his own. He was angry, then sullen, then tearful, then drunk, then violent and then gone. He drank a bottle of whisky and stumbled in front of a lorry carrying frozen foods on the M6. Grace did not know why it was the M6 and she did not care. Or rather, she felt she had already lost him back in April. The details of her husband's subsequent breakdown did not resonate until many years later and, when they did, she wept with an intense, if brief, wave of guilt. Poor Joe. It had been worse for him after all.

She had half feared Hana giving her a grandchild, of

reliving those days of nappies and tantrums and snot-strewn snuggles that would remind her of Tom, and then she had been indignant on her daughter's behalf that Hana's selfish husband had not wanted a child, and then relieved that such a dreadful marriage had not yielded one. Having Hana home was cosy and helpful and mostly harmonious – but it wasn't putting a baby in the family. Now her daughter was with this Ed and she was hopeful, if nervous. For all the pain a child can bring, her daughter deserved some unconditional love, she thought, and her Hana would make a wonderful mother, she had practised, after all, for so long on Ryan.

'So, Ed will come for Sunday lunch if you like,' Hana said.

'This Sunday?' Grace said.

'Yes, this Sunday,' Hana said. 'He's…'

'What? Is he a vegan person? There's lots of that around and, if he is, you'll have to help me out.'

'No, he's… really nice and he likes beef.'

Grace was so relieved, it was only hours later she wondered what Hana had been about to say.

Both women independently phoned Ryan to tell him to be there.

'I want to come too,' Naomi said. She was joking but, on reflection, Ryan thought it a fine idea. Her presence would remove some of the spotlight from Ed, defuse his potential embarrassment at being the centre of attention.

'Have you warned Ed about Grandpa?' Grace asked Hana as they peeled potatoes together.

'No, I don't think that's fair, to tell people what to think.

Ed might have his own grumpy grannie for all I know and by comparison Grandpa could be excellent company. So, Mam, don't feel the need to apologize for him.'

Grace sensed an agenda but she could not fathom what it was, so she changed the subject.

'I've met this Naomi, you know,' she said. 'She's very tall and she's his lodger.'

'And his friend,' Hana said.

Grace sniffed sharply. Her children were ganging up on her, she could tell, but it was hard to stay cross. It was going to be such a lovely lunch.

Ryan and Naomi arrived first. Naomi awkwardly handed Grace a small orchid and said, 'Thank you for having me,' unable to stop herself sounding like she was eight-years-old. Ryan had brought a large carrier bag of booze. He had been certain beer and wine were necessities but then, as he plonked it on the table, wondered if maybe Ed was teetotal and whether he should hide it all until he found out.

'Very nice smells coming from your kitchen,' Naomi said, wondering at how roast dinners were an all-year-round dish and should have been the last thing she wanted on a muggy August day.

'Hope you are hungry, my dear,' Grace said, distracted, as Hana had left to meet Ed from the train over half an hour ago. But then the key flickered in the lock and in walked her daughter and her new friend.

Everyone shook hands apart from Grandpa, who had dozed off in the heat untroubled by the additional voices. Ryan suggested they sit in the garden, which was small but with room enough to cater for the five of them. Or rather the four of them as Grace meddled nervously over the hob wondering why she had been so keen to meet Ed when now she felt so timid and fearful of saying the wrong thing.

Ed was in his late forties. This was not so ridiculous, thought Ryan, given Hana was nearly forty, but he had the air of someone who has lived a life whereas Ryan felt he was still getting started. Still, he liked the way Hana hung on his every word and how he clasped her hand from time to time, but then he wondered if Hana was too quiet and Ed too talkative. Naomi glugged back the wine with a ferocity that did not suit the suburban blandness of the occasion and as they moved inside to the dining table, Ryan felt he was in a dream where everything was off kilter.

Naomi walked in ahead of Ed and Ryan noted that they were same height. Exactly the same height. Behind them, Hana also noticed they were the same height and she flushed with an unwanted wave of possessiveness and cursed herself for not wearing heels.

In the seven steps it took Ed and Naomi to reach the dining table from the small patio, Naomi's long bobbed hair brushed Ed's chin and their limbs mingled sensuously, lightly. Hana was certain her boyfriend breathed in Naomi's scent, no doubt an alluring mix of summer sweat and a Chanel perfume. Perhaps she had rubbed coconut tanning lotion onto her elegant neck. Hana squinted to see if there were any hairs poking out from under her bare armpits but she wore her pink vest top to perfection.

As Ryan and Grace brought out the plated beef and the

bowls of roast potatoes and baby carrots, Hana sat feeling the odd one out as Naomi spoke about her studies. There was nothing Hana felt she could contribute and what made it worse was that, although they were talking about science, Naomi made it sound like seductive poetry. She spoke of the spotted lanternfly, its love of apples and hops and how people were on constant alert in New York in case it reached the Big Apple from Pennsylvania.

'Biodiversity,' Ed said, leaving the word hanging in the air before adding, 'I don't think that existed when I chose my degree. Pharmacology, that was my choice, and it sounds like the strict uncle of the daring and reckless young biodiversity.'

Naomi turned to Hana.

'What did you study?' she asked, and at that precise moment Hana hated her.

'I didn't,' she said flatly.

Ed covered her hand.

'Hana decided to travel and she more than likely learned more doing that than we did in our laboratories and lecture theatres,' he said.

He was being kind but she flinched at how they were 'our' laboratories, '*their*' lecture halls. Ed had not yet poured gravy over his food and he was already half of a perfect couple. She pictured Naomi and Ed flying to Stockholm or Geneva or wherever you had to bloody get to in order to collect Nobel prizes for saving the Granny Smith.

'I need to travel more,' Naomi said and she was about to quiz Hana about her wanderings but Grace and Ryan had sat down and she remembered this was supposed to be a lunch for Ed's integration, so she took another gulp of wine and smiled benignly at them all.

Hana had supposed she would be embarrassed or annoyed by how her mother interacted with Ed but now she was grateful for the way Grace made assumptions about them being in a serious relationship.

'So, excuse a nosy mother, Ed, but indulge me and tell me how you met Hana exactly.'

Ed threw his head back and laughed.

'She hasn't told you?' he said.

Grace glanced between her daughter and her boyfriend. Hana flushed and looked at her plate. She did not know how he would tell the story.

'I was searching, in vain – because I don't have the knack for it – for a way to take a half-decent snap of the rocks and the sea – a very twinkly sea – and I stumble upon this woman I had not yet spoken to, although I had noticed her, and I mean *literally* stumble upon her because she is crouched down pulling up her shorts having found a not-so-private spot after all for a pee.'

Naomi spluttered with laughter and Ryan smiled politely.

'That sounds a dreadful way to be starting off,' Grace said.

'Ah, but she was surrounded by these swaying pink flowers and long grass and it was so ludicrous that we both chuckled at the same time and I told her she was the most beautiful woman on an interrupted toilet break I had ever seen and she said, well, at least it hadn't happened on a side street off Tottenham Court Road, and I decided there and then I wanted to complete the day's walking with her.'

Hana looked up. Grace was almost tearful, Ryan was

looking relieved and Naomi was making patterns in her gravy with the quartered potato on the end of her fork. At the other end of the room, Grandpa made happy spluttering snorting snoring sounds.

'I made her wash her hands at the first pub we came to,' Ed added and Hana punched his arm, glad to have an excuse to make proprietary physical contact with him in front of the Amazonian Naomi (who was now bored and sleepy but had a feeling she was trapped for at least another hour or so).

'That's what they say, isn't it?' Naomi slurred. 'You find love when you are least expecting it and I for one have never expected to find it while taking a piss.'

Naomi waved her glass in the air and continued: 'You see, me and Ryan have found love but not the toilet.' She frowned. She had expected something wittier to emerge from her mouth.

Grace's dark eyes became glistening and beady.

'What's this, then, Ryan, about finding love?'

Ryan was busy kicking Naomi under the table.

'I have found nothing, Mam, nothing at all. Me and Naomi have both spotted people we quite like but don't know very well, that's all. I'll help clear the table.'

Hana spotted a denouement, a trump card.

'We'll help too,' she said, 'and Naomi can have a snooze next to Grandpa.'

Naomi did snooze, but later, on the Tube ride home, her chin resting on her crossed arms over her bag. She was too tall to rest on Ryan's shoulders. He scanned the carriage, automatically, and sighed. Even though he knew Millie to be peculiar he had not shaken off his obsession. In a way, he thought, it had become a deeper infatuation, one that was more layered, more complex. There might be a reasonable explanation for her day underground, there might be a fantastical one, but either way, it was worth knowing, wasn't it? And what did he have to lose if he found out? He brightened. He had nothing to lose. He did not have her, did not know her. If it all goes wrong, he thought, I am no worse off.

'You're very bouncy,' Naomi said later as Ryan zipped through the washing-up, having made them omelettes for a supper they were not hungry for.

'You're very bounceless,' he replied.

'I'm going to not drink at all next week, not a drop,' she said. She stood to look out of the window. The children next door were playing pat ball badly in their pyjamas and the sound of it was less irritating when you could see what was making it.

'There are lots of photos of you as a boy in your mum's house,' Naomi said. 'I mean, loads.'

'They're mostly of Tom,' Ryan said. 'We looked similar so it's hard to tell but they're mostly of him.'

'Oh, right,' Naomi said. She knew he had a brother, briefly, but had half forgotten it.

'I'm not sure I would want to be surrounded by pictures of someone who had died,' she said. 'I don't mean it's creepy, I just think it would be like a permanent advertisement for unhappiness. I mean, every day your mum is reminded of a son who has gone.'

Ryan had thought the same for a long time but had eventually decided that for his mother the photographs did not provoke melancholy because the sadness would be with her whether there were reminders around the house or not.

'It's fine,' was all he said to Naomi. 'She's a very brave woman.'

'And are you a brave boy?' Naomi asked. 'Have you given up on your girl?'

They both sat down.

'OK, let's brainstorm,' he said. 'I've decided not to give up, at least not until I know for sure if she is a bit crazy.'

'Excellent,' Naomi said. 'You do realize you do not need to follow her again.'

Naomi tapped her fingers against her lap as Ryan frowned.

'I certainly never want a day like that again,' he said. 'She never stopped travelling. It spooked me. And it was exhausting. And I found out nothing, so why do you look so pleased with yourself?'

'OK,' she said. 'She stopped for lunch, didn't she? Well, you can miss out the morning session of aimless Tube rides and go straight to the…'

'It was a restaurant at Waterloo.'

'Yup, there you are, you go to Waterloo for lunch and sit on the same table and ask her something.'

'She might never have lunch there again.'

'So? If she never has lunch there again then you've wasted a few lunch hours. Try it a few times first at least. Don't be so pessimistic. And I know you get a longer lunch break on Wednesdays so just go on Wednesdays to start with.'

'Oh, I don't know. It all sounds like I could get arrested for being predatory.'

'No, no, no,' she said. 'I think it's romantic and mysterious and I'm jealous. I'm all out of clever ways to woo Cappi.' She paused. 'Shit, I don't even know he'll definitely be here for the new term.'

*

Ed had been gallant, Hana thought, to stay until Grandpa woke up. Grace had made gooey meringues, as they were more summery than cake, to be served with a fruit salad. The serving of them roused Grandpa and Grace led him to the bathroom so he could freshen up, maybe sit at the table for a change, meet Hana's friend.

As he returned, Ed stood and shook his hand. Hana held her breath. Grandpa grasped Ed's hand firmly, warmly. 'My, you must be Merv's son. You are most welcome, lad.'

Ed had subconsciously prepared himself for an old man's casual racism but not for mistaken identity. He glanced at Hana, unsure if he was supposed to contradict her grandfather.

'This is Ed, Grandpa, I met him on one of my walking holidays.'

'Yes, yes,' Grandpa said impatiently, 'Merv's lad. Spitting image.'

Ed shrugged. His father was a distant memory but he was pretty sure he had been called Kenneth.

'What the hell are these?' Grandpa added as he bit into a meringue. 'It's sticking to my teeth.'

Grace darted to her feet, removed his plate and brought a shop-bought muffin from the kitchen.

Ed tried not to smile. Hana grimaced apologetically. He winked at her. She exhaled. Grandpa studiously devoured his cake, asked for a fresh pot of tea, peered out the window suspiciously and announced he would take a nap as if that was something unusual, then shuffled back to his chair.

Before he closed his eyes, he called out, 'Give my best to your family.'

'Absolutely,' Ed said.

Ed asked for extra meringue and told Grace she was an excellent cook. As he stood to leave he noticed the tears running down Grandpa's cheeks. He was moved, believing the old man to be lost in reverie about the mysterious Merv, while also hoping he did not have to meet him again and have to pretend he was someone else's son.

He noticed there were many more photographs of Ryan than Hana on the narrow hall walls but then spotted one of a young Hana with a toddler and a baby. He was about to ask about it but thought twice. There had been a sadness in Grace that mirrored the sadness of his own mother, and there had been warmth in the house but also a hollowness. He would not be overly keen to return.

There had been a rapping at the door. It was Tilda, a neighbour, breathless and agitated. She told Grace she would stay with Hana and Ryan while Grace went to the hospital.

'I'm sure he's fine, a bad bump on the head maybe, but you'll want to be there.'

Be there just in case, thought Grace, and in a daze she found herself at Joe's side, both of them staring in disbelief at the still-crumpled Tom while Tilda fed the agitated Ryan, now desperate for his banana, some chocolate from her handbag.

If she could take it back she would. 'How did you let him run into a freezer? What's he doing, running into a falling freezer? Did he have to be running so fast? Why were you not holding his hand? Did you not tell him to look where he was going?'

Grace kept the photographs out of love but also as a penance, a reminder that she was not the only one who suffered.

Chapter 9

Ryan mulled over the idea of spending his Wednesday lunches in Waterloo station. He decided he had four options. He could follow her again; he could give up on her completely; he could keep making little trips to Waterloo; or he could just speak to her while she was sat on the Piccadilly line with him.

There was an oversized novelty dice in one of kitchen drawers. He decided to let fate decree what happened next. He rolled a five. Five had not been allocated a fate. Other than procrastination. He would procrastinate. His days were taken up by postgrads and professors and meetings in his labs. Soon there would be the influx of undergraduates that meant broken flasks and spilled ethanol. Soon it would be autumn and that would mark half a year of hoping to catch the same train as the candyfloss girl.

Paul had an interview at Brunel, then met him after work.

'They want me to start in January; well, they want me now, but I can't leave Seville until Christmas.'

Ryan was impressed if not surprised. Everyone wanted Paul. He was a very good lecturer and he churned out papers that people wanted to discuss. Right now, no one could mention Fabry disease without using Paul's name in the same sentence.

He had a way of owning genetic disorders. He had an aura. The driest of topics became scintillating simply because he could smile while explaining them. This, it transpired, was a rare skill. The smiling scientist, that was Paul.

He was staying in a hotel at Heathrow and insisted he meet Ryan at Acton Town the following morning so that he could take a peek at Millie.

'You're kidding,' Ryan said.

'No, I'm intrigued. I think we should follow her together.'

'She's not always on the train, and no, we shouldn't.'

'I have a feeling,' Paul said.

He was already on the platform holding a tray with takeaway flat whites as Ryan alighted, five minutes earlier than usual.

'She wasn't on that one, then?' Paul said.

'No,' Ryan said, 'but you can move to London and bring me coffee every morning anyway.'

They stood on the platform, Paul relaxed, Ryan agitated.

'This is fun,' Paul said.

'No, it isn't,' Ryan said.

The next train pulled in. Ryan could not see her so Paul tugged at his jumper, dragging him back onto the platform.

'We'll wait,' he said, sipping his coffee.

It did not occur to Ryan to lie. He had never lied to Paul and so when he saw her on the next train – tucked into the corner of the front carriage – he simply nodded to his friend. There were no seats for them but they could see her clearly enough, her eyes closed, her hands on her lap, her nearly red hair loose as if in celebration of the change in season.

Paul was surprised. The woman was slender but not, to him, in an appealing way, and while her hair was distinctive, it did not strike him as particularly interesting, although he could see a sort of prettiness that for someone else might be captivating.

The train whizzed into South Kensington station and Ryan shuffled off, annoyed as he always was by those who tried to board before those leaving had alighted, speaking to Paul as if he was on his shoulder, but Paul remained in the carriage and gave Ryan the thumbs-up as he stared incredulously back at him through the window.

Gordon was still running the bridge club so Naomi could not attend it but she could time being nearby when it ended, just in case Cappi was back on board. He wasn't. But she knew he was back at the university. She had seen him on the stairs. She had seen him on the stairs and yet her heart had not skipped the anticipated beat and in that moment she knew there had been a dilution in her yearning – and the dilution had been down to the man she had met in a fairly drab house not too far from Wembley where a grandpa had snored in an armchair, the baby carrots had been smothered with chopped parsley and she had drunk so much her head span all evening. Inevitably, she thought, that man is out of bounds. I will never lust after someone who is free and lusts after me.

They sat in a pub defined by its shiny wooden pews and booths, low doorframes and fine ales.

'Tell me you didn't.'

'I didn't.'

'Oh Christ, you did.'

'I did.'

There was a silence. It was companionable but nervy.

'Oh, just tell me.'

Paul leaned forward.

'North, south, east, west, emerging for lunch at Paddington,' he said in the voice of the man who reads the shipping forecast on the radio.

'And you were desperate for a piss by then, I bet,' Ryan said.

'I went when she went,' he said, sounding pleased with himself.

'And then?'

'Oh, well, and then I lost her. Or maybe she lost me. We won't know until you've dated her a few times and you've come clean.'

'What do you think is going on with her?'

'Not a damned clue, mate. She is sort of efficient about it, like she is going somewhere specific but that somewhere keeps changing. She is very calm, very patient when she reaches a platform, sort of assesses it like – I don't know – like she is deciding if it is clean enough.'

'Do you think she is… off limits?'

Paul laughed.

'She ought to be but no, weirdly, no she isn't.'

Ryan was quiet.

'So?' Paul said after a minute or so.

'So. Looks like she could eat at any station so I'm relieved I didn't waste any lunch hours trekking to Waterloo. Might be weeks before she goes there again. I think I need a new strategy. Maybe I should spill a drink on her; pretend I'm reading whatever book she's reading.'

'If it was me,' Paul said, 'I'd give it one more go on the Tube. See it through to the end. I don't know why, feels it needs to be that way.'

Ryan gurned into his beer.

'Yeah, maybe.' And then they settled into talk of Spain, the tapas bars of Seville, the flaws in tiki taka football, Paul's impending move to London and yet another genetic disorder he had his eye on.

'There is work on genetically engineering mosquitoes out of existence at your place,' Paul said, 'so I might ask for a meeting and do some research there. Aww, I might be inches from your lab, mate; we can wave at each other through the glass every day. We could commute in together.'

And so the conversation ended as it had begun, with tales of the Underground and the girl who never got off it.

In the end several London universities agreed to share Paul. It was better than not having him at all and each of them believed after half an academic year he would choose just one of them as his base, his home, the place that would bear their name when his next paper was published. He flew back to Spain, with the warm glow of plans well made and of having kept open all the options he liked. He was a hard worker but on this particular late-September evening, had you peered through the window of his spacious second-floor flat on the outskirts of Seville, you would have found him sprawled on the floor with a pink highlighter pen, gazing at an enlarged map of the London Underground.

Paul retraced the route Millie had taken to Paddington,

convinced he would see a pattern or logic that had eluded him. If this was a tale of the supernatural, he thought, the highlighter pen would spell out a message.

Leave me alone.

Help me.

How do I get to Madame Tussauds?

He chuckled to himself and then stood to look at the bigger picture. Just in case there really was a pattern or a message and he became vaguely aware that his heartbeat had quickened. He so wanted there to be some sense to this but there was none. If you were generous about it then you could claim Millie had travelled in the shape of a spiral, but the truth was that her route was a mess. It was random. It was the journey of a woman killing time until lunch.

He shook his head and thought if there was a message it was that he must not kill time until he could leave Spain for London. Paul liked very much the fact that whenever he left a university no one at it was relieved to see the back of him. Every single city so far had asked him to stay, to reconsider. Those he had tutored gave him gifts, bought him dinner, those in charge had tried to negotiate without seeming desperate.

He was told, again and again – in modern, bright rooms, in cloistered ancient ones – he would be welcomed back at any time, but how he *adored* the anticipation of the next place, the different architecture, the different sounds and echoes, the new people, the altered dynamics, the smells of a new city, the finding of the most aesthetically pleasing route from his new home to the campus. He had known deep down for a while that he would end up in London near Ryan.

He had not been jealous of his best mate's relationship with

Ellen. In fact, he had liked how easily the three of them could hang out, sometimes with a girl he was dating, sometimes not. He never seemed to stay with one girl for very long. He, like Ryan, had not quite understood the meaning of death. One day Ellen was laughing in the bar, being taught how to play pool, proving rather adept at it – potting three balls in a row and wagging her finger at him and Ryan – and then, a day later, she was in a car, driven by her mother, and was thrown through the windscreen while taking off her jumper because the car was too warm and because her mother was an idiot.

It was sudden and brutal and surreal. Where there had been two, there had been three, and then there were two again. Paul had dated a junior doctor in Toronto who disconcertingly held her booze better than he did. One evening she'd narrowed her eyes as she settled into her armchair and told him he had been frozen in time the day Ellen died, unable to fall in love, unable to commit because he was aware more sharply than most that relationships can snap in half, that it is better not to become too happy, too settled, too content. She had taken yet another a sip of her single malt, paused, breathed in and told him there was a reason he flitted from city to city, from continent to continent.

Paul had deliberately remained impassive. He told her that all she had said would make sense if it was Ryan who was the wanderlust professor. It was Ryan's girlfriend who had been killed, not his. That, she said, made it worse. Paul had been clear-headed enough to see Ryan's pain, his fragility, for what it was, to know that men can suffer in love so they had better not fall too deep.

He and the junior doctor split up a week later. She said

he was being predicable. He told her it was a self-fulfilling prophecy. Still, he thought, as he played with the lid of his marker pen, she had been nice, the doctor, and maybe she had a point all along because he felt no regret at all that they never saw each other again, not even accidentally. He had stopped it before they fell in too deep.

The Underground map glimmered in the orange-tinged late-afternoon light that suffused his living room. Paul had desecrated it with his pink pseudo-spirals. The map was a design of acute beauty, he thought, and as he stared at the scroll he noticed the river Thames was marked on it and he wondered if it had always been there, on the map, because he was certain he had been in London one day and studied a Tube map without the river there. But he could summon no good reason why the river would be included one day and left off on another.

Perhaps, he thought, Millie simply loved the Underground, or was a secret traveller – the way there were secret shoppers and secret diners. Perhaps she was being paid to monitor the service, the contentment of passengers. Perhaps she was being paid to look for fare dodgers or graffiti artists or drunks. There had to be a reason.

There had to be a reason because Ryan had not been much interested in anyone after Ellen and, yes, it was not inconceivable that he had fixated upon Millie because she was mysterious and perhaps unobtainable and therefore safe, but Paul felt things were coming together for his friend. Paul would be with him soon and surely, by Christmas, Ryan would have found a way to buy the woman known as Millie a coffee.

Chapter 10

Naomi sat at the end of the long white refectory table, peeling the foil lid from the top of an apricot yoghurt. It made a plopping sound and a small splash of it hit her black shirt as Cappi sat down opposite her. She did not notice him, she was too busy licking her index finger and rubbing at the tiny stain. Which meant when she did look up it was to see the tall Italian staring at the damp patch near her cleavage.

'Excuse,' he said nervously and she thought his voice was far too reedy for the size of him. 'I miss you not at the bridge,' he said and she stared into his eyes. She would have done the refectory washing-up for free for a fortnight to have had him say that a month ago.

'Yeah, well, Gordon was a bit of a creep,' she said.

'Oh,' Cappi said. 'I only went once this time. Ah, we can, ah, go for a walk and a drink and dinner this weekend maybe?'

He did not appear terribly sure that this was possible, and Naomi could tell it had taken him courage to ask. It sounded as if he had been playing bridge to see her and she had been playing bridge to see him. A wave of crashing sadness engulfed her for a split second. She cursed his timidity and her own lack of courage. Right now, she was not all that keen on a walk with this shy Italian, let alone a drink or dinner.

'That would be really nice,' she said.

Cappi beamed but said nothing.

'Saturday?' she said. 'The nicest walks start here anyway so I'll meet you by the main entrance at three? On Saturday?'

Cappi took her hand, the one that had been rubbing at the splurted yoghurt, and kissed it.

Naomi inwardly groaned. 'Mamma fucking mia.'

She was there on the dot of three, though, wearing her old, comfortable Doc Martens, another dark shirt, a clean one, and her best cashmere jumper casually wrapped around her waist. Cappi took her hand but she pulled it away.

'OK, we are not going to be friends if you kiss my hand again. Kiss my cheek, kiss my ass, but not my hand.'

She said this with a beaming smile lest he inwardly crumpled. Maybe, she thought, he is not a natural hand kisser, maybe he is just really, really nervous and deep down is a cool guy. There was a moment then when neither of them moved or breathed as he absorbed her words and she waited to find out how he would cope with them.

He placed his hands in his trouser pockets and took a step back.

'Are you a… lesbian?' he said.

Naomi blinked and then took a step back herself as she unleashed a clanging peal of laughter.

'Yes,' she shouted, 'yes, please!' And she turned on her heel and walked towards the park and the Serpentine, where she would buy herself an ice cream and try to not weep tears of self-pity.

'So, you know how Cappi thinks you're gay,' she said later as Ryan pottered about the kitchen. 'Well, he now also thinks I'm gay. I think the guy is an obsessive homophobe.'

'And?' Ryan said.

For a few seconds, Naomi wondered if he knew. If he knew she had fallen for Hana's Ed, that her crush on Cappi had been extinguished by a new love interest. But Ryan's expression was one of concerned innocence. Poor Naomi.

'And, to be honest, I'd gone off him anyway. Really.'

Ryan slammed down the pan he had been scouring.

'We are becoming quite ludicrous,' he said. 'Let's do something stupid. Spend money we don't have. Go to a show or something. Or a casino. Or a club.'

They ended up at a small cinema that specialized in subtitled erotica, giggling at the self-reverential nudity and lack of plot until, suddenly bored, they walked out before the end of the film and went to eat at a cramped, overpriced restaurant in Soho that was packed with brooding couples and dripping candles.

'Why are we here?' Naomi asked.

'To be deliberately self-destructive,' Ryan said. 'To allow a steak costing £24.50 to take our minds off our romantic issues.'

'But I want the monkfish costing £26,' she said.

'Then let's have them both,' he said.

'And Châteauneuf-du-Pape,' she said. 'I've heard of that one. It's posh.'

Once they had accepted the ridiculous expenditure their spontaneous Saturday night's entertainment would be costing them, they relaxed.

'Is the Cappi thing dead now?' Ryan asked.

'Yup. Is the Tube-train-girl thing still alive?'

'Oh, I don't know. It's all a bit fantastical and idiotic.'

'But intriguing. I mean, a lot more fascinating than a parody of an Italian lover who thinks it's cool to kiss the back of your hand. Have you seen her lately?'

'I saw her yesterday, in fact,' Ryan said with a smirk that was meant to convey a self-deprecating smugness.

'And?'

'Jesus, there are no more *ands*. I've followed her, Paul's followed her, and she doesn't get off the damned thing. Except to have lunch. We know she eats. We know she's had lunch at Paddington and at Waterloo. I'm prepared to go out on a limb here and say I bet she's had lunch at Euston.'

'Oh, no,' Naomi said. 'Euston's horrible. No one eats there through choice.'

'Ah, but no one sits on the Tube all day through choice, either. So I reckon she *does* dine at Euston.'

Naomi chewed through a green bean. A pricy green bean that tasted, she thought, no better than her mother's green beans.

'But that's what's interesting, isn't it? It's the choice. We don't need to know where she gets off, we need to know why she doesn't. Maybe she has no choice.'

The waiter looked mildly disgusted when they each paid half the bill. It was the sort of place a man brought a woman to show off or to end a relationship. Either way, it was usually the man who paid while the candles flickered in the faces of delight or sorrow.

The faces of Ryan and Naomi were slack with booze and too much rich food as Ryan thought he might take a day off soon. Chance his luck. Give it another go. Solve the mystery; and when he did so he would most definitely not kiss the back of Millie's hand.

He could not bring himself to book off a day he did not need to have free, so resolved to text Naomi to tell his boss he was sick the next time Millie was on his train. That day was a full three weeks after the expensive Saturday. There was a chill in the air and he had the sense she was there less often. He had not made a chart of his sightings of her but the cooler the days, the less likely he was to sit opposite her. The Tube was full of passengers in parkas and pullovers. There was a rather stunning woman scrutinizing her phone wearing a scarlet woollen coat and matching lipstick and a small gaggle of girls in prep-school uniform wearing blue felt hats with a bold pink stripe. In the corner sat Millie wearing a dark green quilted jacket. She looked up as the girls giggled and asked their teacher if anyone needed her seat. The teacher smiled and shook her head and then Millie caught Ryan's eye. He smiled too and she looked away, then back down at her book, without a flicker of recognition. He took sidelong glances and saw her caress the cover of her novel after she had reached its denouement.

Four hours later he sidled into her booth high above the platform at Waterloo.

'Is it OK if we share?' he said gently.

His ears buzzed with the nerves he felt. His peripheral vision was shot to pieces, the mezzanine-level shoppers and diners were two-dimensional, disfigured fuzzy-felt figures walking as marionettes might walk, bobbing exaggeratedly.

He wondered if he should stand up again and wished he had not spoken in the first place.

'Of course,' she replied, and so he did not stand. He remained still, waiting for the buzzing to ebb away.

She had been asked this question many times before and only once had it led to an unpleasant lunch when a woman, in her sixties perhaps – or maybe younger because her features were bloated and mottled by years of too much booze and cigarettes – had sat down and taken her acquiescence to mean she wanted company. The woman had been angry with her day, angry with her life, and her bitterness had seeped into Millie's pasta parcels. Even the waiter had noticed and gave Millie a sympathetic grimace as she pushed the half-eaten plate of food to one side.

Ryan studied the menu, occasionally darting a glance in her direction. She had taken off her coat and was wearing a subdued blue soft cotton long-sleeve T-shirt. The waiter was reasonably new and had not seen Millie before.

'You two ready to order?' he asked with the jolly twang of an Italian who had learned American English.

'We are not together,' Millie said neutrally. 'Please, could I have the dolcelatte and walnut salad and a fresh orange juice?'

'We're not together but I'd like the same,' Ryan said. 'But with garlic bread.'

'OK,' said the waiter, 'I wish all customers made my life so simple.'

'Hey,' Ryan said. 'I've just worked it out. I saw you on the Piccadilly line this morning.'

She lifted her face and looked at him steadily as the buzzing in his ears returned to taunt his rehearsed line.

'Well, that's a coincidence, I suppose,' she said.

There was a silence as Ryan rejected every possible next sentence. He could not ask her what train she was catching because he was fairly sure she was not catching one and that might make her uncomfortable. He could not say he recognized her because she was so pretty because that would make him sound corny or horny or like a pervert.

Her phone vibrated and she sat back and read a message and scrolled for a few seconds before putting it back in her bag.

Ryan slowly rolled back his shirtsleeves, wondering for the first time in his life if his forearms were too hairy or too slim. She smiled, he was sure of it.

'It's warmer now,' he said.

'Hmm,' she said. 'That's why I went for a salad.'

The waiter placed their juices in front of them. Ryan was certain he winked at him as he did so. He took a sip at the same time she did.

'This is like the opposite of speed dating,' he said, trying very hard to sound intelligent and relaxed.

'Have you been speed dating?'

'No. It sounds nasty.'

'Mc neither.'

She looked down at the concourse, at the uneven rows of people staring at the departure boards, waiting for their platform to be announced. A murmuring had begun and so she looked at the boards too and saw the words 'delayed' and 'cancelled' repeated across them.

'What's happening?' Ryan said, hopeful that the station would be in lockdown, that they would be forced to sit together for longer.

'They never say why, but there's a problem on most lines, it looks like. Leaves made soggy by this odd rainforest weather in November perhaps.'

'Humidity is definitely an issue. I've had to roll up my sleeves. You've taken off your coat.'

'Will you miss a meeting or something?' she asked him and he was startled into a gormless silence.

He had worried for so long about what to say to her that he had not considered what she might say to him.

'No, I'll be fine,' he said lamely, hating himself.

'OK,' she said, biting into a walnut. 'Me too.'

He could not prevent himself from frowning. She was so reasonable, witty, normal, beautiful – so why was she about to disappear back underground? As he chewed on his last bite of garlic bread he had a brainwave.

'I'm going to the bookshop,' he said. 'I don't suppose you are too? That would be another, very nice, coincidence.'

She smiled and delved into her bag, pushed a nearly red curl behind her left ear, and pulled out the novel he had seen her close with a sense of sad finality that morning.

'I finished this on the train,' she said. 'I thought it would last longer. So, that's not a bad idea at all.'

'Let me,' he said as the waiter brought two bills. 'You've made what would have been a dull bite to eat a very pleasant lunch.'

'No,' she said. 'I could say the same so let's pay for our own.'

But he was floating now, surprised and happy.

'In that case, let's do this again and then you can pay.'

She shrugged and pulled on her coat. As they stood she

offered her him her hand and he froze, remembering Naomi's abhorrence at Cappi's big mistake.

'I'm Sylvie,' she said, amused.

'I – sorry, I was thinking of, sorry, I'm Ryan.'

They approached the bookshop in companionable silence and split up once they walked through the door. Ryan mooched among the bestsellers, occasionally glancing around to see where she was, wondering if he needed to actually buy a book, wondering if he did whether she would think him lowbrow and dull. But he had said he needed to buy one so he had better buy one. He decided the safest bet was to buy Hana a novel, the sort that had an old watercolour on its cover and was labelled a classic. He chose an Edith Wharton simply because its illustration was so very corseted. He would give it to her at Christmas, pretend it was from Grandpa. To give her two novels she had not asked for in one year would be weird.

He timed his arrival at the cash desk to dovetail with Sylvie's.

'It's for my sister,' he said as she peered at the cover.

'Oh, you must give her this too. I've no room at home for all the books I get through.'

She handed him *The Shadow of Ashlydyat*, the very heavy novel she had finished at Blackfriars. It was by Mrs Henry Wood. He remembered ordering *East Lynne* for Hana. That had been by the same author. This was the moment to shine.

'Didn't she write *East Lynne*?' he said but, instead of seeming impressed, Sylvie looked at him guardedly.

'I think so,' she said. 'Anyway, maybe you can say hello

next time we are on the same train and then we can arrange for another lunch.'

She sounded more brusque now, in a hurry to leave, but he was uncertain what it was that had caused the mood to alter.

'Where are you off to?' he said lightly, but she did not answer. She walked instead towards the escalators that led to an array of Tube lines as if she knew exactly where she was going, and maybe she did, he thought, but he doubted it.

He felt deflated and was unwilling to head back onto the Underground immediately. He returned to the bookshop where, towards the back of the room, was Ellen, her head bowed as she traced her fingers across a stack of paperbacks.

Ryan blinked. He knew it was not a co-incidence. An elderly man walked in front of him. Ryan tilted his head to look past him. Ellen's jumper was being worn by a skinny teenage boy.

'Oh my God, you never did,' Naomi said

'Oh but I did,' he said. 'But of course, as it went so well, it had to end badly.'

'You kissed her bloody hand, didn't you?'

He could not help but laugh, but when he explained the exchange in the bookshop, Naomi nodded seriously.

'Ah, I see.'

'Well, do please explain because I don't.'

Naomi spread out her arms, rotated her wrists and wrinkled her nose.

o much. Like in
s known Andie
ly known him for
because he knows
ed. Blokes like you
nk about it. Think

Items on Loan

Library name: Portadown Library
User name: Miss Anita Wishart

Author: Rudd, Alyson,
Title: Eleven lines to somewhere
Item ID: C903973771
Date due: 11/8/2022,23:59
Date charged: 21/7/2022, 14:17

LibrariesNI
++++++++++++++++++++++++
Make your life easier
++*+*+*+*+*+*+*+*+*+*+
Email notifications are sent two days before item due dates
Ask staff to sign up for email

'It's like, well, it's like, you know tr... *Groundhog Day* when Bill Murray h... MacDowell for ten years and she has on... two days. He thinks he can impress her ... what ice creams she likes but she is spooked... don't know Mrs Henley Whateverface. Thi... about it and watch *Groundhog Day*.'

'Seen it,' he said, pouting.

'See it again,' she said.

Chapter 11

Sylvie had headed serenely towards the Bakerloo line after their lunch. Ryan had been familiar in a hard-to-pin-down-why sort of way. He had been by the far the most attractive and pleasant person to have ever struck up a conversation with her at a railway station but, also, he had seemed to be hiding something and she was perturbed. People were complicated; people were sometimes kind while being cruel. She was too busy, anyway, to be side-tracked by him and whether he was kind or cruel. She travelled to Oxford Circus. She could have sat down but she chose to stand, to sway with the bends that were peculiar to the Bakerloo, a noisy, squeaking line that she sometimes felt was used by people who failed to take their journeys seriously. She walked, slowly, to the Central line and travelled as far as Lancaster Gate. She sat on a bench and took out her new book, which was not by Mrs Henry Wood. It was *A Passage to India*, a novel she had been meaning to read for some time but was only now in the mood to begin.

She had been sat down for twenty minutes and seen five eastbound trains come and go when a short, trim man with a neat beard, aged around fifty, sat down next to her and, in the lull between an emptying and filling-up platform, asked her if she wanted to go with him to a nearby hotel.

'You look ready,' he said and her heart froze.

'Go away,' she said in a low voice.

'No,' he said as, for reasons best known him, he felt empowered, fairly sure he would get what he wanted.

She stared at the open page of her book, which was about Dr Aziz and his poetry, but the letters were jumbled. She turned the page all the same while the man stroked his knee and she felt her stomach tighten. The next train approached and she did not lift her eyes from her book. The doors opened and still she did not move. The man shuffled slightly, smugly acknowledging that by staying put the girl was coming round to the idea of a liaison, but then she leaped from the seat, her book still open, and darted into the carriage just as the doors began to close. As she exhaled a tall man in a smart dark suit glanced at her quizzically and a taller, younger man with a shock of white hair buried his head in his hands, unable to accept that sudden movements were not connected to him. Someone was letting him know he had spent too much money today.

Sylvie felt exposed, that all eyes were upon her now, that she was a misfit. It maddened her that an older man had believed it acceptable to try to pick her up. What signals had she given him by being sat quietly reading a classic novel? Her brow wrinkled at the notion that there were no safe spaces any more. She had assumed that anyone sat, absorbed in a book, was as close to invisible as you could become without a magic cloak. And Ryan, come to think of it, had seen nothing to stop him from flirting with her even though she had not looked up at him until he spoke. She began to grind her teeth in annoyance. A woman alone could not be alone, it would appear. They all think they can own you, help you, pester you, intimidate you. Only when the trains were moving was she safely in a bubble of isolation, but she could not be in motion the whole day long. It was essential she stopped from time to time, maybe for an hour, maybe for three, to give a station her time, although if anyone asked why she would not be sure of the reasoning. Her routine had not been decided by her. It had been decided for her. Most of what she did was done on instinct, after all, and where that came from, she did not know either. Her life held so little logic these days that sometimes she wanted to peer into the Tube tunnels and shriek into the darkness.

Is this all becoming untenable, she thought. What is it I am waiting for?

Eight months earlier...

'Don't go straight home,' he had said. 'Wait. I'll buy you a drink.'

He would probably be saying the same thing to her replacement in a few weeks' time.

There was a map on the wall near the ticket machines at King's Cross. The whole of London was there and accessible. She daydreamed a little, wondering if her next job would take her to an office in the City or the West End. She reached out and placed her forefinger upon Holborn station as if it were an eyesore. A job near the building she had been escorted from that morning was out of the question. She would need a fresh start and she scanned the Tube map. St James's Park would be nice. Green Park would be nice. She frowned. Were they two stations serving the same stretch of park? She did not know. She smiled, aware that she was prevaricating; aware, also, that she had done too little exploring of London since moving here to work. She needed to go home, begin the search for a new employer and a job that was not so time-consuming so that she could enjoy the metropolis.

The map told her she could catch a train that took her directly to Eastcote station and home or she might need to change at Baker Street. The platform was what she would term mildly busy. She walked towards the rear end of it, where a young woman, a small, compact woman in a long, layered skirt, was there too, holding a package tightly.

The woman turned to look at her. There was a recognition in the woman's face, she had turned as if she and Sylvie had an appointment and the strange thing was that Sylvie felt the same way. The young woman's large brown eyes flickered to life and Sylvie had to bury an urge to say hello as the beginning of the underground breeze stirred a sweet wrapper and sent a charcoal-coloured mouse scurrying into a hole. The skirt began to billow, Sylvie's hair was fluttering as their eyes met, and the young woman thought to herself that she had been found by an angel and that she could, just maybe, find some peace.

Chapter 12

There had been peace, a stillness, when Franklyn left for university, Sylvie reflected as she settled in for a long haul on the Bakerloo line. Sylvie had held her breath, or so it seemed to her, all the way back from the airport. Her mother had cried snottily, trying to smile and say jolly things while her father fiddled with the radio – a crackling voice told them about a wicket taken at the Oval. Sylvie was numb. She had so looked forward to Frank leaving, to having the undivided attention of her parents, but it seemed they would spend all the hours she hoped were hers bemoaning his absence.

'Oh, it feels so strange,' her mother had said when they had been home for just ten minutes. Sylvie had to agree. Her brother had gone out a lot but there was a definite, tangible emptincss. A stillness. A stillness she knew, then, she would not be able to shatter. She went to her room and nestled into the pile of plump cushions on her bed with an Agatha Christie, her easy read in between tackling *The Mill on the Floss*. Outside, bees hummed in the August heat. Later, her mother would potter in the garden and her father would unfurl the crossword. Nothing would change except they would miss their darling Franklyn, and she pictured endless meals where the conversation would be all about how he was faring.

Sure enough, that evening, they sat at the kitchen table, speculating on the standards of his fellow scholarship undergraduates in Florida, how certain he had been about what he wanted, how he would enjoy every minute.

'You're very quiet, Sylvie,' said her father, 'missing your big brother already?'

She nodded without making eye contact, annoyed that her parents assumed she shared their emotions, miffed that they had not even considered how the absence of their son could mean a new, improved relationship with their daughter. Out of spite, more than interest, she cleared her throat.

'I'd like to study in America too. What do you think?' she said.

'My, she *is* missing her brother, isn't she?' her mother replied, and Sylvie quietly growled as her parents moved on to discussing when they would fly out to visit their son.

'Christmas is too soon, don't you think?' her mother said in a tone which conveyed that Christmas was leaving it too long.

Sylvie rolled her eyes. She did not much like the heat and she certainly was not keen on substituting the frost of a Berkshire December for Santa in the sunshine. All the same, from the age of twelve she would spend three Christmases in a row in Tampa and hated them mostly because she became aware that she was just too young to be considered an asset, too young for her brother's friends to flirt with her, too young to interestingly fill the void when Franklyn had to dash off, leaving his family to fend for themselves at the crab shack.

Worst of all was that the family car, back in Berkshire, now sported a bumper sticker celebrating the sunshine state.

As far as Sylvie was concerned her parents might as well write on the boot of the car that their eldest child was a superstar soccer prodigy on a sports scholarship abroad and their pride in him was beyond measure. Convinced there was no point trying to compete, she let her studies slip and became an average student unlikely to win a scholarship anywhere. Her parents barely noticed.

She was, though, put in charge of the school musical – or at least of its admin and ticketing and props – which led to her head teacher suggesting she should take courses that could lead to her being an executive PA or office manager. Given this was the most interest in her life anyone had shown for a while, Sylvie responded with gusto and, by the age of twenty-one, was earning much more than any of her friends or peers. Even at twenty-three, when many of them had left university and found jobs, she still earned more. It turned out she was very good at organizing things. It turned out she rather liked the gratitude of her bosses, of being told an event or meeting would not have run so smoothly but for her talents. It turned out she was brighter than her parents knew and when she changed jobs she picked up the new rhythms of a new sector with ease. She was good at what she did – and now she had been sacked.

Perhaps it should not have shocked her so. Her boss had been volatile. Initially he had been distant and then grateful and then attentive. Had she really been dismissed because she had removed his hand from her thigh? He had taken it well at the time, she thought. She had even praised herself for how well she had navigated the whole male ego dilemma. She had not made a complaint about him. She had not stopped smiling when she said good morning to him. She had told Catherine about it but Catherine had slept with her boss and not suffered for then *not* sleeping with him. She wondered if other women her age confided such problems to their mothers rather than not so very close colleagues. It would have been nice to have a mother who was wise and worldly, but mostly it would have been nice to have a mother who was caring enough to be aghast at what had happened to her daughter, to be protective, possibly angry. Sylvie could have forgiven her mother all manner of poor advice had it been delivered out of love, but her mother's contributions were uninspired out of a lack of interest.

She guessed that Catherine would have had fun at the Lancaster Gate man's expense. That she would have told him she would indeed like to go to a hotel with him, have followed him up the escalator, maybe even out into the street, maybe even into the hotel bar to order an expensive cocktail she could throw into his lap. Catherine might even have gone further but she hoped not. Catherine's boss had been far less revolting than Dirt Lancaster and now she would have to find another station to settle down in before heading home. She plumped for Bethnal Green but for the whole ninety minutes that she stayed there she was agitated. Lancaster Gate nagged at her as unfinished business. Maybe she was not near the end at all. This could be, still, the beginning of a very long quest.

*

Isak's life was a quest funded by Andrew. His money, or rather his allowance, came from the fact that his stepfather was big in the City. His mother had met Andrew when Isak was twelve and sufficiently difficult to mean it was hard for her to make friends and forge romantic relationships. So she did not mention her son until Andrew had flown her to London for dinner and a musical and their relationship appeared to be something real. She had braced herself for a tight smile and a cursory kiss goodnight but Andrew had toasted her son – her awkward, sometimes frightening, sometimes frightened son – and said he would like very much one day, if she deemed it appropriate, to meet him. It was one of the nicest things anyone had ever said to her and now Isak was twenty and, thanks to Andrew, receiving the best care, which intermittently allowed him the freedom to roam the capital looking for clothes. Isak was a man-child with no future but Andrew never drew attention to the open-ended nature of his financial support. Isak was Isak. They never argued about him. Andrew viewed him as an extension of Ulla. It was, for him, as natural as buying her insurance for her car. If Isak was contained, coping, content, then Ulla would smile, run her hands through Andrew's hair and he would be, at last, happy.

Chapter 13

The weekday mornings were different now. Ryan was not even sure if he wanted to travel in the first carriage any more. He could smile and say hi and she might look right through him, the odd man who knew the works of Mrs Henry Wood. She might smile back, though. He bit his lip. He had made one mistake, just one. Everything else about their modest lunch at Waterloo had been fine. Better than fine once the buzzing in his ears had ceased. Millie, now Sylvie, was real, for a start, and still as beautiful; she owed him a salad and over that salad she would him tell why she stayed underground for so long and it would be reasonable or maybe even wonderful. Maybe.

For the first three subsequent commutes he could not eat any breakfast. He was sick with nerves, but when a full week had passed with no sighting he calmed down and forced himself to feel fatalistic. After two weeks he was not so much worried as sad. After four he began to suspect she was avoiding the salad.

Paul arrived in London two weeks before Christmas to sort out his accommodation.

‘I am,’ he announced, ‘like the curry or funny tea women have when they want to give birth. Now I am here she will reappear.’

The two men did not have a set tradition but when feasible would visit each other’s family homes on Christmas Eve or Boxing Day to ease the burden. Grace became giddy then drunk then maudlin every time but would always rally when Paul arrived with a box of expensive chocolates for her, usually from an airport.

Grandpa rallied too, roused by the smell of mincemeat and pastry and stuffing, the random and frequent offers of a festive glass of wine or brandy or sherry. Ed had not asked Hana if she wanted to join some of their fellow ramblers for a festive walking break. Hana would have said she had to be with her mother because there was never any question of a breaking of tradition, but she had expected him to ask all the same.

‘Thank you for the lovely book, Grandpa,’ she said.

‘You’re welcome,’ he said, waving his hand dismissively.

On his lap he had a giant chocolate panettone which he had just unwrapped and was unwilling to share. They all knew he would have a slice as a sort of starter before he tucked into the Christmas cake in front of the Queen.

Hana stood and looked out of the window onto the street. She and Ed had made no arrangement to meet that day but she had a feeling he would pop by to surprise her, that he would not have gone hiking at Christmas without her.

‘It’s drizzling,’ she said. ‘There’s nothing remotely winter wonderland going on out there.’

A car pulled up but it belonged to a relative of the single mother who lived opposite, whose family multiplied with such alarming regularity that even the most ardent socialist could not but help calculate how much she accrued in benefits. Grace glanced over at her daughter and caught a glimpse of the sad version of her Hana, the one who had come home to her in tears, broken and hurt.

She beckoned Ryan into the kitchen.

'Are your sister and Ed still OK? I'm wondering if they're not and she doesn't want to worry me.'

Ryan exhaled. He too had noticed the frown lines on Hana's forehead, the slightly hunched back, the way she checked her phone when it had not made a sound.

'She hasn't said anything to me, Mam, but I'm sure it's just normal stuff, the ebbs and flows of everyday romance.'

Grace planted a kiss on his cheek.

'Get you, Mr Ryan Wordsworth,' she said. 'When will you be bringing a girl home for Christmas?'

Ryan shrugged in an exaggerated manner and patted his stomach.

'I have that I'm-full-to-busting-but-need-a-mince-pie feeling,' he said as the Queen and Grandpa began to speak, one mentioning the Commonwealth, the other demanding to know where his cake was.

Franklyn was home. He had settled in Florida, become a sports physio and had missed the last two Berkshire Christmases altogether but this time brought with him a tanned and leggy girlfriend with perfect teeth. Sylvie felt herself sat in permanent shadow while Brooke hogged all the sunshine and pronounced everything to be so quaint, so awesome, so English.

Her parents had thoughtfully bought Brooke gifts so she too could be handed things to open from under the tree. Never, thought Sylvie, has a notebook from Harrods been greeted with such gleeful enthusiasm. Indeed, the final gift of the unwrapping session was for Brooke. It was a small box containing an engagement ring.

Ah, thought Sylvie, if a girl gets so excited over a green jotting pad, what will she do when proposed to?

A hundred 'oh my Gods' later, Sylvie's father had opened the special-occasion Champagne and her mother was on the phone to her best friend. Far from appearing to think their Christmas had been hijacked her parents were variously touched, honoured, moved or thrilled by the whole escapade. The *pièce de résistance* came when Brooke said she would like the ceremony to be in England. Sylvie smiled. She could tell her soon-to-be sister-in-law was dreaming about a horse-drawn carriage and Windsor Castle. She looked over at Franklyn and realized for the first time that his nearly red hair and English freckles would have gone down a storm with the girls in Tampa.

She wondered if it would alter the mood at all if she chose to finally tell her family she had lost her job back in March. Such was the intense hysteria that she doubted they would hear her if she did, but the fact she had even considered it was another sign that the time she spent underground was finite. It would end. Surely it would end. She popped on her new Jacksonville Jaguars earmuffs and Brooke squealed in delight.

That girl, Sylvie thought, is far too easily pleased.

*

The snow came mid-January. It was not all that pretty and Naomi declared it bargain-basement sleet. It did not stick for long, but it was pesky enough to mean that Ryan had to blink a lot as he shuffled to North Ealing Underground station. He had a meeting with the lab's main chemicals supplier to look forward to and, although he knew the weather meant they would be late, he had to be on time.

She was reading *Bleak House*. It is not weird, he thought, for me to know of other books by Dickens, but he did not comment on it all the same.

'Hi, Sylvie,' he said, 'how are you?'

She looked up, a half-smile on her lips. He had remembered her name, but she had also remembered his.

He had imagined the moment, feared it, been impatient for it, but now it was here he was strangely relaxed.

'I haven't eaten a salad for weeks,' he said, 'you know, in preparation for the next one.'

'I am a woman who pays her debts,' she said. 'Can you be at the same place at 12.30 today?'

He wanted to say of course he could but he knew that would be cutting it fine, even if the Chemical Brothers turned up on time.

She smiled some more.

'Or 1 p.m. if that's easier?'

'Yes,' he said. 'That would be much easier. Great.'

The carriage became clogged and he had to shift a little further from her, making conversation a horribly public affair. No one else was talking at all. She returned to Lady Dedlock, only looking up again when they pulled into South Kensington and he whispered he would see her later. She nodded and as he stepped off the train he realized he was humming an atonal piece of electronica.

The meeting was, as he knew it would be, delayed by snow that did not stick in London but had stuck at a crucial point on the M40. Then there was the small talk about the weather and pleasantries about getting back into the swing of things after Christmas. Ryan found himself tapping the table with the tip of his pen. There was some chat about unavoidable price hikes and a weak joke about having the solution to it. Ryan forced a hurried laugh. It was already noon. At 12.40 he was hurtling through the main doors just as Ed was entering. Hana's Ed. Had he not been so preoccupied, Ryan would have been bemused by his presence but he did not have a spare second in which to become distracted.

'Can't stop, Ed, running late,' he said and he really was. He reckoned he would reach her ten minutes past the hour but there were no delays. A Jubilee line train was waiting for him at Westminster and he spotted her candyfloss hair at 1.05.

She was not alone. The restaurant was busy but the woman sitting opposite Sylvie had asked for the bill and when Ryan sat down she flapped her arms and said, 'Don't worry, I'm practically on my train already.'

'It's not really salad weather, is it?' Sylvie said as the waitress approached.

'I'll have the penne giardinera and an Earl Grey tea,' she said.

'I'll have the same,' Ryan said. 'But with garlic bread.'

'Did you have a nice Christmas? Were you in London?' she asked him.

'Not too bad,' he said. 'It was, let's say, traditional, dull and a little emotional and, oh Christ, what was Ed doing at the uni?'

Sylvie raised an eyebrow but she seemed interested.

Ryan fiddled with a spoon and without knowing where the story would end began to tell her about the lunch in August, how Naomi and Ed had almost towered over Hana, had looked like a couple and had lots in common and right now he was probably doing or saying something that would hurt his sister.

'Hana had a really bad time with a shitty husband and Ed is the first bloke she has seen since then so—'

'So,' Sylvie said, 'you need to find out what he was doing there before you tell your sister anything.'

'Oh, yes, of course. But it's a bit weird. Him being there today, don't you think?'

'Maybe,' she said. 'My brother brought a Tampa girl home and proposed to her in front of me and our parents on Christmas Day. *That* was weird.'

'I have a hunch we are the only sane people in our families,' Ryan said and then guiltily sipped his tea, remembering that for some time he had feared Millie, now Sylvie, and her journeys might turn out to be too weird. She might still be highly peculiar and so he could not yet bring himself to ask where she was going, where she had been that morning, where she would be tomorrow.

'Are you a student?' she asked him.

'No, I run the chemistry labs. I was late meeting you because of a fascinating meeting about the price of nitric acid.' He paused. 'Are you a student?'

She laughed.

‘Long story,’ she said. ‘I’m job hunting right now.’

‘Do you need a job in a chemistry laboratory?’ he said, hoping to sound self-deprecating rather than patronizing.

‘If your lab needed organizing and hosted events and the nitric acid fell out with the, with the… helium, and needed a new cupboard every five minutes, then yes, I could work with you.’

‘Helium is expensive,’ he said, ‘due to inflation.’

She stared at him blankly then spluttered over her pasta.

‘My, that’s so bad it’s almost funny,’ she said. ‘Do you have a joke for every gas and acid and Bunsen burner?’

He nodded sagely.

‘What do you call a clown in jail?’

She pretended to think about it then shook her head.

‘A silicon,’ he said.

‘And all you’re drinking is Earl Grey,’ she said.

‘I have to get back to work,’ he said, ‘but I’d really like to take for you a drink one evening. Early evening perhaps. Friday. This Friday, if you could make that?’

She nodded.

‘Can I take your number to arrange it? We could meet in town or nearer your home?’

‘I’ll meet you there at six,’ she said, pointing to the champagne bar a bit further along from where they were sitting. It was a bar designed for people waiting for trains, for meeting friends off trains, for serving people that starter drink before a big night out or for a last drink before heading home after the theatre. It was not the sort of place he had in mind at all and a wave of claustrophobia briefly engulfed him.

‘We can start there, of course,’ he said, brightening. It was a start, after all. He looked at her hands. She had slim fingers and unpolished nails. A mischievous voice in his head – that sounded suspiciously like Naomi's – told him to reach for her hand and kiss it but he resisted.

'Shall we go halves?' he said but she firmly declined and remained seated as he slid a five-pound note under the salt cellar for the tip.

'See you over there then on Friday at six,' he said.

'Understood,' she said, which seemed to him to be an odd thing to say but perhaps she was teasing him for being overly officious. He walked away towards the escalator trying to appear nonchalant – trying not to appear overjoyed that he could happily take a different Tube line and maybe, just maybe, not ever need to follow her again.

Naomi was in one of the meeting spaces designed for informal academic discussions. She was with a small group of biodiversity postgraduates who were plotting a field trip and she had the sense that someone was watching them. She looked around to spot Ed loitering, hands in his coat pockets. It was a long, heavy dark grey coat that only a tall man could wear well. She signalled to him then pointed at her chest to ask if he was there to see her.

He nodded, not sheepishly, but boldly, smilingly. She held up her hand to indicate 'five minutes' but the discussion broke up before then.

He kissed her cheek. She did not need to stoop; he did not need to stoop.

'I was nearby and thought, well, I've never seen this place.

Thought you could give me a tour and tell me more about your Masters.'

Naomi was struck by how relaxed he was, how natural it seemed to him to seek her out even though they both knew, didn't they, that there had been an inappropriate frisson between them at Grace's lunch.

'First up, I have to tell you I was badly drunk when we met for that hot-day roast lunch and, um, sorry if I was an idiot.'

Ed was genuinely surprised.

'No need for an apology,' he said, 'unless you were making up your life. You made perfect sense and it was refreshing to be able to talk about science and nature to someone who knows what it means and should mean.'

'You're not humouring me?'

'I most certainly am not.'

She gave him the tour, they bumped into a few people she knew and she introduced Ed as 'a friend of mine' even though she did not know his last name. She liked showing off the building but mostly she liked the way they were streamlined, comfortable.

'Oh, you make a divine couple,' Daryl, a short, annoying blond Aussie said as they passed him in a corridor.

They both ignored him.

'And where does Ryan work?' Ed asked and she blushed.

'This way,' she said, trying to slow her breathing, practising in her head how to look innocent when Ryan saw them, but the labs were empty and locked.

'Shame,' Ed said 'but, then again, chemicals are less fascinating to me.'

'Of course,' Naomi said and without thinking added, 'You'll have to give me a tour of your place.'

'I think it would much more fun if we met for dinner,' he said and he confidently took out his phone. 'Give me your number,' he said as if there was no subterfuge, no moral dilemma, no awkwardness, and so she did.

'I've texted you, so you have mine too now,' he said.

She was speechless but to ask about Hana felt immature in the face of his older-man certainty.

'Cool,' she said. 'I'll walk you to the lobby.'

He kissed her on the cheek and as he said goodbye he held her gaze for a second longer than could be considered platonic. Their eyes were dead level.

As she returned to her desk, she glanced at her phone. His text read:

Dinner this Friday, I'll book for 8 p.m.

She was startled, firstly, because his texting technique was incredibly speedy for someone not in their twenties, and secondly, because there was no question mark. He had included a comma, so he had not simply abandoned punctuation or forgotten the question mark. His confidence was appealing. It was, she admitted to herself, sexy. They were meeting on Friday and that was that.

Chapter 14

Both Naomi and Ryan decided to have a quiet night in on Thursday. Both decided to eat simply and without booze.

'I've bought some soups,' Naomi said. 'Do you want to choose one? I like all of them.'

She even heated them up on the hob for them and buttered some ciabatta rolls. As she did so she became vaguely aware that she could not recall ever being so domestic in a kitchen as she was with Ryan. She shuddered as an image popped into her head of her wearing a stiff wipe-clean apron while she kneaded some dough. But she kept on buttering and stirring. She was starting to feel very guilty at interrupting Ryan's family by dating someone his sister so obviously liked. Ryan did not notice.

'I'm meeting Millie, now Sylvie, for a drink after work tomorrow,' he blurted out.

'You'll have to call her MNS for short,' Naomi said, 'or – radical idea – just call her Sylvie. Actually, ask her if her name is really Sylvia. One vowel change and it goes from the name of a spinster to the name of a pretty pixie.'

Ryan shrugged. Her name was the least of his worries. He wondered what would happen if he suggested they leave Waterloo station, walk out into the winter air, cross the bridge and head to the West End. As he thought about their second Waterloo lunch, and he was certain he could recall every word they had exchanged; he remembered he had told her about Ed and Hana.

'Oh, I've just remembered,' he said, 'I saw Ed, Hana's boyfriend, at the uni this week, which was weird.'

Naomi felt betrayed. What was the point of the buttering and stirring if Ryan was just going to put her on the spot like this? She inhaled sharply, then pretended to have butter on her nose and hoped her voice would sound nonchalant as she wiped it away.

'Yes, I forgot to mention it. He was passing and came in to see us but you were out so I gave him the tour.'

Ryan exhaled.

'Oh, good, I was worried he'd come to see you.'

'Nah,' Naomi said. 'I don't think so, I was a bit surprised he remembered we worked at the same place, to be honest, it was a while ago now that I met him at your mum's but, er, are he and Hana still loved up?'

'Not sure really, she seems less happy, maybe it's wobbling. He didn't come over at Christmas and she was a bit upset, I think.'

They slurped at their soup as Naomi processed what Ryan had said. Hana had glared at her, back in the summer, and at the time Naomi had thought it was because she was tipsy and garrulous and unimpressed by the romance of her and Ed's meeting, but now she realized it was really because she was wearing a pink vest, she was as tall as Ed and she was a scientist.

The bar was packed but Ryan found a low table with room for two and waited. This time it was Sylvie who was five minutes late. Her hair was pinned back, loosely, so that a few curly candyfloss strands framed her face.

She peeled off her dove-grey trench coat and sat down at right angles to him in the cramped space. She was wearing a soft wool short-sleeve jumper. She was both wholesomely cuddly and sexy at the same time.

'I don't know what you like so I haven't ordered anything yet,' he said, 'but the cocktails look fun. And don't laugh but I think I'm going to have an Appletini because I watch *Scrubs* a lot and… have you seen it?'

She nodded. 'Good show and yes, JD, he likes Appletinis, I remember that now.'

They took their first sips at the same time, both of them expecting something excruciatingly cloying.

'Maybe in America it's less sophisticated,' she said, 'because it's quite nice really, not too sweet and not as girlie as the show would lead us to believe.'

They discussed *Scrubs* for a while and then other box sets they had in common but to Ryan it seemed they were in a play, avoiding the topics normal people would discuss.

'How's the job hunting going?' he said.

'Not amazingly well,' she said.

He smiled encouragement but she did not expand.

'Are you getting interviews?' he said, wondering now if she

had been wandering around the Underground after getting cold feet or a bad attack of nerves.

'I have had a few but I'm just not…' Here she placed her glass carefully on the napkin on the table. 'I have to finish something first.'

'Something?'

'Yeah, something hard to explain. But it's coming to an end, I think. I hope so anyway.'

'Maybe I can help,' he said.

'Oh, you are helping already. I don't normally let strange men buy me lunch, you know, but I feel I know you or ought to know you for some reason.'

She shook her head as if keen to release more curls. 'Anyway, that's all for another time. Tell me, did your sister like her book? No. Tell me: did you find out about her boyfriend and whether she needs to worry?'

'No, no it's all fine, he was at the uni to see me and my flatmate. Together. A sort of package. I just didn't give him a chance to speak because I was rushing to meet you.'

'You've seen him since, then?'

'Oh, no, but my housemate, Naomi, she explained what happened.'

Sylvie squinted at him. 'OK,' she said in the tone people use when something is far from OK.

'What? What have I said?'

'Think about what you were initially worried about. If he was after Naomi or already seeing her, would she just tell you? Just like that?'

'Yes, I think so,' he said uncertainly. 'Am I being a bit dim?'

She touched his elbow. 'Of course not, I'm just saying it might not be so simple after all. But I hope it is, for your sister's sake.'

'Thank you,' he said. 'Would you like to walk across the river, find something to eat in Covent Garden?'

Sylvie looked startled, as if it had not even occurred to her that the river was crossable.

'I can't think of a good reason to say no,' she said.

The wind bit into them as soon as they saw the water and her hair became scattered and wild. He thought she might just be the most beautiful woman he had ever met and just as he was feeling triumphant that they were outside the remit of Transport for London – that they were just like any other couple on a first date; nervous, keen, hormonal, happy – he felt Ellen's hand on the nape of his neck, her breath close to his ear, reminding him that *she* was the most beautiful girl in the world and he realized why he had been so patient in tracking Sylvie. While she had been a puzzle she had been another ghost, not something to rival Ellen, to test his vow, made all those winters ago, that he would never want anyone else.

Naomi had been alone in Cotton Street most of the day. Staring at her laptop, then at her wardrobe, then at the laptop again. She had done about as much research as it was possible to do on a restaurant. She had peered closely at the six photos on its website and noted that it had lots of internal foliage and fairy lights but that this had been concocted in a classy, urban sort of way. The prices were neither steep nor reasonable, the reviews were mostly extremely positive. The place was large enough not to be labelled intimate but not so huge that it would swallow whole a couple trying to talk quietly.

The main problem was that Naomi was not quite convinced she was on a date and, when she decided for a few minutes that she must be, she realized Ed could not be all that nice a bloke. When she thought about just how nice he *was* she had to conclude that they could not, therefore, be going on a date.

She wore a knee-length dress and suede boots with a two-inch heel because she knew the only times she had stood next to him she had worn two-inch heels and she had liked how level that made them. This was not an evening during which she wanted to be shorter or taller than Ed.

He was stood outside, leaning against the window frame.

'Hello, you,' he said as if they were old friends, old lovers.

'Hello, Ed,' she said as he kissed her on the cheek as smoothly as if they had been married for months or colleagues for years.

He held the door open for her and they were guided to a table where one of them would have their back to the wall and one would be facing it but it was also next to the window so neither of them would be without a view.

'Which side would you like to sit?' he said.

She chose the seat facing the restaurant.

'You look really lovely,' he said.

'Ah, well,' she said, but before she could continue he placed his hand upon hers briefly.

'I have to say this. I am not the sort of bloke who meets someone when with someone else and thinks, oh she's nice, I'll move on. I have never done that. But you blew me away, Naomi. I thought I'd get you out of my system but I couldn't.

Let's face it, I waited nearly six months since first meeting you. Something happened when we walked through that little kitchen, something weird really, like an electric shock. And I felt it again when I came to see you.'

He frowned and paused.

'Look, it's hard to put into words without it sounding like a cheesy song lyric…' he trailed off. He wanted to say, 'But I think I could love you,' but he knew better than that. He knew it would sound needy and off-putting and possibly scary. And maybe untrue. Ed was not sure if he could define love, but he was certainly bewitched.

Naomi ran her fingers along the edge of the menu. She was simultaneously flattered and annoyed.

'What are you saying? Have you split with Hana? Because we met through Hana's brother, my friend, and Hana, I've heard, is totally into you. That is not cool, Ed.'

He sighed.

'It's not cool. I know that but, honestly, I've been trying to let her go gently. I know her story, that she's had a shit time and I'm the first man she's trusted and heck, that's a lot of responsibility. I didn't want that role. I was single, she was nice, and then suddenly I'm in a room with her dotty grandfather who clearly thinks all black men look the same, her over-emotional mother, her protective brother, and trust me that does not bode well for anything remotely romantic – which makes our connection all the more astonishing.'

'Can we order some drinks?' she said and only when she had gulped down half the house aperitif did she respond.

'I'm here, so you know I like you. Actually, to be honest, I had a crush on this guy which died as soon as I met you so yes, I think we have made a connection but we don't make any progress while Hana thinks you are together. You have to find a way to end it so she isn't devastated, and even then it will be tricky because I share a house with her brother.'

She smiled, cheekily. 'So you'd have to put me in a little flat of my own.'

'We could share a flat. I'd move closer to town.'

They both wallowed in the warmth of forbidden flirtation and then roused themselves to order food.

He walked her to the nearest Tube station and as they stood on the platform he took hold of both her hands.

'We're going in opposite directions,' he said, 'and I won't see you again until I've sorted it with Hana.'

'Be kind,' Naomi said. She could see that her train would arrive first and as she looked into his eyes their lips touched because their lips were level and she was as close to swooning as she ever had been in her life.

She looked for a seat but the carriage was full of painted faces and swaying drunks apart from the far corner, where Ryan was sat with a girl with a creamy complexion and nearly red wavy hair. Her first instinct was to get off at the next stop, Piccadilly Circus, but he might see her and become suspicious and she saw no way it would help matters for her to avoid him now. She was about to shuffle over to him but then realized she had the perfect reason for avoiding him: she did not want to spoil their romantic journey home. So, feeling practically virtuous, she pushed against the hordes trying to alight and waited for the next train.

'Is Naomi very tall with a dark bob?' Sylvie asked Ryan.

'Yes,' he said, looking around the carriage. 'Why?'

'Oh, then in that case she was about to come over – she definitely knows you – but thought better of it and got off,' Sylvie said, having seen Naomi and Ed. They had been an eye-catching couple and Sylvie had an eye for pockets of difference on the Underground. And from what Ryan had told her it could only have been Hana's Ed that Naomi was almost but not quite kissing and it was the almost part of it that made them stand out. It was rather beautiful. A piece of slow-motion cinema amid the swirling madness of late-night Tube travel.

Ryan was already unsure what they had eaten that evening, every gesture had felt momentous. He had touched the tips of her fingers, unable to resist but also fearful she would pull away. She had kept her hand there but looked away, shyly. They had played some upbeat Motown in the restaurant and then Marvin Gaye's 'Inner City Blues', which he knew and loved and considered one of the sexiest songs he had ever heard, so when Sylvie had said, 'Oh, do you like this song, I love it,' he had almost slid off his chair with happiness.

Ryan travelled past his stop and walked out of Eastcote station with Sylvie.

'I'd like to walk you to your door but that might sound, I don't know, pushy or corny or something,' he said, hoping she would insist it was neither and, anyway, he still did not have her number.

'That's nice of you but I'm fine to walk from here,' she said. Her breath froze slightly as she spoke and he leaned in but she turned her face to her left so he was forced to kiss her cheek. In the distance a girl laughed and he thought, again, of Ellen.

'Can I give you my number?' he said.

‘Of course,’ she said. ‘And I’ll text you.’

‘Good, that’s good,’ he said, trying not to sound forlorn, and she turned and started to walk down the uninspiring high street, so he turned back into the station and wondered if the evening had been wondrous or deflating. As he neared North Ealing, humming Marvin Gaye, he concluded it had been both, and he was full of gratitude that Naomi had not interrupted their ride home. Great girl, he thought, she deserves to find a great guy.

Ed suggested they meet in Regent’s Park for a London walk. No need for hiking boots, he said in his text. Hana had not seen him for three weeks. She was both excited and nervous. It was icy cold and the sky was a weak blue damaged by long slate-grey clouds. Hana had bought a new coat while trying to convince herself she had not been shopping just for this walk. Now she felt stupid. Her coat was so obviously on its first outing and would tell Ed all on its own how desperately she wanted to keep hold of him. On impulse she looked around her as she walked to the Tube station, took it off and dragged it along the pavement. When on the train she rolled it up and sat on it to give it some creases.

When she found Ed he said: ‘New coat?’

‘No,’ she said. ‘Actually, it needs a clean.’

‘I sort of like this weather,’ Ed said. ‘It makes London feel sharp and fresh, ready for anything.’

Hana looked across the park towards the grand houses that were built like wedding cakes.

‘I prefer Devon though,’ she said.

Ed took her hand.

'Devon was great,' he said and he took a deep breath, a breath so deep he hoped it would tell Hana all she needed to know. 'But I feel we've been drifting apart for a few weeks and maybe this isn't really going anywhere. You must have felt the same thing?'

He hoped he did not sound impatient or that he was talking to a simpleton. He needed to believe she was prepared for this. He was no good at hurting people but that had never stopped him before. Honesty was preferable to deception. It was preferable to compromise.

Hana could not help it, she began trembling. She said nothing. They kept walking.

'Look, it's all my fault,' he said. 'I've let us carry on because I knew you had been through hell but of course you don't want a bloke who feels like that.'

'You mean pity?' she stammered.

'No, of course not, Hana. I mean, I liked you and still do but not quite enough to make us a thing and, well, you deserve more than someone who thinks that way.'

'A thing?'

'Sorry, a relationship. I don't want a long-term commitment.'

She knew she should walk away with dignity but she felt protected in his company even though he was breaking up with her.

'It *is* a new coat,' she said and he smiled uncomfortably.

'Hana, I didn't want to do this via email. I'm old school. I want to give you a hug and wish you every happiness.'

'It's fine,' she said, 'I didn't have any other plans for today anyway.'

'Shall we go for a coffee and warm up?' he said, the guilt of the conversation seeping into his heart.

'No, you can walk me to the Tube and we'll leave it at that,' she said. 'But, be honest, Ed. Does this mean you have met someone else?'

Ed paused, torn between a desire to be honest and to avoid specifics.

The silence wounded Hana. She filled it with panicked thoughts.

'Does this have something to do with Naomi?'

'Do I know a Naomi?' Ed said.

Hana felt her chest tighten.

'Ryan says a Naomi gave you a tour of his university.'

'Oh, yes, right, I'd forgotten. Well, we are not splitting up because of a university tour, I can promise you that.'

'I think perhaps we are,' Hana said and she took off her coat and flung it in the next bin they passed.

Ed hung back and turned on his heel. He had tried his best, he thought.

She looked over her shoulder and watched him retreat. He looked like a film star in his long coat with his long stride and she felt the tears well up. Her only tissues were in her jacket and when Ed turned it was to see the distant figure of Hana retrieving her new coat from the bin and rummaging through its pockets. He was too far away to see how her tears began to sting her cheeks.

He took out his phone.

I am officially unattached but want to be attached to you

he texted without re-reading his words first. He was sure about Naomi, so sure that the genuine anxiety he had felt at hurting Hana evaporated at speed. A couple of teenagers on skateboards approached him as if in a game of chicken but he kept walking the same line and the boys parted with a stifled screech of their wheels and whizzed past him without even touching the tips of his flapping dark grey coat.

Sylvie texted Ryan the day after their walk over Waterloo Bridge. She told him she would like to take it slowly as there were things she needed to sort out. She politely added that she would quite understand if that was a frustration and he did not want to see her again.

Ryan texted her back that slow was good and would the suggestion they meet one Friday towards the middle of February be too impatient of him? He did not tell her so, but he vowed to travel at the other end of the train, to give her space. He would not tell her, either, that he spent long minutes of each day wondering what it was – other than a job – that she needed to sort out.

She was tiring of it. The responsibility had taken its toll. As she tapped her card on entering Eastcote station she was no longer on automatic pilot. She was choosing to do this and was not at all sure she was making the right choice. What, she wondered, if this is not what I was supposed to do and I have wasted all these months? She was cold and miserable. Nothing had changed. She had achieved absolutely nothing and, having kept at bay the idea that she was living a lie, she now was forced to accept it. The things she had to sort out, as she had put it, were hazy now and she wondered how she could wrap up this phase of her existence if she did not know what her task entailed. She was a woman on the move without an itinerary, without solid purpose, and yet she stepped onto the next train, settled into her seat and closed her eyes with a degree of relief.

Chapter 15

Grandpa said he did not want to go to the pub. He was busy.

'You're busy?' Grace said. 'Busy doing what, now?'

He grunted. He was, she saw, busy with the shopping channel. He never bought anything so it was a harmless enough pastime, financially, but he had entered a twilight world where the smiling, chirpy presenters had become his friends. Now and again he soiled himself rather than drag himself away from the TV to visit the bathroom. Grace wondered if this was the beginning of the end or if that had happened years ago.

She heard Hana place her key in the lock and she could feel the reluctance in the action, she could tell her daughter was sad.

'How was Ed?' she asked with forced brightness.

'He dumped me,' Hana said, 'and I threw away my new coat. Twice.'

Grace opened her mouth then closed it again and gave her daughter a hug. At least it had not been Ed who had thrown away her coat. Hana's ex would have done something like that.

'I'll make us all some tea,' she said and Hana surveyed the scene and sighed.

'Can't he watch normal stuff, programmes we could watch with him?'

Grace was torn between the competing needs of those she loved.

'When he drops off, we'll watch a nice film together,' she whispered but Hana had begun to weep and the helpless Grace noticed how, as the tears rolled down her daughter's cheeks, she so resembled her grandfather and, it had to be acknowledged, her father.

Grace stood in front of the kettle. She was troubled. She had worked hard to keep the family from fraying but there was an unravelling now – she could feel it – and the memories she fought hard to suppress began to creep across the kitchen walls like fast-growing ivy. She was in the churchyard, the wind blowing in fitful gusts sometimes of rain, sometimes of sunshine, her black dress-coat rattling at her calves as Tom was lowered into the earth. She refused to hold Joe's hand, refused to look at him, so he was held upright by Grandpa and Grandpa's brother. Later she was disgusted by her husband's tears, the way he was fed beer and whisky, the way he accepted the beer and whisky but refused the sandwiches.

'I can't eat,' he had said but he could drink all right. She put up with him for another week and then told him to go and drink in someone else's house. He could come back, she said, when he was ready to be a good father to his remaining children. He had stopped weeping and stared at her. She had not known it then but that was the moment Joe realized he would never be a good father in her eyes. He had let her firstborn die. His relatives and friends were welcoming at first but his inability to explain what was slowly destroying him meant they tired of his self-pity and long alcoholic hazes. He ran out of places to stay. His mother was poorly, his best friend's wife was pregnant and superstitious and treated him like he was a bad luck charm.

He knocked on his own front door early one June morning and Grace, holding a heavy Ryan on her hip, answered. She did not ask him to come in.

'You smell of drink,' she said.

'Of course I do,' he said. 'It's all I have. It's too hard for me, Gracie.'

She placed Ryan on the carpeted hall floor. He wrapped his arms around her leg.

'Tom used to do that,' Joe said in a gravelly whisper.

'And you think I don't remember,' she said. 'Well, I *do* remember but, amazingly, I manage to remember *and* not touch the drink.'

'You pious bitch,' he muttered as he walked away, swaying slightly.

Now, Grace wondered if she had heard him properly. He might have said 'that's a bit rich'. It was horrible if those were the last words she heard him speak. He had hated her as much as she had hated him. But she did not hate him now. She understood him better these days. His grief was double the dose of hers and hers had been bad enough.

'Mam, he's dropped off, we can watch something if you like,' Hana said. Grace wanted to be alone, to go for a long walk, a long holiday, lie in the sun, meet new people, maybe dance, she used to be a good dancer.

'Whatever you fancy watching, my love,' she said, linking

her arm through Hana's and nestling into her shoulder. My poor Hana, she thought.

Paul was on his phone, sat on the sofa in Ryan's house. His spacious flat in Hammersmith had looked too good to be true and it had turned out that was.

'The noise,' he groaned. 'I'm living beneath the loudest and angriest of angry and loud drug addicts. I need some quiet moments to think and oh, yes, to sleep.'

Naomi, nursing a hot mug of coffee, sat down too quickly and spilled some of her drink onto her lap.

'That sounds awful,' she said. 'Move in here while you sort it out. I've got a friend who, er, who has just split from her man and is begging me to keep her company, so my room is free.'

Paul sat up straight.

'Really? When are you going?'

'Shall we say Sunday?'

'It's a deal, and thanks.'

'What's a deal?' Ryan said as he walked in, and he wondered why Naomi seemed so sheepish but soon forgot about it when he heard Paul would be moving in.

'You do realize, the place will start to smell bad by day three,' Naomi said.

'Wouldn't have it any other way,' Ryan said, looking at the brown smudge on her trousers, 'and Paul's clothes aren't stained.'

*

Naomi could not quite believe how sure she was that she wanted to be with Ed. She sat on the train and pondered her impulsiveness. It was all about the contrast, she decided. All those young excitable students – and then in walked the mature, confident Ed. Cappi had been tall and shy, Ed was tall and composed and possibly a little unknowable. She almost shivered in delight.

'This is not a flat,' Naomi said as she walked through Ed's door. She had tried to play it all down in her head. People shared all the time, it did not have to be a big deal and she was self-aware enough to know she was hungry for excitement, for a dash of recklessness, and being reckless with an older man had to be a safe sort of recklessness, didn't it?

But Ed lived near Plaistow in what could reasonably be termed a big house. It had a front garden with an iron garden gate and one huge two-storey window running through the centre of it; it was unnervingly grown-up and serious that she was stood on its threshold with her belongings.

'I never said I lived in a flat,' he said. 'But I would live in a flat. With you.'

'Are you super rich or something?'

'Sadly not. I am super old, that's all. Got this place cheap at auction fifteen years ago and spent the next thirteen doing it up. I planned for it to take six months. I guess you could say I got side-tracked or I ended up quite liking it here.'

'Are we really still in London?'

'Narnia.'

She had one large suitcase and a laptop bag.

'I'd have helped but you told me to stay away,' he said.

'Oh, we can never tell Ryan about us,' she said matter-of-factly.

'Right,' he said.

'Not unless we are still together in five years' time and then we can have bumped into each other at a party, half recognized each other, that sort of thing.'

'Five years,' he said,

'Or sooner if Hana gets married or something.'

'I don't regret being with Hana,' he said, 'if I hadn't met her I would never have met you.'

They stood, facing each other, in a room with a very high ceiling, letting their lips touch as if on a dare to see who could remain still the longest.

'I know nothing about you,' she said.

'I know almost nothing about you,' he said.

'I'm a homeless student of biodiversity,' she said.

'That, I already knew.'

Chapter 16

Sylvie had either patrolled, monitored or examined the platforms of Marble Arch, Mansion House, Hanger Lane, Golders Green and Arnos Grove between Monday and Friday of the second week in February. She had no checklist and was sure she had covered old ground. She wondered from time to time if she was possessed because the real Sylvie was a whizz at organization. The real Sylvie would have made notes of every route, every station sat at – but there was no order to her travels. It was always done on a hunch, a feeling. Sometimes she loitered with a book. Sometimes she paced back and forth. Now and again, a member of the station staff would ask her what she was doing.

If she had been completely honest she would have told them she had made a late diversion. That she had planned to be at King's Cross but could not make it. She was beginning to understand that she would be underground forever unless she actually did patrol at King's Cross but she had been procrastinating for months. It would soon be a year. A year since. She closed her novel and let the rumble of her southbound Northern line train calm her down. A year since she had stood at the end of the platform and the girl with the large brown eyes had recognized her, or so it seemed.

The girl was petite, her long skirt had billowed in the draught of the tunnels. It was not a parcel she was carrying but a baby. She scooped the baby out of the simple papoose that had kept it hidden and handed it to Sylvie.

Does anyone ever refuse a baby? Sylvie had thought, many times, subsequently.

Of course, she accepted the child. It had, at the time, felt predestined. There had been a connection between them, she had been almost mesmerized by the woman's soft and vulnerable, warm brown eyes. The mother must need to find something in her bag or tie her shoelace or stretch her back, so Sylvie held the baby, a little nervously. She had not held one for a while, not since she had been a babysitter when she was seventeen for the Chappells who had lived next-door-but-one to her parents and liked to go out at least twice a week and to ease their guilt would pay a generous hourly rate to whichever teenager was available to look after their three children.

They had never been real to her, the Chappell kids; she had no view on whether they were cute or intelligent. They were little people to be looked after, little people who could fall out of bed or need a drink or have bad dreams, they were little people who could interrupt her watching *Strictly Come Dancing* or *The X-Factor* while nibbling her way through the stacks of patisserie strawberry tartlets, chocolate cakes and biscuits left by Mr and Mrs Chappell as if they thought she needed fattening up.

So she held the girl's baby and the stranger had given her a sad and grateful smile and then jumped.

Someone had screamed but Sylvie was sure it was not her who screamed, and nor was it the girl. Sylvie instinctively held the baby tightly and stumbled back as if it was still attached to its mother and might be sucked onto the tracks, but a train now occupied the tracks, a train that had hit the girl.

There was much commotion but none of it made sense to Sylvie. A woman in a high-visibility vest placed her arm around her.

'Can you come with me, please?' she had said and so Sylvie had walked with her as other people in similar vests ran past them. Still she held the baby. They walked into a stuffy room with a battered sofa, thin-legged table and chairs. Still Sylvie held the baby and then she vomited so the woman took the baby from her grasp and handed it to a woman in uniform but no high-vis vest who cooed in a low voice and rocked it.

It took a while for Sylvie to remember her own name and address. She was sick a second time and someone gave her a cold flannel.

'Lie down,' the high-vis lady said.

'Gillian and the baby will stay here with you. Take your time.'

Sylvie did not sleep on the battered sofa but fell into a strange state of semi-consciousness, hoping the smell, the noise, the image of the girl's sad eyes would go away. She could hear groaning and realized, with a shudder, she was the one making the sound.

Yet another woman walked in and gave her a brand-new toothbrush and some toothpaste and guided her to a tiny sink.

'You're in shock, sweetheart,' she said and then guided her back to the sofa.

'How are you now? Are you diabetic?'

Sylvie shook her head and was handed a mug of sugared tea as the baby began to wriggle and make mewing noises like a trapped cat.

The high-vis woman reappeared wearing a serious, grown-up expression.

'I know you feel awful,' she said, 'but is this baby your baby or the baby of the woman who jumped?'

'It's hers,' Sylvie said. 'But she wanted me to take it so maybe I had better hold it?'

'Do you know the woman who jumped?'

'No. She smiled at me like she recognized me but I'd never met her. I'm pretty sure I'd never seen her before. I thought she needed to tie her shoes or something.'

'Did she say anything to you? Anything at all?'

Sylvie closed her eyes. The girl had said something. One word. She assumed she was saying thank you but maybe she had said something else.

'Nisha. Yes, that's it, she said "Nisha".'

'And did you, Sylvie, say anything to her?'

Sylvie frowned.

'I didn't know she was going to… so I just held her baby, I had no idea… I said nothing, nothing at all.'

'That's OK, Sylvie.'

'Is she dead now, the girl?'

'We think so,' the high-vis woman said, 'and perhaps if you had not been there, she would have jumped with her baby, so you have done a wonderful thing and saved a life.'

'Why, though? Why jump at all?'

'We might never know. She could have had problems at

home, been suffering a mental illness, post-natal depression, all sorts of sad reasons.'

There were forms that needed filling and when the questions were over, Sylvie looked around the room only to find the baby had vanished.

'We had to get it to a paediatrician quickly for a health check,' the high-vis woman said.

This made sense but Sylvie felt her views were being unnecessarily overlooked.

'She gave the baby to me, I ought to do something to help it,' she said.

'You won't be able to do more than the professionals,' the high-vis woman said gently.

A police car took her home. It was her first time in a police car and the woman driving it was very nice, as was the man sat in the passenger seat, but Sylvie felt miserable. She did not deserve this VIP journey back to her flat. She had been remarkably stupid, it was now clear, not to have guessed what the young woman was about to do, and all it would have taken was one word of kindness to have changed her mind. That night Sylvie became convinced the manner in which she held the baby might have persuaded the young woman to jump. The baby is better off without you, she deserves better than you. The baby must be called Nisha, she thought. Nisha. The sound of her name was like the sound of the rush of air that arrived before a Tube train appears.

'Where had you been heading to?' the woman from the British Transport Police had asked her.

'My, quite a day,' she had said quietly when Sylvie explained how she had lost her job.

'Otherwise I would have been nowhere near King's Cross,' she said, unsure if that was a good or bad thing from Nisha's point of view.

'Look, we'll let you know when we know more,' the constable had said. 'We'll let you know how the baby is and what we think happened, if we can. In the meantime, see your GP if you still feel sick, and don't let this get to you. You were in the right place at the right time to save a baby. There was nothing more you could have done.'

Sylvie doubted that. The next time a stranger smiled sadly at her she would know what to do.

The following morning she had mooched about her flat in her dressing gown tearfully with nowhere to go, with nothing to interrupt her dark thoughts, so she took a long shower, dressed as she would have done for work and took the Tube into town. This cheered her up enormously. If she was needed on the Underground, she would be there. She avoided the platform where it had happened though. Later, she thought, I'll be ready for that later. And ten months later, she still was not ready. Soon she would be out of money. What was she waiting for? It was beginning to look as if she had been waiting for Ryan but he had not needed her help. He had not tried to jump from the food balcony at Waterloo. He had needed to buy a book for his sister, that's all, and he had not needed her to help him with that; and then it dawned on her that perhaps it was she who needed help from him.

*

They met again on the booths hovering above the heads of the scuttling passengers and this time she ordered the garlic bread on his behalf.

'So tell me,' he said, 'what it is you need to sort out. Maybe I can help. I'd like to help.'

'Why?' she said.

There was silence. Their food arrived.

'Good question,' he said. 'I've not been completely honest with you. If I tell you all, will you tell me all?'

'Are you with the police?' she said.

'No,' he said. 'Jeez, no, why? Don't answer that. We'll get to why you thought that.'

Sylvie played with her food. Ryan barely touched his.

'I saw you ages ago, on the Tube, and thought you were really beautiful. Sometimes you'd be on my train and sometimes not and now and again I'd miss my train on purpose in case you were on the next one. I kept thinking I'd pluck up the courage to say hello but I never did and—'

Sylvie interrupted him. 'And then you saw me here. That's not so strange, it's nice, really. I'm flattered, honestly I am. And I was a bit worried about the book but that explains why you knew about Mrs Henry Wood. You'd seen me reading her, hadn't you? Months ago.'

She seemed so relieved that he could not bring himself to continue.

'Yes, I did consider striking up a conversation about one of those books but then I wouldn't see you for a while and you'd be reading a different one. It's hard to keep up with your book club.'

She smiled, she appeared very happy with his story, as if it answered everything, which it did not.

'Your turn?' he said hesitantly.

'Mine is more… awkward,' she said. 'Nowhere near as lovely as yours. You won't like it. You might hate it.'

'I doubt it,' he said.

She sat up straight and pushed a strand of her hair behind her ears. It fell back onto her cheek almost immediately.

'I seem unable to get off the Tube.'

Ryan knew this. He knew he was not supposed to know this. He opened then closed his mouth and at last said: 'Why not?'

'I lost my job. Very unfairly. I wouldn't let my boss have a grope and on the day I lost my job I didn't go straight home. I didn't want to, not immediately, and I ended up at King's Cross. A woman on the platform seemed to recognize me. It was very strange and she handed me her baby. It sort of appeared out of nowhere and I took it. I mean, I held it so she could tie her shoelace or something and she jumped in front of the train. While I held her baby. I puked up a few times, they took the baby away, the police drove me home but I felt dreadful.

'I should have done something else, not just held her baby so she could kill herself, and when I got back on the Tube the next day, I felt better about not avoiding the place, like I was making amends. I don't even know what that means, but I sort of hang around waiting for something to happen. Maybe see someone holding a baby. I don't know. Sometimes I think I'm waiting to go back in time but of late I'm thinking that I am procrastinating, building up the courage to go back to the platform at King's Cross, I don't deliberately avoid the platform where it happened but on the other hand it's never the right time, the right day, to actually go there and so… And so I am stuck on the Underground.'

She had been staring down at the passengers while she spoke, not daring to look him in the eye. As the words flowed she wondered at the stupidity of them. Perhaps, she thought, I have gone mad. Perhaps Ryan is my mental health nurse. Perhaps he is my guiding angel and no one else can see him.

She turned to look at him. He was tapping one thumb against the other as an inner voice scolded him for being as mesmerized by her voice as by her story, for being so grateful to be her confidant. He had to stifle a grin at the realization that he was part of her life now. He calmed his breathing and ordered himself to sound sage and understanding. He had to believe that Sylvie's trauma was not so scary, that Sylvie could be saved, or else how would *she* believe it?

'Maybe I can help,' he said. 'Would you be up for me trying to help?'

She exhaled almost happily.

'We hardly know each other,' she said, 'but I think you can and I am ready to try.'

As Ryan returned to his labs, he wondered at the sensation in the pit of his stomach. It reminded him of the day he signed his mortgage papers. It had been an isolating, grown-up thing to do. He had done it propelled by a maturity he did not realize he possessed and by motivations that he did not quite understand. It had been an act that mapped out his future as an employee with responsibilities and a lack of freedom. It had also been a satisfyingly sensible decision and had given him a sense of propulsion, a sense of having direction in his life.

He had chosen Millie, now Sylvie, and had known on some level all along she was different, fragile and challenging. She was also pretty and funny and someone he wanted in his life. Right now, though, he needed to know if the answer to why she never got off the Underground was an acceptable one. He needed to know what Paul thought about it and he texted him that he had news.

'I would never have guessed that,' Paul said. 'But it's better than her being a trainspotter, isn't it?'

'That's one way of looking at it,' Ryan said, distracted.

A young woman had walked into the pub alone wearing the sort of big cream Nordic knitted jumper Ellen had worn for their only full winter together.

'Do you think me and Ellen would have stayed together, be married by now?' he asked Paul.

He had never asked him that before, although his friend had been waiting for him to ask it for a long time. Now, though, to ask him *now*? Was he asking for permission to leave her behind?

'I think yes, you would, but I don't think that should guide how you live today,' Paul said. 'Except...'

Paul shrugged. He was no expert on relationships. He had no idea if Sylvie would be good for Ryan but he did know it would be no good if he let Ellen be the thing that stopped him being with Sylvie. Ryan was not interested in the 'except'. He had wanted confirmation this was not the life he should be living. It helped him to make sense of the interruptions by Ellen in his thoughts, his dreams and in avatars. She was letting him know that the further from her he travelled, the harder it would be to forget her. He did not want to forget her, he reminded himself, but he wished she could forgive him for still being alive.

'Is it mad of me to want to help Sylvie? Would you do it, if it was you?'

'I'd do it, but as a challenge. My ego would let me think I could kill off her vicious circle, free her from the ogre, find the fucking golden fleece or whatever and I would do it without caring whether it meant an obligation. It might mean she became infatuated with me or resented me. I wouldn't care either way if I succeeded. And I doubt that is very helpful, is it?'

'It's honest,' Ryan laughed, 'but I'm not sure it will be as exciting as all that. My cunning plan so far is to tell her I'll accompany her to the platform she's been avoiding, hold her hand – literally, if necessary – and then we'll walk out into the street with violins playing and she'll be over it.'

'Beautiful,' Paul said, 'naïve, but really fucking beautiful.'

Ryan leaned forward and almost hit the table with his forehead.

'Maybe,' he said, 'it's a test. You know, like *The Truman Show*.'

'Shit,' Paul said, 'we thought you were years off guessing. Can I stop pretending to be mates with you now?'

'Not just yet,' Ryan said. 'I need your rent money to cover my mortgage.'

'I'm paying you rent? When did that happen?'

And they spent the rest of the evening in high spirits, a little drunk, eating kebabs in the street in a blaze of nostalgia for their college days, the gunky sauce running down towards Ryan's elbow as they stood in a puddle of shaved lettuce and underripe diced tomatoes.

'Ellen would say she could be vegetarian if kebabs didn't exist,' one of them recalled but the next day neither was sure which one of them, if it was indeed either of them, had said that out loud.

Chapter 17

A weird deadline entered Ryan's life. Theo and Jenny, his next-door neighbours, were having a party to celebrate Theo's early retirement. Ryan had never been invited to a house party with so much notice before. June. Three months away. He would take Sylvie, the new, free-from-the-past Sylvie. It would form her debut on the world stage after her period of hibernation. Theo and Jenny could give her career advice, Sylvie would meet Paul and Naomi and perhaps even be able to talk about her trauma, her past trauma, her fresh start. Three months.

'The weekend?' she said. 'I don't use the Underground at the weekends. I was commuting when it happened so my peculiar routine follows a commuter's.'

'That's the point, or at least partly the point,' Ryan said. 'I work in the week so it's easier for me to do this on a Saturday or Sunday. But I can book time off if you think it would be easier in the week for you. Really. I do get time off.'

They were sat at their usual banquette. It was a table with which Ryan had a love/hate relationship. It was claustrophobic, very public, very transient, very pasta-based, but it was theirs.

'Or we can go now, right now. I'm covered at the uni today.'

Sylvie tried to smile but could not quite manage it.

'Not now,' she said. 'Saturday is good. Thank you.'

'I've given this some thought and I think it will also help if I meet you at the start, at Eastcote station. Start as we mean to go on, sort of thing.'

He stood on the pavement outside the station at 11 a.m. as arranged. He was wearing black jeans and a black sweater. She was wearing a short black dress under a short black cardigan.

'We look like we're off to a funeral,' he said. She tried to smile again but failed.

'Right, Metropolitan line to Baker Street and then we change, or,' he said, turning to look at the miniature LED screen, 'we can wait another six minutes and get one straight to King's Cross.'

'Let's not wait,' she said and hand in hand they boarded the next train and he felt like Dustin Hoffman in *The Graduate*, rescuing the girl of his dreams; no need for any more words, no need to do or say anything other than travel towards what they needed to escape from. They sat next to each other in silence. She placed her head on his shoulder for a few minutes, in between Northwick Park and Preston Road. He held her hand. It was peaceful.

They navigated the intricacy that is changing trains at Baker Street with relative ease and Ryan forced himself to forget that this was where he had tried and failed to keep up with her. Three stops later they were at King's Cross standing on the eastbound platform. All they had to do was shift to the westbound platform, walk to the end of it and wait for the next train.

'Coffee first?' she said.

'No worries,' he said, keen to sound relaxed.

They sat not far from yet another young musician at the free-for-all piano who was trying his best not to overkill an Eric Satie 'Gymnopédie'.

Ryan thought the piece could easily be called 'Delay'. He asked her about her boss, the pervert, and how it was he could get away with removing her.

'It was,' she said, 'very easy. They gave me more than I would have got if I took them to a tribunal or to court and they did it so… swiftly. It was like the guillotine. I even had to leave there and then like you see in films about Wall Street. I was escorted from the building in a state of shock, I suppose. And I ended up here, cash rich, job poor.'

'That sort of thing doesn't happen in universities; at least I don't think it does, but if it did I'd like to think if the lecturer was the groper then he would be told to leave, not the student he tried it on with. But as you can tell, I can be hopelessly naïve.'

She had to smile now. She had the nerves associated with exam halls not grand station concourses, but he *was* hopelessly naïve and that was, she realized, a large part of his attractiveness to her. He was nothing like the corporate men she had worked with and for; he was earnest, possessed of something akin to purity, a sexy purity. She clung to the phrase. She had found a man with sexy purity, which made her very fortunate. She needed to remember that.

He drained his latte. 'Ready?'

'I'll just use the loo,' she said, touching his arm. 'Wait here.'

He waited, wondering if she would come back and if she did come back whether she would ask for another coffee, then for something to eat, for some fresh air. He decided he would not be too surprised if he sat there for an hour, waiting, eventually wondering if she existed at all or was a test sent by Ellen. Ah, he thought, here she is again, and as a joke to himself – or at least a diversion from his dead girlfriend – he looked at the corners of the café to see if there were cameras all pointed at him for *The Ryan Kennedy Show*.

Sylvie was only gone five minutes in the end. She placed both hands on his shoulders.

'I'm ready if you are,' she said with enforced jollity.

'It'll be fine,' he said. 'And if it isn't quite fine, I'm here.'

He stood up and they headed along the arcade of posh shops towards the entrance to the Underground. There was a huge swell of travellers and very few of them were wearing normal clothes. There were men, women and children in replica football and rugby shirts, a hen party in tutus and tiaras, a tall man in heels and a red leather skirt. There were transatlantic tourists in nasty leisurewear and bright trainers pulling and pushing bulky suitcases wrapped in thick layers of clingfilm. There were four policemen with guns stood to one side watching people in the early stages of revelry: before the booze, before the game, before the triumph and disaster, before the emotions got out of hand, before the abuse, the posturing, the singing, the chanting, the puking, the falling over, the ankles sprained by teetering on platform shoes while drunk, the stabbing. There would be at least one stabbing tonight. The policemen were sure of that.

'You've got to love this city,' Ryan said as he guided her towards the ticket barriers.

He stood behind her on the escalator, aware, suddenly, of how fragile she was physically as well as mentally. Her nearly red and robust hair had distracted him from quite how petite she was.

The westbound Metropolitan line platform was full so they hung back, allowing the throng to ebb in and out of the next train, and then together they walked to the far end of it. Sylvie was acutely aware that somehow this did not count as an exorcism. Saturdays were different. She could easily have been on the underground system of a foreign city for all the familiarity she felt. She stared at the tracks but there was no blood, no traces of the clean-up of a body crushed. There were no traces of emotion either. She was neither fearful nor tearful.

Ryan realized he had not thought about the moment. Was she supposed to cry or shake or, God forbid, wail?

'Is this helping?' he said.

'I don't know,' she said. 'I don't feel anything. It's not the same as it was then. It was quieter. It was sort of in slow motion. There was a hush, believe it or not. I should have brought some flowers.'

'That's probably not allowed,' he said.

'No, you're right.'

He tried to imagine what it must be like to watch someone jump in front of a train but decided he didn't want to. That decision came too late. It was Ellen's face he saw being slammed against a windscreen. He stepped back, wondering if this was all more unsettling for him than it was for Sylvie.

'Do you need longer?' he said.

She shook her head.

'It's so sad though, isn't it?'

'Of course it is, no one would say it wasn't.'

He looked at the clock on the platform display.

'I think we should go for a walk, have some lunch, maybe go to a gallery. What do you think?'

She paused in front of the map of the Tube.

'I've never been to Holland Park,' she said.

'Then let's go,' he said.

They wandered among the grand houses and leafy lanes, dodged the bikes in the park itself and then found a café just off Kensington High Street which was serving Moroccan chicken stew as its daily special, so they ate and they chatted like any couple.

'Thank you,' she said. 'For today. You know the policewoman said I had saved a life, that I was in the right place at the right time and had done a good thing. I didn't believe her but you were in the right place at the right time at Waterloo when you recognized me so maybe there's a pattern to it all, a reason, fate, something.'

'Maybe,' he said. 'I think you had post-traumatic stress and it's rubbish, really, that no one gave you any advice about it. You should probably tell your doctor, you know, get some free counselling on the NHS.'

She clutched the top of her head. 'I should have done that straightaway. I feel pretty stupid now.'

'So, what next?' he asked. 'Job hunting, or did they pay you off with a million quid?'

'I am registered with all sorts of agencies and I think I might do some temping, to ease myself back in.'

'Excellent plan,' he said, thinking, well, this is all going smoothly only we have not even kissed properly yet; but he did not want to try it over a stew.

'Is there an art gallery you've never been to?' he said. 'We could do the famous double whammy of new park, new museum.'

'I can't think. Give me a list.'

He took out his phone and sucked in through his teeth.

'There's lots of them,' he said. 'Tate Britain, Tate Modern, the Serpentine, the National Portrait Gallery, the Royal Academy—'

He was interrupted by a woman on an adjacent table.

'I am so sorry to interrupt,' she said, 'but we have just come from Leighton House Museum. It's five minutes or so from here and it would be a shame, if you are after art, not to go. We loved it.'

'Amazing,' said her friend. 'A hidden treasure.'

'I've never heard of it,' Ryan said,

'Me neither,' Sylvie said.

They left the women in a state of aesthetic martyrdom for having saved their souls from a slog to a big gallery when there had been a smaller, more intriguing one on their doorstep.

The main feature of Leighton House was the Arab Hall, covered in delicate, mostly blue, mosaics arranged around a small patch of water under a golden dome.

'So peaceful,' she said and they kissed, both understanding as it happened that such kisses are rare, that it was unplanned but inevitable, that it was amid beauty, that it was public and safe and that they would have looked a perfect sort of couple.

'Was that your first kiss?' asked a rosy-cheeked attendant.

They both laughed a little too loudly.

'Was it that obvious?' Ryan said.

'Maybe,' she said. 'I collect them. We get quite a few in here.'

'The First Kiss Collector,' Sylvie said later. 'If I was a teacher of English Language I would ask my students to write a story or a poem with that as the title.'

'And all the boys would make it about snooker and all the girls would make it about Justin Bieber.'

'That's sexist,' Sylvie said, 'and I was thinking the students would be in sixth form and they would have chosen English and they would all write something moving or tender or sad.'

'Hmm,' Ryan said, 'or it could be a thriller or a story about zombies.'

She punched him. 'You are being deliberately blokey,' she said. 'I will always remember our first First Kiss Collector.'

'I want to meet our first Second Kiss Collector,' he said and she giggled and they kissed in front of a busy pub and then guessed that their Second Kiss Collector was the young bloke with the crazy-old-man beard.

'Is it Appletini hour?' he said. 'Or we could catch a film, or do you need to get home?'

'Imagine,' she said, 'if we reached the cinema and there was a film called *The First Kiss Collector*.'

'I'd prefer *The Third Kiss Collector*,' he said and a few minutes later she pinched his arm and asked him when he would stop counting.

'I'm guessing after twenty, then it gets boring,' he said so she pinched him again. As they walked, constantly nudging each other, Sylvie slowly became aware that she felt carefree, but only in the way someone on holiday from a tough job might be carefree. The job – the Underground – was still there in the background. She had been to the platform but the anticipated sense of an ending, of a job done, was missing. She was happy right now, but she was not liberated.

'You're ironing and you're humming,' Paul said. 'That is not natural.'

'Sylvie is cooking me a Friday-night dinner,' Ryan said. 'At her flat.'

'But it's Monday. Rein it in, mate, you'll be yapping like a dog in heat by Friday.'

'Lovely image, thank you, Paul.'

'Oh, I've got the antidote: you can come to my open lecture on Thursday. Seeing how I'm delivering it a full ninety-second walk from your office I don't see how you can avoid it.'

Paul's lectures were legendary and usually involved members of the public with no expertise in genetics piling in and lending the whole event rock-star status.

'I want a front-row seat with a piece of paper stuck on it saying "Reserved for R. Kennedy".'

'And Sylvie, don't you want to impress her with the hottest ticket in town?'

Ryan sent her a message asking if a front-row seat at a genetic-solution-to-malaria lecture was worth her dashing away from her new job for, and to his surprise she said that it was.

The lecture theatre was jam-packed with undergraduates, postgraduates, lecturers, visiting lecturers and curious outsiders. An incognito TV producer was there too, to see whether Paul was the next smiling, screen-friendly and handsome scientist she had heard he could be.

There was a low hum peculiar to educational expectation. It was, Ryan thought, similar to the feel of a room just before a famous stand-up comedian entered it – except it was sober, contained the rustling of notepads and possessed a smugness that comes with knowing the world is about to become a better place.

Paul was not the least bit nervous. Had the hall been half empty he might have stammered and lost the desire to tell jokes and the ability to tell them well but a packed audience meant validation and that in turn boosted his conviction in the message. A packed audience meant they would get his jokes, they wanted to get his jokes and indeed would compete with each other to prove they understood the nuances contained in them, but Paul started with a knock-knock joke. It settled the room, forced them to interact and was, the TV producer noted, a success because of Paul's timing.

'Amos who?' chanted the audience and they all began laughing as Paul looked at them as if to say, 'You don't actually need me to complete the joke, do you?' But he did anyway with a wry smile that told of genius to come.

As he said, 'A mosquito,' Sylvie turned to Ryan in their front-row seats and whispered, 'Do you write his jokes too?'

Ryan whispered back that of course he did and then the laughter ebbed so he and Sylvie and everyone else settled back for the ride. Ryan was unable to stop feeling smug that he had had a part in the blossoming of the wondrous, witty being by his side, and he settled back to pay rapt attention to his friend.

There were no slides, no videos, just Paul and his science and his passion. The TV producer even shed a small tear of triumph as she pictured launching him on BBC primetime, while Sylvie wondered if he was already on TV because he looked familiar. Paul even received a standing ovation, which churned a portion of envy among some but few begrudged him his reception.

There was a small surge of bodies towards the stage. People were keen to either show off that they had understood the lecture or keen simply to shake Paul's hand. The producer hung back, watching carefully in case he disappeared.

Sylvie surveyed the room and saw Naomi, who was stood next to Ed. She recognized them both instantly, noted their restrained intimacy.

'There will be a sort of procession to a pub now,' Ryan told her. 'But we don't have to go.'

'Have you told people about me?' she said, suddenly conscious of the fact that while she was comfortable with Ryan, and he with her, she might be considered a freak by others.

'A bit,' Ryan said, unsure if he should lie or not. 'But it's fine, all fine, you mustn't worry. Trust me.'

She slipped her hand into his and he squeezed it then relaxed his grip as he spotted Naomi with Ed.

'Look who I found,' Naomi said and Sylvie held her breath, wondering if Ryan would be fooled.

'Good to see you again, Ed. Are you joining us for a drink?'

Naomi chewed the inside of her cheek as Ed accepted, even though Ryan's tone was guarded. Sylvie could not help thinking they would at least provide a distraction if she was to become the focus of attention.

Like the Pied Piper, Paul walked with his followers towards the pub. The producer decided to pounce before Paul began boozing. She introduced herself firmly and not a little seductively, produced her card and then her phone and asked for his number. Those who had been in conversation with Paul at that moment stood back a little in deference, as if watching him turn water into wine, for he certainly took the producer's intervention in his stride. With no trace of delight or mistrust or self-doubt he reeled off his number before asking if she was joining the pack in the pub. She smiled and said she would call him the next day and retreated smugly as Paul's acolytes stared after her with barely disguised nosiness.

Naomi had been full of swagger earlier in the day. Hana was not her responsibility, she kept telling herself, but she was Ryan's sister and Naomi was fonder of Ryan than she really knew.

'Ed was desperate to meet Paul and see him in action,' Naomi said weakly to Ryan, an element of guilt seeping, possibly imperceptibly, out of the pores of her skin.

This was not a lie. Ed's involvement with Naomi had reignited his passion for research and underlined for him that his work had become a treadmill lacking vigour. But Ed had also seen Paul's lecture as an opportunity for his and Naomi's relationship to become something she no longer had to hide.

'I also wanted to come along so I could ask Naomi out for a drink,' he said. She groaned involuntarily. 'And she said she would, although I'm hoping this isn't it.'

'It might be,' she growled but Ryan misunderstood.

'Hey,' he said, 'people move on. It's not as if Naomi is the reason you and Hana split up.'

'There you go,' Ed said. 'No one's embarrassed but you, Naomi.'

Sylvie noticed how Naomi glared back at him and how that glare softened to a knowing flirtation, but Ryan had turned to speak to a tall, willowy woman in her fifties who was wearing a long russet knitted skirt and matching jumper who would not have looked out of place in an Edward Hopper painting.

It meant Sylvie was left with only Ed and Naomi within easy earshot and, as the two women were stymied by their knowledge of the other, Ed was left to indulge in a soliloquy about how he was considering going back into education, inspired by Naomi's hungry insects and Paul's deadly ones, and then, realizing he had monopolized the space, he smiled at Sylvie.

'You look like you dashed here straight from the office,' he said.

There were plenty of lies involved but nothing too complicated. Sylvie had told the agency she had been diverted from work because her mother had been ill – but in remission now, thank you – and as she had an excellent reference from her previous employer, no one appeared all that bothered about her near-year-long absence from the job market. She was a temp, and no one cared too much about temps. By their very nature they would work in bursts and it saved a degree of awkwardness if, when the permanent member of staff returned, the temp had felt temporary.

The handover was smooth. Sylvie was covering for Clara, who was heavily pregnant in a jolly, rosebuds-on-her-smock sort of way, and the office was friendly enough but it had been hard to leave the Tube. Physically hard. The ride up the escalator had been a suction on her vital organs. She had reached street level at Moorgate and found it hard to breathe and when she returned to the Underground at 6 p.m. she felt not the spasm of guilt she anticipated but a deep sense of ugly bereavement.

The next day was worse, not better, and Sylvie was frightened by the compulsion – frightened that it was so visceral, that her ignoring of it caused her to feel hot and anxious and torn in two. Clara was leaving early on her last day in the office but before heading off to her afternoon-tea treat, she found time to tell Sylvie that she looked unwell and must leave early too.

When Thursday morning came, Sylvie dressed for the office but she trembled as she did so, partly out of self-loathing, and partly out of a prescience that her world was about to collapse just as she had been rebuilding it. She mouthed a mantra as she walked towards Eastcote station. Get to the office; meet Ryan after.

When the doors opened at Moorgate she remained seated. She was glued to the seat via a cord that ran from the nape of her neck. To struggle would make her conspicuous. She was by now feeling panicked, so she did not stand, she did not make a move towards the doors and, once they had closed, the air circulated again in the carriage and her ears felt as if they had emerged from being under water. At Liverpool Street she was able to seamlessly alight and change to the Central line. She was both relieved and disgusted with herself. She knew what her day held now. Stay below; meet Ryan after.

*

On the Friday, the day after Paul's triumphant lecture, she cooked for her new boyfriend. He had disliked her high street so was pleasantly surprised by her home. Sylvie lived on the first floor of a pretty terraced house that had been converted into two flats with the owner occupying the ground floor and its garden. Sylvie opened the front door to him and then tapped on another front door to the left of it inside the narrow hall.

'Trish, this is Ryan, Ryan this is technically my landlady but also my dear friend Trish, and I promised she could meet you.'

'Sorry, Ryan,' she said. 'But I was insistent. And you have to come in and have a drink with me.'

They stayed for twenty-five minutes, mainly because Trish had put some crisps in a bowl and chilled some beers and wine and it seemed rude to cut the visit any shorter. If Trish knew about Sylvie's strange year then she hid it well and the talk was mainly of Sylvie's predecessors in the upstairs flat, one of whom had been a bigamist with a mail-order bride.

'Presumably he thought it didn't count, being mail order,' Ryan said.

He had been valiant. It was not an enjoyable twenty-five minutes. Trish was intelligent enough and, as landladies went, from his past experience of the land of bedsits, clearly fair and quite possibly generous, but Ryan found it hard to look the woman in the eye. Her face was uneven and her skin blotchy. It was impossible to tell if she was forty-five or closer to sixty. She was quite clearly an alcoholic and yet Sylvie did not squirm when Trish opened what was undoubtedly an unnecessary second bottle as they were about to leave.

The woman was, he thought, in love with Sylvie. She gazed at her intently, nodded intently when Sylvie spoke. She stroked Sylvie's arm and told Ryan to 'just look at that hair' three times. The subtext was not hard to fathom. Trish had been pretty once; there were photographs on her shelves to prove it. She had been a receptionist for a commercial radio station, married a presenter, given up work to have their child, been divorced by him for his new co-host, had turned bitterly to booze and then, somewhere along the way, she lost the bile but had been unable to shed the prop of alcohol. The child was there, in the photographs, but he guessed the daughter had little to do with her bloated mother these days and Sylvie was a substitute. It irked Ryan that Sylvie was so relaxed in that ground-floor flat while being stared at so hungrily, with such need. The room had stifled him. He could smell the vinegar of wine dregs mixed with the cheap scented candle being used to mask it. For a brief second he could see his mother sneering in distaste at the smell of ale in their home.

He wanted Sylvie to roll her eyes when Trish finally closed her door so they could climb the stairs but she merely murmured, 'Poor Trish, such a nice woman,' which left him feeling uncharitable. Even so, he refused to let the woman dominate any more of his evening so he pretended not to hear what Sylvie had said and instead found himself asking her if she always wore the same perfume and gurning at himself for being so uninteresting.

Sylvie had recreated the Moroccan chicken dish and he declared hers much the nicer, although he found it hard to digest because she did not seem to want to talk about her new job. He honestly was not at all sure he could handle it if she was back underground, except she confessed that she had never really left it after they had made love in a room that smelled of jasmine and on cream sheets that made Sylvie and her nearly red hair look like part of a Botticelli painting.

'We'll sort it,' he said, but had not a clue how.

'I won't blame you if you want to bail; we can part as friends,' she said, not moving from the bed, and he shook his head. This was all too beautiful for the Tube to be allowed to spoil it.

'It's too late for friends,' he said and lay back down, both enchanted and dispirited and then enchanted again as she shook her hair as if it was full of sugar shards that needed to be released before they could embrace once more, and he wondered how it was he could be so happy and so worried at the same time.

Hana was sat with her mother and grandfather. Both women were becoming frustrated with their lives. There was no carriage clock on the mantelpiece but both of them heard one ticking as Grandpa fell into a post-Battenberg doze, some of the pink sponge lodged in the folds of his lovingly hand-washed cardigan.

Grace was hesitant to ask her daughter about her holiday plans, *any* plans. Hana was bitter these days, snappy. Her pain with the sloth had been deeply felt but expressed quietly. Her disappointment in Ed was brittle and angry with a barely disguised layer of self-loathing, for she had adored him and he had not adored her. Grace could see that she adored him still.

Grace was annoyed too. She had nurtured her daughter

back to emotional health after her divorce, made living with Grandpa seem like fun when it was very hard work. She had sheltered Hana from most of the trickier visits to the bathroom, the bathtimes, the pyjama struggles on his bad days. She had made it all about cake and TV and weekly outings to the pub. She had made sure she smiled when she would have preferred to scowl and swear; she had encouraged Hana to go out even though she missed her terribly when she did. Grace's life had become Grandpa-centric just before Hana moved back in and the monotony and loneliness of it had been bearable because it was shared with someone she truly loved. Grace was fond of Joe's father, he had suffered as she had suffered, and he had no one else but her to care if he ate enough parkin loaf, but he was not her father. She did not love him unconditionally.

It was duty and a shared awful sadness that kept him in the armchair in front of the shopping channel. It was duty and love that had given her the energy to rebuild Hana's shattered confidence, encourage her to go walking, to find new friends. The discovery of Ed was a bonus and while a part of Grace feared Hana announcing she was leaving home again, mostly it was what she wanted for her daughter – even if the prospect of endless bouncy voices extolling the virtues of a knife sharpener or a yoga mat or a limited-edition charm bracelet filled her with hollow dread. And now she would have to start building Hana's self-esteem again. But it was tougher this time, for some reason.

She decided to take the plunge.

'I could do with a break,' she said. 'We could go somewhere together if you could bear it, my sweetheart?'

Hana turned to her slowly while pointing at Grandpa.

'Ryan can stay and he can pay for some help,' Grace said. 'He has offered, you know.'

Hana was not so angry that she wanted to hurt her mother but she had thought she and Ed would be spending the Easter break walking in Cornwall and then travelling abroad in the summer. She had daydreamed about their elegant, minimalist, grown-up wedding, about a surprise baby when she was forty-two that would give Grace a new burst of life and purpose. But now Hana was expected to climb down from the cloud of fertile happiness and engage in the life of a barren spinster supping tea on a terrace in Bournemouth or Torquay.

'Where do you fancy going?' she said gloomily.

'Las Vegas,' Grace said and Hana spluttered her coffee. 'I've been saving up,' her mother added. 'I want to see the Grand Canyon as well.'

Hana was so surprised that she stopped thinking about Ed for a full twenty seconds.

'You're on, Mam,' she said, not believing for a moment they would do it but certainly intrigued enough to fall into line.

Grace allowed herself a small smile. She had no idea at all if she would like Vegas and had never thought about going. It had been an inspired spur-of-the-moment suggestion in case her daughter had been dreading the prospect of a holiday that would include them strolling along Blackpool Pier towards a cabaret show or eating fish and chips in the blustery breeze of Lyme Regis.

Still, she stole a guilty glance towards Grandpa, who had been silently weeping but had now stopped. The tear stains on his cheeks were such a regular occurrence, she thought, that there would come a day when she would not quite be able to erase them. Like a glacier taking centuries to leave a scar on the landscape, the tracks of Grandpa's tears would become a permanent feature of his plump and jowly face. She had no real idea of why he wept but she could sympathize. If she was to sit in the same chair each day with the luxury of time in which to reminisce about her life before Tom was taken from her, she too would weep so hard her cheeks would become as chapped and sore as her soul.

On the other side of London, Naomi turned towards Ed.

'It's still based on a lie,' she said, but not crossly.

'No, it isn't. You were loyal and honourable and would not fondle me until I had made it clear to Hana it was over. We did not overlap. We did not deceive. We are in the clear, young lady.'

'You know what I mean. I'm still sleeping on a mate's sofa bed as far as Ryan is concerned.'

'We are simply a few weeks out of sync with reality, that's all. In a few months, no one will care, just like nobody cares what A level results you got a year later or whether you saw Radiohead live or not.'

'I guess,' she said and for the first time she wondered if it was such a good thing that Ed was so eloquent and persuasive in absolving them of any wrongdoing whatsoever. Oh, but Naomi so liked their dead-level kisses, the way strangers gawped at them as they strode along the pavements of Lilliput London. They had both worn black jeans the day before as they headed to the cinema and she had noted the envy in the eyes of a pretty woman of average height whose hot drink had dribbled on to her neatly wrapped pale coral scarf as she had stopped mid-sip to assess a relationship that she could only dream of having.

The woman reminded Naomi of Hana and how smitten she had been with Ed. She knew that, she could understand that, and she conceded, with a spasm of guilt, that just one, rather ludicrous, lunch had ruined everything for a woman who deserved better.

Chapter 18

Paul dragged Ryan off for yet another Friday-night curry. He had missed the ability to easily find a decent Keema Masala while abroad and was still in his childlike, glad-to-be-back-in-London phase. He was a mixture of contentedness and excitability and very good company, aware that teasing Ryan too heavily about finally sleeping with Sylvie would ruin the evening, but unable, all the same, to stop congratulating him.

'You know, you did say part of the reason for coming back was to find women who would get your jokes,' Ryan said, keen for his sex life not to dominate the conversation.

'Not true. No one is ever going to truly like my jokes but I want to be able to impersonate Lord Percy Percy and not be treated like an imbecile. Shared humour, it's not much to ask for. OK, why are looking so pleased with yourself?'

'Sylvie was happy to try an Appletini, so I get it. It's vital for any healthy relationship to be able to order an homage cocktail.'

'God, yes,' Paul said. 'And what's the score with her? One minute she's a bit, um, dubious, the next she's back at work, then sat next to you at my lecture smiling at all the right moments, smiling at you, and you're getting envious looks from the geeks using your labs. What did you do exactly to turn a mystery into a relationship?'

Ryan tried to appear confident and nonchalant but Paul knew him too well.

'Ah, what couldn't you do?'

'Don't get me wrong, she's great, I like her a lot, and she did get a job after we, you know, visited the scene of the crime, so to speak, but she's jacked it in and she's back on the Tube.'

'As in, back on the booze? She's addicted?'

'No, no of course not. It's like OCD or something. She calls it a commitment. It's like she still blames herself and is doing it as a punishment.'

Paul nodded and chewed and nodded again. He was fascinated by the woman he too had followed underground.

'You thought – she thought, in fact – that going to the platform where it happened would give her closure, and it almost did by the sound of it. But there's something else. It was a sound guess to think she needed to see the place but,' and here Paul adopted a Northern Irish accent, 'unfortunately not the right one.'

Ryan laughed.

'You see, shared humour. Roy Walker, *Catchphrase*, I salute you.'

'So any idea what the real catchphrase for Sylvie is?' Ryan asked once Paul had stopped repeating the phrase, 'Good answer, but not the right one.'

'She'll know it,' Paul said, suddenly serious. 'Only she can know it, really.'

*

Sylvie was about to board the mainline train to Reading, having not visited her parents since Christmas. She collected her ticket from the foyer at Paddington, bought herself a large coffee and some dark chocolate, settled into her seat and tried to think about nothing. All her life she had hoped her parents would express more interest in the minutiae of her life but currently their lack of curiosity was a blessing. She would be vague and they would not care for her to elaborate. She could have spent the entire journey daydreaming about Ryan but she knew he was disappointed in her. She was quite convinced he would vanish, spooked, from her life and she was angry she could not summon the courage to prevent it.

She had stopped restyling her bedroom nine years ago and it was stuck in time now with its Paul Smith-style wallpaper and matt grey desk. 'I was virtually a tomboy,' she chuckled to herself but of course when compared to her brother's room hers was mightily feminine. Franklyn had sports memorabilia galore and myriad posters and cards of famous sportsmen from football, rugby, cricket, baseball and American football over every square inch of the place. Not one woman, she thought, not even a cheerleader.

Brooke could have been a cheerleader. She would have to ask her next time they met. Or maybe not. Franklyn had become someone who suited his name. Her family had not one single link to the United States before they named their firstborn after a famous president. It was as if every morning the toddler Franklyn and then the young Franklyn and then the teenage Franklyn – never Frank, never Frankie – had woken up and vowed to do more to ensure he could gain passage to America. His hair had been more of a strawberry colour at Christmas, kissed by the Florida sun. His kids would probably be called Todd and Madison. He phoned home while Sylvie was there but not because he knew she was. He was calling to ask his mother to sort out the wedding for June.

'June next year?' Sylvie heard her mother say as if that would be pushing it if they wanted to luxuriate in the various choices of venue.

'The wedding,' she said as she ended the call, 'will be in seven weeks. Brooke, apparently, is distraught. She is pregnant.'

As the evening unfolded, Sylvie became aware that her mother too was distraught. She was being denied not only a year or more of planning and anticipation – of having the time to change her mind on whether the napkins should be a shade of apricot or peach – but also the speculation of when her Franklyn would become a father. It was all happening too quickly and, all at once, and she was quietly furious. So furious that she turned to her daughter, eyes glinting, later in the evening.

'Don't *you* dare pull a stunt like this,' she said and Sylvie was annoyed that she felt an unfurling of pride that her mother wanted her to have the perfect, chaste wedding day, if only for herself.

The upside was that questions about Sylvie's career were at their absolute minimum as her mother ordered her to hurtle through various websites to help find the fairy-tale English venue Brooke was hoping for.

'Oh, the invitations,' she groaned, 'that's a month's work we'll have to pack into a few days.'

Sylvie found herself offering to liaise with Brooke and Franklyn over the guest list and to be in charge of the printing.

Her mother paused, weighing up the loss of power over the practicalities, and decided to graciously accept, even adding a 'thank you, darling' that her daughter lapped up thirstily. As Sylvie retired to bed her mother stood to give her a kiss on the cheek.

'We make a good team in an emergency,' she said and although they had never teamed up before Sylvie subconsciously created a personal history in which she and her mother had rescued soufflés from deflating, found petrol stations just as the dashboard warning sign flashed that they were out of fuel and had pulled a puppy from a sticky pond.

She emailed Franklyn that night, adopting a deliberately officious tone so he would know she was in charge. Of all her relatives, it was, curiously, her brother who knew best that she was extremely adept at organization. He would calm Brooke and tell her they were in good hands. He would give her Sylvie's contact details and before too long she would be a de facto wedding planner.

On Sunday evening her father drove her to the station, his eyes cloudy from the boredom the wedding talk had induced. He would sorely have liked to discuss the weekend's cricket and Sylvie, having managed to forge a connection with her mother, decided to do the same with her dad. Years of sports chat at the dining table had left her with a residual knowledge of the ebbs and flows of the season and so she asked him if he had enjoyed his recent trip to Lord's. Her father was too grateful for the opportunity to expound to a captive audience to bother wondering why his daughter cared.

As she climbed out of the car, her parting shot as she

closed the door was, 'I don't think we were truly ready for draft system in cricket.'

Her father drove home a little perplexed but also a little proud. He had a daughter but she liked her sport, of course she did, he was a great dad. Enlightened, probably. He had watched her play netball once.

'We're off to Vegas next month,' Hana told Ryan that Sunday.

For a moment he thought she meant her and Ed were going away together and he flushed as he remembered Ed had hooked up with Naomi and that was, in a roundabout way, his fault.

'Yes,' chimed in Grace, 'we're hitting the slot machines.'

Ryan looked from one to the other, wondering if he was missing the joke, and then he looked from one to the other and across at his grandfather, wondering if it was he, Ryan, who *was* the joke.

The women saw the panic in his eyes.

'We've looked at home help and if you can get back here by 6.30 each night of the fortnight and be here at the weekend, it's doable and not too expensive,' Hana said firmly.

Ryan opened his mouth and closed it again so Hana added that he could buy in evening cover but that was up to him and how much he could afford to pay for it.

'Mam deserves a break, don't you think?' she said without smiling.

'Have I said I won't be here?' he asked and to make a point to Hana he kissed Grace on the cheek.

Grace was speechless, her heart a turbulent mix of gratitude, love, guilt and worry. Eventually she smiled.

'My word, Las Vegas,' she said.

Hana was stirred by Ryan's stoicism and understood at that moment that she had been blaming her little brother for the end of Ed.

'Oh, Ryan,' she said, embracing him awkwardly. 'I should have discussed it with you, I'm sorry.'

'Look!' shouted Grandpa excitedly and they all looked, expecting to see some terrible atrocity in Berlin or Paris, but it was Tiffany, his new love, on the shopping channel with a new hairdo.

At four, Ryan left to meet Sylvie. He had been full of ideas and energy about ways to end her commitment but was now deflated at having a grandparent to worry about as well. He almost welcomed being sat in Trish's Sauvignon-scented maisonette with both women extending sympathy, but neither of them thought he should even want to end this particular commitment to his grandfather. It was almost scary to be in a predicament that no one in the world believed he should be able to avoid. He was at the mercy of some sort of universal moral code.

'I'll visit you,' Sylvie said. 'Help you get him to bed.'

Ryan sighed. He had known it was coming. He had to try to be grateful it was just a fortnight. Sylvie, had, after all, been trapped for a year and without the weight of morality behind her. She was alone. He vowed to be less self-pitying and then, after a short, companionable silence, he blinked with an idea.

'Sylvie, I'll come with you one day next week and you can talk me through what happens so we can devise a way out of it,' he said.

'That's thoughtful but I'd be too embarrassed, really,' she said. 'The whole thing is embarrassing.'

'No,' he said firmly. 'It isn't. It's a problem that needs solving, that's all. And we'll solve it.'

He met her outside Eastcote on a day of weak sunshine accompanied by a weak, lukewarm breeze.

'This is silly,' she said, 'there's no need for you to waste your day as well.'

'It's not a waste, it's the opposite of waste,' he said as he handed her a Cadbury's Creme Egg. 'We are being constructive.'

'Is this my breakfast?'

'No, but it's comforting to have one handy, I always think,' he said.

They boarded a Metropolitan line train.

'How do you decide which train to catch?' he asked.

'I take the first one, that's all. I don't set out with a plan other than to get into the heart of the Underground before changing.'

'How do you know when it's time to change?'

She shrugged.

'I don't know that I know, it just happens, like when you realize you're filling the kettle but you did it automatically.'

They sat in silence until Liverpool Street.

'Time to be on the move,' she said.

'Do you know where you are headed now?'

'Not really. I just follow my nose.'

'Are you looking for anything, or someone, a sign perhaps?'

She did not answer. She was pondering the question. She led him towards the Central line. They could head out of town or towards its centre. What made her decide which direction? She chose west and looked around intently. There was a short woman with long brown hair in front of them. Was there always a woman ahead of her? Was she looking for the mother with brown eyes? Her eyes welled up and she felt in her pocket for a tissue. People did not cry on the Underground. Not even those desperate enough to step in front of a train.

The woman in the long skirt had not cried and she had known what she was about to do or why else hand over her child? Sylvie could not comprehend the premeditation of it, the accompanying calmness. She could not comprehend how she had been a part of it. An accomplice. She wondered if she was punishing herself by turning herself into the ghost of the suicide victim, doomed to wander the Underground until— She rubbed her forehead. That was the question. What signal was she waiting for that would free her from this absurd ritual? There was something inside her, she could feel it, tightly wound, waiting for the key or a code to release the tension and the compulsion. She thought Ryan was the key and then she thought, if not Ryan, then he at least would find it and she knew he was trying and she was grateful but if this was to be her great love affair then it had better stop being so absurd pretty soon.

They lunched at one of their Waterloo booths. It was chilly. The half-hearted sunshine could not permeate the glass roof and those around them scurried with more speed than usual. The departure board updated itself almost petulantly as if to say, 'I am so busy today, too may trains, not enough platforms, keep up people, pay attention, blink and you'll miss where you need to be.' Commuters and holidaymakers strained their necks, parents chased runaway toddlers, a buggy tipped over under the weight of its bags, a large woman in a low-cut scarlet velvet dress belted out something operatic in front of a collection bucket, the queue at Starbucks spread out onto the station foyer. Their waiter winked. He had served them before.

'Are you ever tempted to catch a mainline train?' Ryan asked.

'Never,' she said. 'I think I can sit here or at another station for lunch because that's what I did on the day it happened. But I'm not recreating that day, not really. I'm searching, I think, but for something else.'

Ryan nodded encouragingly.

'What? What are you looking for?'

'A reason perhaps. I don't know. Why would a young mother do that? If I had not been there would she have jumped with her baby? And if she would then I have to be here, don't I? Maybe that's it.'

Sylvie did not sound convinced but she wanted Ryan to believe they were making progress. He could tell she was trying to please him but she had given him an idea.

'Can I choose where we go next?' he said.

'We can try that,' she said and he led her onto the Northern line to Euston where they changed for the one stop to King's Cross.

There was a stooped man helping anyone whose ticket would not open the gates and, when there was a gap in the flow of passengers, Ryan asked if there was anyone in charge he could speak to.

He expected a stare of incredulity or a flat-out refusal but the man led him to an office.

'Stan, there's a customer needs to see you,' he said and then he returned to the ticket barriers.

Stan was stocky and wearing a stocky tie on a short-sleeved white shirt. He did not stand up but he smiled and asked how he could help. Sylvie instinctively stood in Ryan's shadow, nervous about what was to unfold.

'A year ago, my girlfriend here witnessed a woman jump in front of a train at this station and she was handed the woman's baby just before she did so. This has been hard for Sylvie to come to terms with. I wondered if we could have any information about the mother and the baby because I feel strongly that if Sylvie knew more about why such a dreadful thing happened, she could move on.'

The stocky man nodded his stocky neck.

'Terrible tragedy,' he said as if he used that phrase at least once a day. 'Look, give me your details and I'll see who you should speak to. It might be the family don't want to give any information, but you never know. If it was me, I'd be mightily grateful this young woman had been there to take the baby, but you never know.'

Ryan led her up into the integrated shopping mall.

'Do you feel able to leave? To go home, or go for a walk?'

She gazed at the people flocking to the Tube concourse. She wanted to join them, alone, but she fought against it.

'Let's try,' she said and they walked hand in hand onto the street where the sunshine had summoned courage of its own and had warmed the air so that it was the most buoyant of spring days. They meandered and were fortunate to end up in Bloomsbury, which was bursting with daffodils and a Dickensian beauty. She knew how badly he wanted her to say he had found her an escape route, that she could tell this was the beginning of the end, but she did not want to lie and so she remained quiet. It might be the beginning, but she was by no means sure of it.

'It's so peaceful here,' he said. 'London is amazing, don't you think?'

She was too busy fighting the urge to drag him into Russell Square station to absorb the wonders of the Georgian architecture but she was glad to be with him and so she did the only thing that felt honest and kissed him with more passion than she ever had before.

Ryan heard nothing for ten days from stocky-man Stan but just as he was considering composing a brusque email, he received a message apologizing for the delay and suggesting that Sylvie should speak to a Jonny Smalling at the social services department that had found emergency foster care for the baby while the suicide was investigated.

Stan was right, it should not be him who made the call, it should be Sylvie, but instinctively Ryan made the call anyway.

Jonny was sympathetic but not overly so. He had the manner of a man who hears sad stories every working day. His specialism was emergencies, not their year-old repercussions, but he remembered the incident and said he doubted it was breaking anyone's trust to tell Ryan that the child had been reunited with its grandparents.

'But could Sylvie meet them, see for herself that the baby is well, that she did a good thing? She seems to blame herself for the mother dying for some reason. Or at least she is tied up in knots about whether the mother would still have jumped if she hadn't been there. What I am trying to say is that while it seems obvious to most of us that my girlfriend saved a baby's life by being in the right place at the right time, she worries she was in the wrong place and did the wrong thing and was blind to what was unfolding in front of her. Do you see what I'm saying?'

Jonny said Ryan made perfect sense and would ask the family for some co-operation but had a hunch they would not be keen.

'It's ruining her life,' Ryan said, a touch embarrassed by the melodrama of his assertion. 'Could you tell them that at least?'

'I'll do what I can,' Jonny said and Ryan could hear the professional barrier in his tone of voice and he wondered if people like Jonny ever cried at soppy films.

The wait this time was much longer. Sylvie went back to her old routine and Ryan prepared himself for two weeks at home with Grandpa.

'We're off to America, Grandpa,' the women said. 'Won't be long.'

'Get me some of that Madeira cake,' he said. 'I like that one, no surprises in a Madeira cake.'

Ryan waved his mother and sister off at the front door.

'He thinks you're off to the supermarket,' he said.

'No need to worry him,' Grace said and she gave her son a tight hug, the warmth of which meant Ryan felt strong and generous for at least ten minutes. But with his sister and mother gone, the house felt cold and unfamiliar and he noticed, and then became irritated by, his grandpa's whistling way of breathing.

'Grandpa,' he said, 'how about we go to your local this afternoon? You haven't been for a bit. They'll be missing you.'

Grandpa, to Ryan's surprise, turned off the TV.

'My word, you look like Joe,' he said and the tears fell and Ryan wondered why on earth none of them had realized that Grandpa regularly wept because his only child had stepped in front of a speeding truck in the prime of his life.

Ryan handed him one of the many freshly laundered and ironed cotton handkerchiefs Grace had left in the drawer of the small sideboard next to the television, but as his grandfather simply held it, Ryan wiped his cheeks and nose for him. It was the most tender he could remember being with another man.

'Tell me about Joe,' he said. 'I don't remember Dad much at all.'

Grandpa grunted. 'Let me move to the table,' he said and Ryan smiled and filled the kettle and assessed the array of cakes Grace had left under her little mesh cake tent or wrapped in clingfilm on top of the iridescently clean worktop. He had been warned against placing a choice in front of Grandpa but decided there was no harm in a couple of options, so he put two slices of ginger loaf and two chunks of a plain strawberry-jam-filled Victoria sponge on a large plate next to two side plates.

Grandpa peered at them suspiciously but hungrily.

'Not joining me?' he said and Ryan chuckled as he sat down to learn about his father free of the worry of what the telling and reminiscing might do to Grace.

'Very bright boy was our Joe, good at mending things, building things. Elsa couldn't have any more so we spoiled him a bit. I remember he was suspended from school. He was twelve and he got into a fight. Wouldn't tell us what that fight was about and then a few weeks later he gave your grandmother a wooden jewellery box he had made for her, decorated with a few hearts, and she got all tearful, she did, and Joe said that was what the fight had been about. A few lads had teased him about the hearts. Called him a fairy. Ha, well, his mother cried proper after that, she did. Loved him to bits.'

'Not sure I could make a wooden box,' Ryan said.

'Oh, it was a beautiful thing, very fine craftsmanship.'

'Could I see it, is it somewhere in your room?'

Grandpa steadily masticated on his Victoria sponge, then swallowed dramatically.

'I threw it away,' he said. 'I threw it away with lots of other things I shouldn't have thrown away when Joe did what he did. I was angry, son, so very angry.'

Another tear slid down his face and Ryan was at a loss to know what to say. He felt as if his mother had left him in charge of something potentially faulty, like a gas fire or a hairdryer, and told him not to touch it, but he had used it and it had set fire to the entire house. He was meddling with Grandpa's emotions, interfering with his routine. When Grace came home it might be to find a dreadful mess.

'I'm sorry, Grandpa,' Ryan said. 'I'm making you upset.'

'Don't be silly, lad, do you think I'm not always upset? Do you think I don't think about our Joe and poor Tommy unless someone asks me about them?'

Ryan refilled their mugs, wondering if Grandpa was now so emotionally agitated he would be better off taking a nap. He wondered about his father and the pain he must have felt to have wanted to end his life. Not once had he been indignant that he was not motivation enough for his father to stay alive. Hana, though, had suffered that indignation for them both, and, he suspected, still did. Maybe they both needed a drink.

'Shall we go to the pub now?' he asked Grandpa.

'What, straight after cake?' Grandpa scoffed. 'The whisky would curdle in my gut. Let's play some dominoes instead. While the cat's away.'

Ryan laughed out loud. The idea that playing dominoes was breaking all the rules was ludicrous but to Grandpa it was something for the men to do without the background wittering of the women. To his surprise, Ryan discovered he enjoyed the game. He wondered if he had played it as a child with his grandfather, so comfortable was it to be sat opposite him, running his fingers along the smooth edges of a double six. The pieces were probably Victorian, he thought, and he wondered how it was he knew exactly where he would find the oblong wooden box even though he could not recall when he had last played, if at all. They took turns in finding a match in a companionable silence punctured by Grandpa's grunts of triumphalism. Surely, it was a game of pure luck, Ryan thought, and yet he was being trounced. Grandpa was the first to win ten rounds so he leaned back as pleased with himself as he would have been had he just defeated Gary Kasparov at chess.

'Bone and ebony,' he said, holding a double three. 'Belonged to my father. I have an idea he told me they were made of elephant tusks but later confessed it was just cow bone. I much preferred playing with them when I thought they were made of ivory. Can't buy ivory stuff now. I know that from the girls on telly.' Grandpa leaned in conspiratorially. 'It's illegal.'

Ryan suppressed a smile and nodded as if being let in on a big secret, but he pondered if the shopping channel informed his grandfather that cakes were wicked, then would stop he eating them? Was the channel his new religion? What would win in the battle of ideologies? he wondered. Cake or shopping for unnecessary imperishables?

'I was being serious, you know, about you settling down,' Grandpa said. 'And I know why you haven't.'

Ryan sighed and smiled.

'Do you now, Grandpa?'

His grandfather leaned forward again, knocking over the double three he had balanced upright on the table. Ryan was taken aback; Grandpa looked, in a flash, ten years younger.

'You were in love with a girl and I confess right here and now I can't remember her name but I do know she died while you were away, studying, and I know that she's with you still.'

Ryan was unnerved and his throat dried. He looked towards the window and thought he saw her, smiling, just for a second, and then, his face paler than usual against his dark curls, he turned back to look at the old man.

'She's not telling you to wait for her or to join her,' he said. 'I don't know much but I do know that. The dead we love are not cruel to us.'

There was a long silence as Ryan slid the dominoes around the table.

'Then why is she here?' he said. 'Because, it has, she has, you know, made it hard for me to be with someone.'

'I think,' he said, carefully, 'I think maybe you had something so strong that it carried on, that's all. She's just a reminder of a deep love, a rare love, at an impressionable age that should have carried on. It's a great shame, lad, it really is, but it's not a warning. It's a reminder of happiness, that's all.'

Chapter 19

Jonny Smalling looked through the paperwork and decided it was not unreasonable for him to request to see how the child was getting along. He already knew that the girl, Nisha, now just over a year old, was looked after by her grandmother and there was no father on the scene.

He knocked at their front door. It was opened by a young teenage girl who stood there, mouth agape, as he explained who he was. She shut the door on him very carefully as if not wanting to offend him or anyone in the house – or draw to the attention of anyone who might be passing the fact they had an official-looking visitor – and he heard a muffled exchange before the door reopened, softly, and the young girl asked him to follow her into the kitchen, where a tiny woman in her forties was chopping onions.

Jonny asked how she was and she shook her head and muttered that it was a terrible thing to have happened to her family.

'And where is baby Nisha?'

The woman pointed to the long narrow garden beyond the kitchen window where another teenage girl was placing

Nisha on a miniature pink plastic slide, singing 'Whoosh!' as the baby descended, and then repeating the operation.

'She looks very healthy and happy. I wonder if you could help me with something, Mrs Mannan? The young lady who was handed Nisha that day on the Underground is very traumatized, still rather upset, and it might help her to meet you and Nisha, to see how good can still come from such a sad thing. What do you think? Perhaps you have wondered about meeting her; it might be good for you too.'

Nisha was by now in the kitchen being held by her young aunt who said nothing but looked intently at her mother with intelligent and, Jonny thought, defiant eyes.

'No, no,' the mother said. 'That would be impossible.'

'It's your decision, of course,' Jonny said, aware that Mrs Mannan had not weighed up what he had said to her, that she had heard only something that implied prying, that would entail opening her home or her heart, the piercing of long-held secrets.

'Maybe you could think about it and let me know if you have a change of heart? It's just to help a young woman out, that's all.'

Jonny spoke with a degree of perceptible, if professional, sadness; the sadness of a man who knows his words are not being digested but deflected. He waited ten days and then sent an email to Ryan.

> The family are very private and I am unable to do more than I already have without crossing various ethical boundaries but perhaps you could tell Sylvie that the baby is healthy and well cared for and has a pair of what appear to be devoted young aunts.

Ryan slammed his fist onto his desk. 'Very private,' he muttered.

She insisted she find the house herself and he was surprised that he was pacing the floor, waiting for the knock. At last it came.

'Grandpa, this is my friend Sylvie,' he said.

'Pleased to meet you, young lady. I had a cousin called Sylvia. Long dead now.'

Ryan smiled apologetically.

'You'll be Sylvia from now on, I'm afraid.'

'I don't mind. It has happened before and will happen again.'

'I've never asked about your name. You're the first Sylvie I've ever met or heard of. It's pretty.'

'Hmm, my mother loved these Enid Blyton *Faraway Tree* books and there was a fairy called Silky. She wanted to call me that but my dad intervened, thankfully. They compromised on Sylvie but she's still been annoyed that my hair is curly ever since.'

Ryan wound a strand of her hair around his index finger, released it and let it bounce.

'Lovebirds,' shouted Grandpa, 'how's that dinner you promised coming along?'

Ryan had been pelting his grandfather with questions, one of which had been why he would eat cake and no proper lunch and often no proper supper. The answer was not so mysterious. He did not like the things Grace thought he liked – because he had once tried them – or the things Grace thought he ought to like, and so Ryan had asked him what he would really like.

'Corned beef patties,' he said.

'And that's it? Nothing else?'

'You asked and I've told you, son.'

They sat at the table. Grandpa ignored the steamed broccoli and corn on the cob and began to use his fork to break up his corned beef potato cake. Ryan and Sylvie watched on, nervously. They had followed a recipe to the letter but were not at all sure the patties would taste as he expected them to.

'Supposed to be crispier but not bad at all,' he said, grinning, but after about ten minutes he became withdrawn, hobbled to his chair and with the sort of grand sigh only old and tired men can summon he sat down and turned on the TV. He ignored the temptations of Tiffany and instead found the snooker.

'Ah,' Ryan said, 'he does like men in tight trousers poking at a white ball with a stick.'

'You're not a fan, then?' Sylvie said. 'Because you could pretend. To make him happy. We'll pretend together.'

The rest of the evening was spent with Sylvie and Ryan asking questions about Ronnie O'Sullivan and how he compared to the greats of yesteryear, and Grandpa cheered up and began to enjoy himself enormously. Sylvie smiled to herself. She had won over her father with cricket and was now doing the same with Ryan's grandpa and snooker.

'My brother's getting married,' she whispered to Ryan. 'Want to come and meet *my* grandpa?'

*

Sylvie's mother insisted her daughter stay the night before to help with the last-minute hitches that were bound to crop up on the morning of the wedding but there were none. Unsurprisingly, as Sylvie was very good at organizing events to go off without a hitch. Ryan sat with her on his right and her grandfather, an elegant eighty-year-old, on his left. He had thick pure-white hair that curled in a similar manner to Sylvie's hair and spoke with clipped precision. Ryan could not imagine him gobbling angel cake and letting the crumbs rest in the folds of his sweater.

Ryan had made his way to the church sharing a taxi with a couple who were so clearly off to a wedding that Ryan could not resist asking them if they were attending the same one. Sylvie had greeted him looking, he thought, like a 1950s film star and she had whispered, with clarity, in his ear.

'No one here knows about the Tube and, by the way, I am flat broke so if you'd rather pretend to be my friend and not my boyfriend, I'll understand.'

She could not give him the chance to reply. Her mother, ignoring Ryan, grabbed her daughter's hand and pulled her back into the church. Now he was sat, waiting for the speeches, and wondering how he was supposed to pull Sylvie out from the Underground and back to work if not even the family of the dead girl would help him.

He knew he ought to be grateful that Sylvie's mother displayed a marked lack of curiosity as to the nature of his relationship with her daughter; if there had been nudges and winks that it would be his and Sylvie's turn next to face a congregation while making vows he would have been embarrassed. Instead he was indignant on Sylvie's behalf that she was treated like a secretary her father had borrowed from his office for the day to ensure the tanned and sporty Franklyn's big day went off without a hitch.

He hardly spoke to her as she was constantly being quizzed about all matter of detail that sounded inconsequential to Ryan but of intense importance to the bride and her new mother-in-law. The pre- and post-wedding-breakfast mingling was less awkward for him than it might have been, thanks to the couple who had shared his ridc, although the more champagne the woman, Anna, drank, the more overtly she flirted with him. By the time the band started up she was whispering in Ryan's ear.

'Danny's chin, it's weak, had you noticed that? He tries to hide it with that bloody goatee thing. Your chin is so perfect.'

Danny stoically and smilingly rolled his eyes like a man in love. Like a man who might even have put up with Anna sticking her tongue down Ryan's throat. Ryan wondered what their morning after would be like. Would Anna apologize or despise her lover all the more for not becoming angry, for not punching Ryan to the floor to show that a man with a weak chin can be just as manly as the next? Ryan wondered if Sylvie would ever behave this way and whether, if she were to be a flirty, nasty drunk, he would decide to accept it as meekly as Danny.

As Franklyn and Brooke danced another slow dance with steps that were suspiciously rehearsed, Ryan felt he was being watched. He scanned the ballroom and saw Ellen sat at the furthest table raising her glass in his direction. She raised it slowly, sardonically, as if to convey: *Really, Ryan? Are you having fun? Really?*

His heart stopped beating and the band stopped playing, leaving a dull buzzing in his ears, but he did not look away. They gazed across at each other, unblinking, until his view was blocked by two colliding waiters and, in the seconds it took for them to uncoil, Ellen was gone and in her place was yet another sun-kissed Floridian who looked remarkably similar to Brooke, her white teeth gleaming at every possible opportunity.

Ryan knew she was not really there, the girl in a cable-knit sweater amid all the strappy and strapless dresses and perfect smiles, but still, he also knew that he had not summoned Ellen into his imagination. That was entirely her doing.

Chapter 20

Jonny, feeling close to suffocated by paperwork, grumpy because he had not been able to go for a run for five days, annoyed by the amount of sick leave two of his staff had taken in the past month, was told there was a young woman to see him. He hauled himself from his desk and grimaced at how stodgy he felt. How lardy.

'I'd like to meet the lady, the one who my sister gave Nisha to. I'd like her to meet Nisha. I heard what you told my mother. It's not fair. None of what happened's fair but maybe I can help or sommat.'

Jonny asked Riya how old she was, knowing she would be under eighteen and that he would be unable to help her intervene.

'My sister was still sixteen when she got pregnant and dumped,' Riya said, 'and it killed her. How can me being seventeen worry you? Don't be stupid.'

Jonny did not quite snap. He was a stickler for rules and regulations but this young woman's indignant intelligence and her desire to be helpful where her family had been insular moved him in a way he was rarely moved or allowed himself to be moved.

'I shouldn't do this, but I can see you are trying to do the right thing. I have an email address for who I think is the woman's partner. You can contact him and then go from there. Is that OK?'

Riya smiled. It was a sad, graceful smile with a faint hint of cheekiness and Jonny winced as he thought of her sister being smashed apart by a train at the same age. Jaya had probably silently suffered post-natal depression, he thought, and had had her heart broken by a bloke who did not know or care that he had a daughter.

'Do you have access to a phone, a laptop?' he asked her, not knowing what he would suggest if she did not, but she smiled cheekily again.

'The advantage of havin' a sister who kills herself is that I get an iPhone,' she said, her voice both sneering and tremulous. 'And the chance to take A levels. And no hints of an arranged marriage either. We've gone modern.'

The weekends were wonderful. Ryan and Sylvie were carefree and spontaneous and he knew people looked at them, possibly enviously, and saw a perfect couple, tactile and in love, and he wanted to think of it as love but he was not sure if it could be, with Ellen's whispers in the air.

'This is crazy,' he said. 'You are, well, you are funny and clever and gorgeous but—'

She placed her finger on his lips.

'I am none of those things. I am the "but". And I have an annoying "but" to tell you. I think I'm going to have to give up my flat and move in with my parents. I've been meaning to talk to you about it. I did try at Franklyn's wedding. I'm not broke like some people say it when they have overspent on a holiday and need to go easy for a month. I have, literally, run out of money. I'm a mess. I'm sorry. I know you've tried, you've been patient with me, but it's hopeless. I'm what they call a hopeless case.'

They were walking along the South Bank in the sparkling Thames sunshine, past a merry-go-round, towards the Millennium Bridge. He stopped and stood in front of her.

'Move in with me,' he said. 'Move in with me and get a weekend job or something in the evenings, just till we sort you out.'

She turned pale.

'I wasn't hinting for that,' she hissed gently. 'If we ever live together I want it to be for something more meaningful than my shitty finances.'

He thought she might cry but instead she became dry-eyed and thin-lipped. He tried not to smile. She looked like a six-year-old about to have a tantrum.

'OK, I get it,' he said. 'This isn't the most romantic moment we've had. But think about it. I know what's going on. Your parents don't know. Who is best placed to help? Me. Who really wants to help? Me. Who would be on cloud nine if you moved in to Cotton Lane? Me.'

A week later she had moved in. Trish gave her back her deposit in full and waived the rent for the remainder of the month on the proviso that Sylvie still popped round. Had Sylvie admitted to Trish the parlous state of her finances, the older woman might easily have offered to take much less rent, so eagerly did she wait for the sound of Sylvie's key in their shared front door. Ryan had been wrong. Trish was not in love with Sylvie and nor did she think of her as a surrogate daughter. The appeal of Sylvie for Trish was that such a delightfully delicate creature could walk into her living room without a trace of disgust or disapproval. Sylvie would smile and laugh and look her in the eye as an equal. There was no pity, she never looked at the photographs and then back at Trish with a slight shake of the head. Trish could never see behind Sylvie's eyes the question: *Oh, Trish, what have you done to yourself?*

Sylvie had never told her to pull herself together and, when they were together, Trish was transported back to the days when she used to sit in the foyer of the building that housed the radio stations and would chat to presenters, producers, the sales teams, the chirpy, hopeful assistants, the deliverymen who needed a signature and who would frown if they were not also given a smile. She even knew several by name and one or two would linger, chat about the weather, the traffic or even politics. Trish, though, believed herself destined for bigger fish and sure enough landed a presenter. She often wondered what her life would be like now had she gone on a date with Mike. He had worn leather trousers sometimes and had a nice smile – and now Sylvie's smile was leaving and she dreaded the interviews for her successor. Unless by some miracle Mike turned up looking for a home, but even if he did, he would not recognize her and she would not dare tell him she had once been sufficiently attractive to be the public face of a prestigious media outlet. That night, at around 2 a.m., she decided to watch, again, *Misery*, and she fell asleep dreaming of poor Mike, tied to what had been Sylvie's bed, her prisoner until he stopped squirming at her mottled nose.

The night before Sylvie moved in to Cotton Lane, Ryan paced the living room in front of an amused Paul.

'What if she's still wandering around the bloody Underground when she's forty? This could be a nightmare.'

'You'll sort it together, mate, I'm sure of it.'

Paul was, in any case, relieved. He had started to look for his own flat. It was time he bought somewhere, took root, accepted he liked London and London liked him. He had been invited to a screen test for a programme provisionally called *The Human Code*. He had gained the impression there was only one person being auditioned. Without him there would be no *Human Code*. The word 'vehicle' had been mentioned so often he pictured himself in a van with a megaphone roaming Britain educating anyone within earshot about their DNA and asking for any twins in the neighbourhood to come forward, that triplets would be given free cupcakes and matching T-shirts.

'Also, Paul, mate, she doesn't know that you know. Do you think I should tell her you do know?'

Paul remembered the not-quite-spirals Sylvie had made on his Tube map that glowed in the Spanish sun.

'Yeah. Because she'll be able to tell eventually. Tell her we are inseparable best buddies and I even know you've got one of your old teddy bears in your cupboard.'

'At least he's not on my bed.'

'You are a cruel bastard, Ryan.'

Ryan was not much cheered.

'Hey, mate, you got the girl. Remember that.'

*

Trish drove Sylvie and her belongings over to Ealing, gave her a long maternal hug, her jumper stinking of cigarettes, and drove away again. Ryan did not have space in his heart to sneer at Trish; he was far too relieved that she had delivered Sylvie in one piece, so convinced was he that the landlady would have gulped down half a bottle of wine before getting behind the wheel.

Sylvie waved her off then turned to Ryan as if she had noticed he had smelled the air in front of Trish's face for signs of alcohol.

'She drinks too much. She smokes too much. Did you notice the puffiness to her face? It has steadily expanded since I first met her. Sometimes she spends the night on her sofa because she has reached a sort of stupor. All because of a man. I'd rather do what I do than replace it with drink. And underneath all of it there is a tender, bright but damaged woman who cannot move on.'

Ryan said nothing. It was one more reason to be disturbed by Trish. This woman had provided Sylvie with an unpalatable alternative. Of course riding the Underground was preferable to an ever-blossoming nose and cheeks blotched with purple veins but that was not real life. No one was ever supposed to choose between being Trish and being Sylvie. They were supposed to choose *not* to be Trish and not to be Sylvie and he did not much like the idea that a Sylvie without her trains would be a lush with nearly red lank hair and a pink-tipped chin.

Sylvie unpacked self-consciously and Ryan noted how it was as if she had arrived at a convalescent home rather than her boyfriend's house. She was fragile but self-contained. It was probably at the heart of why he could not break the spell. She was resolute. She was tough. She was just obstinate about the wrong things.

He was in the middle of explaining the quirks of the hot-water system when Chic's 'Le Freak' boomed through the wall. They both laughed. Ryan had forgotten it was the evening of Theo's party and it was now clear it would be more pleasant to be part of it than suffer the muffled and annoying version through the bricks.

There were about thirty people at the gathering including the Mizwas from Number 6, who were stood stony-faced in the corner but were in fact delighted to have been invited. Theo and Jenny made a fuss of Sylvie, and Jenny kept touching her hair and scrunching it up in her hands. Theo had not quite retired but had reinvented himself and bought a musty vinyl record store he planned to reinvigorate. By the end of the evening it had been decided that Sylvie would help out in the store on Saturday afternoons and Sunday mornings. Quietly, Ryan had told Theo she would need payment and Theo had said of course, she would be an asset, although he had no idea why she would be all that useful bar the fact she was rather pretty.

Theo gave it some thought, though, and was pleased he had engineered a way that Sylvie would be an asset. On her first day he stood in front of her and wiggled comically.

'Smoke and mirrors,' he said and gave her a sheet of paper with a list of music genres.

'Choose one you know a little bit about already or could imagine being knowledgeable about. Go on. Maybe you'd like to be Vinyl Vibe's film-score expert?'

She scanned the list and frowned.

'My skillset is organizing, Theo. Why don't I organize promotional events, memorabilia, mugs and posters. And man the till of course. You'd get more out of me that way.'

Theo clapped his hands.

'Fantastic stuff,' he said. 'Fantastic.'

Ryan sat in the pub with Paul and groaned.

'I've created a monster,' he said. 'Sylvie is much, much happier with her Underground vigil now she has a weekend job. I've given her a routine, I've made her peculiarities acceptable. She is happier with trawling the Tube now than before I met her.'

His phone vibrated and he read an email from someone called Riya.

'OK,' he said. 'This might help.'

'I've got some good news,' he firmly told Sylvie later that day. 'We're going to meet the baby you saved and its auntie. It might bring you some closure. This is very good news. Excellent, in fact.'

'All right,' she said, 'you don't have to give it the hard sell. I'd like to see the baby.'

They met at a café in Ravenscourt Park. Nisha was in a pushchair but wriggling to get out.

Sylvie had bought her a gift of a child's tambourine and the toddler ran in circles bashing it against her shoulder and the top of her head. They all smiled.

'You're my hero,' Riya said bluntly. 'I think my sister was gonna jump with Nisha but saw that you were a good person, like an angel maybe, cos you look like an angel – do people tell you that? – and so she changed her mind.'

Sylvie felt momentarily weak but also grateful.

'I thought you might hate me for not saving your sister,' she said.

'Nah, that's dumb, that is. She was ill, my sister. No one done nothing about it cos of the whole ghostin' thing, and so she killed herself.'

Ryan and Sylvie did not mean to, but they frowned, perplexed, not grasping the reason for Jaya's desperation. Riya sighed. Her teachers had told her she would receive better grades if she spelled out the obvious.

'I know *you* know,' Miss Cox had said, 'but the examiner doesn't know you know anything.'

'Our family,' Riya said, 'is a *little* weird.' Here she smiled encouragingly, so Ryan and Sylvie nodded.

'Jaya was quite clever, I think, but most important is she's the firstborn and we're all girls and Dad has taken money, a loan thing, from this cousin. That's how he affords the house and a car, but Dad's a hard worker and turns that car –' Jaya paused for effect and then imitated her father's voice – 'into our minicab business, the Harlesden Hire Service.'

The tambourine tinkled and Riya's expression lost some of its mischievousness.

'Anyway, you don't need to know the detail and, man, is it boring or what, but our cousin has a son who's supposed to marry Jaya. It's part of the loan, see?'

Ryan and Sylvie nodded some more.

'But me and Jaya look at his photo and he's a toad. No question. But Mum and Dad ask her all the same if she wants to marry him and I'm listening in and I'm so proud of her cos she tells them he's a toad and anyway she already has a boyfriend.'

Ryan remembered why he never watched *EastEnders*; Sylvie pictured Jaya being bold, Jaya being in love.

'Mum tells her she's too young to have a boyfriend and Jaya, she says – ' Riya snorted with laughter ' – and Jaya says, "What? Too young for a boyfriend but old enough for a husband?" Priceless.'

'Oh dear,' Sylvie said, 'was she forced to marry the toad?'

Riya looked at her somewhat patronizingly.

'No,' she said, curtly. 'Dad had been saving up to repay the loan anyway.'

'Ah,' Ryan and Sylvie said in unison although they were still confused.

'Exactly,' Riya said. 'End of, except my sister is pregnant and none of us met her boyfriend and Mum and Dad were a bit annoyed about the ghostin'.'

'Ghosting?' Ryan asked.

'This guy, he says he loves her and he shags her and then he disappears, whoosh, gone, so we all pretend he never existed but, like, maybe, my sister missed him… but we never spoke about it.'

Riya looked away, briefly, and Sylvie thought she saw the teenager's eyes moisten.

'We were all, like, besotted with Nisha except for Jaya. She just became really boring and slept all the time and said she had headaches. I think we thought we were doing her a favour letting her be lazy but now I think she was, you know, ill.'

Ryan and Sylvie stared at Riya, trying to imagine how isolated Jaya must have felt.

They sat without speaking, the only sound the tinkling of the tinny tambourine.

'Anyways, my parents don't know I'm here but I thought you should know how it was.'

Ryan stopped himself from beaming. It would have been inappropriate but he wanted to high-five this young girl. She had handed them the golden ticket. She had given Sylvie a route out of the Underground. She had provided the tragedy with an ending. Surely now Sylvie would see that she had done only good. She had not failed; she had saved a life. He looked at Sylvie watching Nisha, who had sat down on the path and was staring at them all with large brown twinkling eyes.

'Has this all made your life difficult?' Sylvie asked Riya.

The girl shook her head.

'They're scared now. Scared of being strict, scared of not being strict enough, scared of not listening. She was real nice, my sister, nicer even than Mum. I wish she'd told me she was, like, that desperate.'

Sylvie could see Jaya's face even now. It had been desperate, of course it had, but at the time, she did not know what desperation, that kind of desperation, looked like. To Sylvie she had looked like someone who needed to tie a shoelace. A shoelace. The memory of that moment, of her dim-witted conclusion that the woman – who was not even really a woman, but a child herself – had needed to stoop down to fiddle with her shoes, filled Sylvie with self-disgust so wretched she could feel vomit forming at the back of her throat.

Riya and Ryan looked at her suspiciously and so she swallowed firmly and blinked away the angry tears that had begun to sting her eyes. She coughed.

'I'm sorry,' she said. 'It's not about what I feel. Your family must be torn apart, Riya.'

Riya said nothing. From the moment her sister had died, her family had been offered solace and gifts. They had also been the subject of furtive disapproval and some ghoulish curiosity. All of them had felt guilt and the only blessing was that none of them took it out on Nisha. The baby was a second chance.

They parted awkwardly. Sylvie gave Riya a gentle hug and watched as she pushed the pram up the incline of the path towards the bus stop.

Ryan put his arm around Sylvie and she was grateful he could love her, a woman who had mistaken desperation for a loose shoe. Her interminable journeys on the Tube were an appropriate punishment, she thought. She deserved to be trapped. Riya and little Nisha had shown her that much. It was not ridiculous, it was not inexplicable. She belonged underground. She was so wrapped up in her demeaning conclusions that she did not properly hear what Ryan was saying as he encircled her with his embrace.

'You could try again,' he said, his eyes bright, his cheeks aflame with something approaching religious fervour. 'Tomorrow you could try not getting on the Tube.'

Sylvie heard simply the words 'the Tube' and she nodded the way an Edwardian accomplice to murder would nod when condemned to death.

Chapter 21

Grace returned to a different world, one in which her son had a girlfriend and her father-in-law demanded corned beef patties. She was hesitant to ask to meet Sylvie given what had happened when she had met Ed. Unlike Ryan, Grace had seen that lunch as a tipping point that had gone against her daughter.

America had been a joy littered with Hana's small doses of self-pity. Grace was built on foundations of guilt and so she took on board a tad more. It was her fault Ed had walked away. She had pushed him into the realm of serious relationships – the realm where you met interfering mothers and doddery grandparents and were expected to visit all of them on Christmas Day. Grace did not want the same fate to befall Ryan.

'Grandpa keeps mentioning Sylvia,' she told her son over the phone. 'She made quite the impression, she did.'

'You'll have to meet her,' Ryan said vaguely.

'Maybe you could swing by, as they say, just to say hi to Grandpa,' she said. 'I'm a poor substitute these days for you younger crowd.'

'Maybe we can get him down the pub one night this week, what do you reckon, Mam?' Ryan said.

'He'd like that,' she said.

'I'm happy right here,' he said but Grace was not about to give up.

'They are coming especially to take you to your pub,' she said as she unbuttoned his cardigan over which he had spilled a little tea.

'Get off me, woman,' he said but she ignored him and in the nick of time had him wearing a clean cardigan that smelled of lavender fabric conditioner.

'I smell like a poof,' he said.

'You can't say that,' she said.

'I just bloody did,' he said as Ryan and Sylvie entered the room.

Grandpa greeted Sylvie like an old friend and Grace experienced a twinge of jealousy, which only served to turn up the amp on her guilt levels, but she had to acknowledge that Grandpa acted as a welcome buffer and made meeting his son's girlfriend less of an awkward moment for her. It meant there was less chance of her saying something annoying, of becoming inadvertently possessive.

They made it to the pub seamlessly, Grandpa flanked by Ryan and Sylvie, which meant there was no need for Grace to ruin it all by linking her son's arm and sending what she knew would have been all the wrong signals. She dropped back a step or two and had anyone been watching her closely they would have seen her face illuminated by a benign selflessness, only for the warmth of her smile to ebb and be replaced, ever so slowly, by a forced brightness, a brittle half-smile. Ryan had placed his hand upon the small of Sylvie's back. That was all, but it shocked Grace. She had so wanted him to find someone, to fall in love – but now she was not so sure she was ready to lose another son. She pinched her own arm as punishment for she had said, under her breath, 'It's not fair.'

Once inside Grandpa held court explaining to Sylvie how the pub business worked. It was mostly nonsense but it was just so good to see him out of the house that Ryan and Grace nodded along and let him warble on. It was a warm evening and the lounge bar became stuffy. Grandpa stood to take off his cardigan. Ryan thought he heard the rumble of thunder but then realized the sound was in his head and that something bad was about to happen.

'Sit back down, Grandpa,' he said, his voice tremulous. 'And let me help you with your cardigan.'

The old man smiled at him with such tenderness. Ryan wondered if he was, in that moment, playing the part of Joe, that Grandpa could see Joe as he used to be before it all went wrong. Or that maybe he was Tom and Joc and Ryan. He was all the old man's sons.

'I remember now,' Grandpa said very quietly.

Ryan pulled the man's sleeves down gently, folded the cardigan and handed it to Grace.

'I think we should get you outside into the air,' he said but his grandfather slumped, falling against the table, sending the glasses flying.

'Is he OK?' the barman shouted. 'Want me to call an ambulance?'

'He might have just fainted,' Ryan said, knowing he was lying. 'It is hot in here.'

Sylvie placed a cushion under Grandpa's head and felt his breath on her fingers.

Grace ran her hand through his hair.

'Can you hear me, Grandpa?' she said but he appeared to be fast asleep. 'Maybe call that ambulance,' she said.

'Already did,' said the young barman, astonished at how calmly the scene had unfolded. He was reminded of a school trip to a gallery in Dulwich. He and his classmates had been made to stand before a giant canvas upon which was the depiction of an old man dying in the arms of his many serene children.

Grandpa was still breathing when he arrived at the hospital but an hour and half later, the doctor – a doctor that Grandpa would have called a poof, thought Ryan – pronounced him dead. That thought prevented him from crying for about three minutes and then he gave up and wept openly with Sylvie sat on one side and his mother on the other. Grace remained dry-eyed. She wept only for Tom. She had wept once for Joe but had regretted it. They were wasted tears.

'What did he remember?' she asked vacantly.

Ryan knew. He had remembered Ellen's name.

Hana was waiting for them back at the house. She was pale and had done her sobbing alone – got it out of the way, she thought, ready to be practical and helpful, but Grace was already in crisis-management mode. The adrenalin had kicked in. The phone calls to relatives on Joe's side who had shown no interest at all in the widowed old man would have to be made.

'They'll probably be expecting that he left them some

money,' she muttered. 'None of my business if he did but I hope for sure he did no such thing. Now then, Sylvie, I want you to take Ryan home, make sure he eats something later on and he's not on his own when he wakes up.'

Ryan did not argue. He could not bear to look at the empty armchair.

Sylvie had convinced Ryan she was weaning herself off her routine. She would stay behind when he went off to the university and then, ten minutes later, walk to the station. She told Ryan she waited two hours and that she curtailed her meanderings too and that she would keep diluting them day after day. This was not a complete fabrication. She reckoned she had shortened her life underground by twenty minutes each day but there was no sense in which that twenty minutes was becoming thirty and then forty. It had remained at twenty for eight full days until Grandpa died and then she had to stay inside the Cotton Lane house until Ryan was ready to face the world.

'You can't stay off work because a grandparent dies,' he said but, still, he did not get dressed. Sylvie felt twitchy.

'Maybe you should go in and if you feel too wobbly you can leave early,' she said. 'They'll appreciate that you tried, at least. And then you can see your mum this evening.'

He showered slowly and dressed even slower. Sylvie began to lose the feeling in her fingers.

'Phone me,' she said, 'let me know how you're coping.'

She flopped onto her seat on the Piccadilly line train with undisguised relief and kept as much of her journey as possible to the overground sections of each line in case Ryan phoned her, which he did at three o'clock. She was at Chiswick Park.

'Are you on a train?' he asked.

'Yes, just on my way home now,' she said. 'Not been out for long.'

'See you there, then,' he said and so she really did have to change at Acton Town and head back to North Ealing, her fingers numb once more, her equilibrium disturbed.

'Not like you to be home this early,' Jenny said from her front garden. 'Anything we can do, let us know,' she said when Sylvie explained, her neighbour mistaking Sylvie's agitation for concern for her boyfriend.

That evening two cards were pushed through the letterbox. One from Theo and Jenny, the other from the Mizwas in which they wrote a long, very serious message of condolence.

'That's, er, kind of them,' Ryan said. He was starting to feel a bit of a fraud. His grandpa was old. There was no need to be so distraught but he could not help it and he was worried that he would end up sat in his mother's house crying while Hana and Grace were efficient and useful and practical.

'You don't have to go,' Sylvie said. 'You need some quiet time, some space perhaps.'

He placed his head on her lap.

'I'm sorry,' he said, not entirely sure how needy he might be becoming.

'Shh,' she said, slowly starting to breathe normally because it was Friday and tomorrow she was excused the Tube and she could start to forget about what a suffocating day it had been.

Hana knew it hardly mattered to anyone any more but she wore black and stood with her mother at the door of the small local church. A woman who looked very like Naomi walked towards them alongside Ryan and Sylvie. It was Naomi. No one had told her Ed now lived with Naomi, mainly because Naomi had not yet told Ryan quite how serious her relationship with him was, but Hana knew deep down this tall, bobbed woman had taken him from her. She decided if she chatted to Sylvie long enough, Naomi would walk past her and she would not need to speak to her, to look up at her face.

There were two rows of petty officers and ex-petty officers at the back of the church, representing Grandpa's stint in the Royal Navy. It was not a time he ever talked about and Grace was touched they were there, filling the place, lending their confident, robust, non-trembling voices to the hymns. She knew instinctively that when she asked if they wanted to come back to the house that they would refuse, disappear smartly into the summer rain, duty done.

Ryan breathed in a scent he knew he would never forget. His mother's and Sylvie's perfumes mingled with a damp and stale mustiness as he turned to stare at his girlfriend who sang 'Abide with Me' in a gentle, pitch-perfect voice. Behind him he could hear someone blowing their nose. He decided it would be too rude to turn around but when the service had ended, there was no one there and so he whispered to Sylvie that maybe Grandpa had a secret lover.

She smiled at him and held his gaze. She could not tell him she was failing, that seeing Jaya's daughter had not had the magical effect Ryan assumed it would. She could not tell him because she did not fully understand why the spell had not been broken. It was she that was broken. Broken and broke. Working at a record store to fund an endless commute. She had never smoked but she assumed the Tube was her nicotine, her addiction. Clearly it was not just about routine, it was a form of punishment. Riya had done her best to absolve her of the need to atone, yet still something pulled her beneath London's streets. She was still searching for something, or perhaps waiting for it. That was still how it felt, most of the time, that she was expected. The Underground was not now a terrifying place for her, not at all, it welcomed her, soothed her the way an unsuitable lover might insist on unstinting devotion. And it felt right, morally acceptable. She had mistaken distress and desperation for the need to deal with a shoelace. This was her punishment, to see strangers' faces every day until the moment came when she had served her time. It is not necessarily a life sentence, she thought, it is just that I have not been given any dates. It is not about length of sentence, it is about a revelation. Something would happen, one day, and the spell would be broken, but she might have to wait a long, long time.

And now she was lying. She had somehow moved in with a man she had met at a mainline station, whose hair was curly and nearly black, who had a vulnerable smile, intelligent eyes, elegant hands and believed in her, had faith she could close the chapter – and not just faith, he had worked hard to solve the puzzle. He had found the dead woman's sister, he had made sure she had stroked the cheek of the dead woman's child, and still it was not enough. It was not anything. Whatever it was waiting for her underground it was not now part of how Jaya's family coped. It was not, after all, necessary for her to know the baby was growing and gurgling, toddling enchantingly and was loved and its aunt was grateful Sylvie had been there to hold her in the worst of moments.

Ryan, she knew, thought she sat in all those carriages reliving the moment, that she was haunted, and she had been at first. Now, though, she could travel lightly. She could read her book and not need to re-read the same sentence five times. She could think about her mother, her old boss, whether she needed to buy milk. She could pass a woman in a sari and not hyperventilate. She could feel the rush of the approaching trains and keep her pulse steady. She had even, thanks to Ryan, stood in the same spot where Jaya had jumped to her death, felt the same air. She could be mundane. She could not, however, leave.

As they left the church she wondered if this was now her life; a part-time job, lying about her days, waiting for Ryan to find out, to give up on her. Grace linked her arm.

'It's wonderful, it is, that Grandpa met you before he left us,' she said. 'He'd be glad to have known his Ryan was happy.'

Sylvie said nothing and Grace bit her lip. She was doing it again. She had pushed away Ed and now she was piling it on too thick with Sylvie. Maybe she was doing so on purpose. She needed to reel it in, find more selfless love, not let it ebb into self-pity. Grace patted Sylvie's arm.

'Forgive my babbling,' she said. 'I'm on the emotional side today.'

'No, don't be silly,' Sylvie said. 'I'm so pleased I met Ryan's grandfather and I liked him straightaway.'

'The house will feel strange, that's for sure,' Grace said and Sylvie noted that she sounded far from overemotional, that she sounded like a woman who could cope with the sky falling in, that she sounded like someone she would like to confide in but knew she never would.

There were vol-au-vents from Marks and Spencer and copious

amounts of beer and wine, as if Grace had been expecting those uniformed men after all. Hana watched as Naomi grew steadily drunk and she found herself humming the 'I'm gonna drink myself to death' line from a Florence and the Machine song. Naomi was statuesque, just like Florence. Hana held firm to the side of the table to prevent herself from edging towards Naomi to ask her if she was happy with Ed. No one had said a word, not a single word, but she knew. She could picture him in the park striding away from her and towards his new lover, his coat flapping as if applauding his choice of new woman.

She was shaken from her bitter reverie by Naomi's self-indulgent laughter.

'I can't believe you two,' she was saying to Ryan and Sylvie. 'I never thought it would actually, you know, happen.'

'Why not?' Sylvie said, squeezing Ryan's arm, which, she thought, felt tense.

'Because,' Naomi said in a sing-song voice, 'because, you weren't *real*.'

The room went silent. Naomi pointed her wine glass towards the ceiling as if readying herself for a long revelatory speech but Hana – sensing the imminent wrecking, in the exact same spot, of another relationship – interrupted her flow.

'You look ready to toast Grandpa, Naomi,' she said loudly, if shakily, 'and I think that's a wonderful idea.'

Ryan grasped the moment and almost shouted, 'Yes, a toast to Grandpa,' and they all stared at the empty chair except for Naomi, who wore the expression of someone who had woken up in the wrong house.

'I wasn't sure about the toast,' Grace said later, when everyone had left and she and Hana were washing and drying the glasses.

'It was that Naomi,' Hana said. 'Unpleasant woman, can't seem to handle her drink.'

'Very tall, though,' Grace said and Hana sighed.

'I thought only Paul knew,' she said as they turned into Cotton Lane. She had vowed not to say anything, not on the day he had buried his grandfather, but she blurted it out anyway.

Ryan felt the buzzing in his ears. He always did, it seemed, when panicked or upset. Or caught out. He had told Sylvie the palatable truth. He had told her that Paul knew about the suicide and how she was stuck on the Underground. He had not told her that Paul had once followed her all the way to Paddington. He had not told her that the man she lived with, her new, understanding boyfriend, had stalked her several times before that. He had not told her that Naomi had suggested he do so.

'I mentioned to Naomi that there was a woman on my train in the mornings who was very attractive, that's all. I guess it is unusual to see a stranger and then end up living with them.'

'Oh,' Sylvie said. 'I forgot that part. You did recognize me, didn't you, when you saw me at Waterloo?'

There was a silence. Ryan would not have described it as companionable.

'I never asked,' she said, 'but why were you at Waterloo that day? You never take a train out of London.'

'I do sometimes,' he said defensively. 'Not sure now, but I think I had to visit Southampton Uni.'

'Had you been or were you about to go?'

‘About to go, but not that bothered when I saw you,’ he said and he wondered at how easily he lied and how real the lie felt. If he truly had been expected at a meeting on the south coast he would have happily been late in order to speak to the woman who used to be Millie. That, he decided, meant it wasn’t a lie at all and he could picture himself looking at his watch, realizing he would miss the meeting and not minding much at all.

They had reached the house but were loitering outside, enjoying the way the evening was warmer than the day had been, that the light was clinging on with small charges of energy as each cloud shrunk.

She pressed her forehead into his neck.

‘I’m sorry,’ she said. ‘This is your grandfather’s day and it’s not your fault I am a mess. I’m just so embarrassed sometimes to think how others see me.’

‘But you’re getting there,’ he said. ‘We’re weaning you off it, aren’t we?’

She stiffened and, like Ryan, opted for a half-truth, for a lie that felt like it should be real, could be real.

‘A bit more slowly than I’d like,’ she said, ‘but definitely getting there.’

She was ashamed of her lack of progress but she was also avoiding full disclosure because she could not bear for him to be disappointed. He deserved better than the little she had achieved and so she convinced herself that as long as she intended to leave the Tube eventually it was not an out-and-out lie to tell him she was reducing her hours on it.

Ryan was putting his key in the door when Theo appeared in the half-light.

'I'm doing what?' Theo said, staring at Sylvie in a startled manner.

'Oh,' she said, 'you got my email? Well, I did a lot of research and this is an effective way to get your name out there.'

Theo turned to Ryan.

'I'm sponsoring a band,' he said incredulously. 'I've never sponsored a band before.'

'Most people have never sponsored a band before,' Ryan said, amused. 'It sounds more relevant than you sponsoring a biscuit.'

Theo scratched his head.

'I've got a Half Man Half Biscuit album in the shop,' he said and Sylvie and Ryan both looked at him as if he were a child.

'That's nice,' Ryan said.

'*Trouble Over Bridgwater*, it's called,' Theo said. 'Get it?'

'Yes, Theo,' they said in unison.

The Mizwa family appeared. They had heard that Paul and perhaps Ryan and Sylvie were clever and had taken to blurting out questions about whether they would be allowed to stay in Britain.

In the end Paul had – in the hope of stopping their cycle of confusion – declared that he would personally fight for them to stay should it ever come to that but that simply resulted in them deliberately bumping into the occupants of Number 4 to smile and comment on the weather so that they would never be far from their neighbours' thoughts.

When the Mizwas had gone back indoors Theo looked at Ryan and Sylvie's clothes suspiciously and then he groaned.

'Sorry, sorry,' he said. 'It was the funeral today, wasn't it, and there's me making daft puns.'

'Not your pun really though, is it?' Ryan said.

'True,' he said. 'Anyway, I'll leave you in peace. Er, was it a good turn-out?'

Ryan had no idea what constituted a good turn-out for an old man's funeral but he knew Grace had been pleased.

'Yes, thank you,' he said.

Theo returned to his house jauntily, walking in time to music playing in his head.

'Surprisingly likeable bloke,' Ryan said.

'You don't have to work with him,' Sylvie said, laughing, and they entered Number 4 with hardly any trace of guilt from the fibs they had told each other.

The doorbell rang almost immediately. It was Theo, looking sheepish.

'Clean forgot there was a parcel for you in my living room.'

'Must be for Paul,' Ryan said but the label had his name on it.

He and Sylvie stood side by side gazing at its contents; an eight-piece microfibre dusting kit. It had been bought for them by Grandpa a few hours before he died. It was his first and last purchase of anything from the shopping channel.

It was not Grandpa's last act of generosity towards Ryan. He had left both him and Hana almost £12,000 each and Grace had been bequeathed double that. None of them had any idea he had any savings at all. Aware that Sylvie had spent all her pay-off from the consultancy that had unceremoniously made her redundant, Ryan's first thought was to give her the money. His second thought was that to do so might serve to prolong the Underground agony. Even so, the small inheritance brought him no joy. He did not want to slowly fritter it away on bills and booze and nor did he want to blow it all in one go on a big holiday. He opened a savings account which offered a beyond mediocre level of interest and felt queasy about having done something he believed to be middle-aged.

He could not bring himself to throw away the dusting kit but knew he was unlikely to ever use it. He hid it at the back of a cupboard. Seeing it made him maudlin. He wanted there to be a hidden joke, something only he and his Grandpa would understand, or a message, but all it told him was that Grandpa had come to really, really love the shopping channel.

When Ryan was in the middle of a particularly gloomy mood, Paul told him he was moving out and Ryan suffered a pang of lost adolescence. He wanted in that moment not to have to worry about Sylvie, not to have a set of dusters. He almost wanted, he realized, to be back in that state of wondering if he would ever speak to her, and it scared him that he had, without keeping tabs on it, grown up and entered a world that was complicated and ever-changing. It was a world in which people died, where people fell in love only to be hurt, where people were lonely and turned to drink, where all the exciting things happened to others.

'And where do stars of stage and screen live these days?' he asked Paul.

'It seems I have a weakness for balconies,' he said, 'and I've found a flat in Barons Court with, wait for it, a balcony.'

Ryan smiled.

'You know, when my mum finds out the first thing she'll

think of is that you must not get drunk on your balcony, and that means the first thing I thought of was that you must not get drunk on your balcony and fall off it.'

'I refuse to let you ruin my excitement,' Paul said and Ryan noted how his friend was indeed in such good spirits he would no doubt smile even if he did find himself falling from a great height.

'But tell Grace there is a big bush underneath to break my fall. In the meantime, I have a hot date with my producer.' And with that Paul returned to his room to change into a crisp new shirt, leaving Ryan to wonder if he could eat pizza and beer and do nothing much at all now that he lived with what he had at least constructed to be the woman of his dreams.

She was also, in a different sort of way, the woman of Theo's dreams. What had started as a vanity project was beginning to resemble a viable business. People were talking about Vinyl Vibes. Theo would be in the local café and spot a classy flyer. He had even overheard a couple in the queue talking about it. He'd seen someone wearing a VV T-shirt. And now he was an impresario. He was sponsoring a band; he was giving musicians the means to play to a live audience. The remarkable part was that Sylvie appeared to have little interest and certainly no passion for music. She was motivated by the project, by the tying of loose ends, by the smell of success, by the act of making something out of nothing but an idea.

The room at the back of the pub was pretty basic but acoustically acceptable and, as Sylvie pointed out, it was three doors down from Theo's shop. Theo covered the room rental, paid a small fee to the band and bought their drinks. Entrance was free but everyone was given a glossy card advertising Vinyl

Vibes which gave them £2 off their first album purchase. Sylvie said it was all about joined-up thinking, that the public were already predisposed towards VV because of the free music and the £2 would be the tipping point to entice them to the store. Once inside they would be welcome to browse and end up thinking of the place not as a shop but as a sweet break in the day, a comforting spot to listen to music played the old-fashioned way, to investigate new bands and relive favourite sounds. Sylvie guaranteed that those who did not actually buy a record would buy a branded mug or T-shirt and return, soon, to buy something more substantial.

As the weeks passed, Theo noted she was spot on. He was slowly growing a loyal customer base and his greatest joy was that it comprised all ages. Mainly male, admittedly, but all ages, which prompted Sylvie to introduce seductively packaged gift tokens so that women could buy difficult-to-buy-for men a birthday present they actually wanted. Come Christmas, she said, he would struggle to keep up with demand. Except, she added, that she would anticipate that demand and ensure he never ran out. Theo stared at her in adoration, this angel with a flair for the right direction, the efficient email.

Come Christmas, she thought, I should be free of the Underground, but she did not really believe it. She was reducing her hours on the Tube but not by much. It tugged at her as if it were part of her veins and ligaments and she was reminded of sci-fi films in which humans become part machine. She was part of the network of tunnels now. They sucked her down and kept her there and she knew the tunnels were waiting for something just as she was waiting for something but she did not know what it was. As she cleansed her skin each evening and looked at the dark grey dirt on the cotton-wool pads it was a bedtime reminder of her failings. When the breeze of the oncoming Tube trains caught her hair it was not a refreshing moment at all but a further pollution of her weak soul.

The producer laughed at Paul's jokes.

'You're funny,' she said, 'we need to get that across on the screen.'

The producer kissed him and Paul sighed the sigh of a man who was being proven right at every turn. Love was better with a shared sense of humour. Love was better in London. Love was better on a balcony even without the scent of oranges.

They were interrupted – as they both caught the whiff of a nearby balcony barbecue – by the estate agent, who told him he was a buyer's dream and the place could be his in six weeks. Paul looked down and thought of Grace. There was no bush, just a white pavement, four floors down.

'Would I die if you threw me over?' the producer asked.

'Paralysed,' he replied confidently. 'Which would be far worse. So don't make me angry.'

She clung to him in mock panic while wondering how long they would remain a couple once he was a household name and regularly being offered unfettered sex by eighteen-year-olds studying biology and eighteen-year-olds not studying anything at all.

'Back to mine?' she said as the agent looked at his watch.

Chapter 22

Hana had always assumed her mother needed her to help with Grandpa and that once Grandpa and his reluctant shuffling to the bathroom were no more, she would move out. On the other hand, it would be cruel to leave Grace alone in the house of memories and so the two women continued to live together. Just for a little while longer, thought Hana, but she made no real effort to look for somewhere else to live. The end of the romance with Ed had left her fragile, defensive and insecure. When she received a round-robin email about another walking holiday she deleted it immediately as if walking holidays had nothing to do with her. The woman who had been caught short in sight of the sea and been able to laugh about it with the best-looking-by-far man in the group had vanished. In her place was the divorcee who found little in the world funny and was mistrustful of men no matter how handsome, no matter how friendly, no matter how they both liked hiking and the way the first sight of the sea after a slow fifteen-mile slog was as refreshing as a glass of cool lemonade.

Grace thought it was time she tested to see if she could live alone but could sense her daughter was not ready to do the same. It began to worry her, though, that the day would come when she was sat in an armchair, needing help to reach the toilet, and it would be Hana who was holding her arm, wiping her chin, phoning the doctor. By that point no one would want Hana, she would not meet another Ed, she would never again grab a rucksack and head to the hills.

Her Ryan prompted sweeter thoughts; or rather, bittersweet ones. His girlfriend was so pretty, Grace was sure she had featured on a set of coasters she had bought her mother many years ago. Grace had noted how self-contained Sylvie was, unlikely to be the sort that would natter to her, and just her, over a cup of tea, but most women of that generation and education were neither the chattering nor confiding kind. They were distant and clever and hid their emotions but Grace did not mind as long as Sylvie was loyal to her son and made him happy and she was almost sure she did. Except Grace had caught him gazing at Sylvie with what she could only describe as confusion. There was a complication there, she was sure of it, but she had no idea how significant it was. She pinched her hand as she wondered if perhaps the relationship would start to falter and to cheer him up she and Hana would whisk him away on holiday, just the three of them together; it was all she had left.

In her daydreams she tried to plan Ryan's wedding, all the while knowing that if Ryan was to marry she would not be part of the co-ordination committee. In any case, she would invariably end up fantasizing about Hana having a second wedding day; a quiet, classy affair that Grace would take charge of and execute beautifully. She looked at the empty chair and stifled a potential sob. For the first time she acknowledged that Grandpa had been like a child to her, fulfilling her need to nurture, and it was nurturing that had always taken her mind off Tom. If only she had been the one to pop out that day. He would have held her hand as they splashed in puddles. She wondered, too often, if she had pieced it together as it truly had unfolded.

The double doors of the block of flats were already open and there was a small ramp in place so that Glenn, the man from the department store, could take away the big old heavy broken chest freezer. She never forgot that his name was Glenn. Just as Tom reached his top speed, the fastest he had ever, ever run in his life, out came Glenn and the freezer. Glenn did not see Tom, not that it mattered. Glenn did not deliberately allow the freezer to slide and topple from the too-flimsy ramp.

Tom did not see the freezer, why would he? He had eyes only for his dad, checking that he could see how fast he was today. Joe did not see the freezer in freefall. His view was momentarily blocked by a vibrant forsythia. An elderly man, puffing on his tenth fag of the day, had been on the path, had seen the young boy running towards him, had smiled at his joy in life, and the elderly man had shouted 'Hey' in a gulping, frantic way to Glenn, and Glenn had turned towards him just as Tom collided with the freezer, or rather, the freezer collided with him.

When he passed the forsythia, Joe experienced that jolt every parent feels at least once in their life. The jolt of 'Where are they?' Tom was not there. There were two blokes and an old freezer. Where was Tom? He hurdled the flower bed.

'Have you seen a—' and then he saw. Collapsed on the

paving slabs. Collapsed and not crying. A younger man and a much older one and now a passing fourteen-year-old boy heaving a massive chest to one side of a tiny body.

'Don't move him!' someone shouted. So he kissed him instead and whispered, 'Hang on in there, son.'

How did she know Joe said that? It had become part of her, by now, as she felt her way through the narrative. Joe must have told her on one of the many occasions she had completely ignored him.

In the aftermath – when Hana and Ryan were being fed and put to bed, or soothed when poorly, or nervous over homework – there was no space in her head for Tom. She had a purpose, a reason to live; there were people who needed her. Now it was just Hana and she did not want Hana to need her. She wanted Hana to go walking again, go loving again, but she had closed up, just as she had after the nasty piece of work she married showed his true colours. Grace leaned on the armchair. There was a dark patch on the headrest which had been stained by Grandpa's Brylcreem and she bent down to smell it and closed her eyes. She could almost hear his voice and was surprised that it reminded her of Joe, who would call out to her whenever the children squabbled or stumbled or said they were hungry. He was quite useless really, she thought. Why on earth did she think he was capable of taking young Tom to the shops?

It always ended this way, her reminiscences of Joe. She would become angry at his incompetence and forget what it was she fell for in him in the first place. But she would never had had Tom if she had not fallen for Joe, and all that was good in her life now was a consequence of meeting him. All that was bad was down to him too and that was inevitably the trump card. She and Grandpa never spoke about him, not really, not unless Grandpa forgot he was dead. They did not need to speak; they were united in the pain of having sons who had been hit, squished, bludgeoned.

She picked up her phone and, carefully, using just her index finger, sent a text message to Ryan.

Is there anyone at your work who would like to be dating your sister? We need to cheer her up and I don't know anyone who can

Ryan was sat in the refectory, watching Naomi walk towards him with a tray of what looked like chips and baked beans.

'Nothing else I fancied,' she said. 'How's Cotton Lane without me these days?'

'Different,' he said. 'We see an awful lot more of the neighbours.'

He looked down at his phone.

'My mum wants me to find Hana a man,' he said absently and he did not see how Naomi blushed.

'Cappi?' she said and they both laughed a little self-consciously for the Italian now glowered when he spied Naomi and looked nervously at the floor whenever he passed by Ryan.

Sylvie was on the Jubilee line contemplating changing to the Central line and having lunch at Liverpool Street. She had no idea why she constructed these elaborate plans. She was increasingly of the view that the most comfortable she felt was on the banquette at Waterloo where she would half hope and half dread Ryan appearing. She knew the menu intimately but chose more economically these days. She knew she really ought to make a sandwich at home and eat it on a train or a platform but she could not rid herself of the notion that to do so would be to debase her journeys. Her daily commute to nowhere was an honourable endeavour. She did not know why she should label it honourable, not when it was a form of punishment, but she knew it deserved better than for her to skulk in a corner munching at tuna on granary.

The next day Ryan rubbed his hands together.

'I'm being spontaneous,' he said. 'I've got the day off.'

He looked at her intently. She met his eyes.

'But I don't have the day off,' she said.

There was a long silence in which she hoped he would smile, stroke her arm, leave it at that, but he sighed deeply.

'This can't go on,' he said. 'You know that, surely?'

'Are you asking me to leave you, to move out?' she said trying hard not to whisper but she could not summon the energy for anything that might constitute normal volume.

Ryan groaned.

'That's just it,' he said. 'Why does it always have to be so dramatic? Why can't you…?'

The silence returned.

'I'd like us to have a day together,' he said at last, 'a normal, slightly indulgent day. A day that does not revolve around the Tube.'

She curled up, her arms around her knees, her nearly red hair falling over her face.

'So would I.'

'Well, then, let's try, let's see what happens if you don't spend the day on trains.'

Her chest tightened and she could feel pinpricks of sweat forming on her shoulders.

'I mean,' he continued, 'you're diluting the time already – you must feel stronger about it.'

'Is this an ultimatum?' she asked, trying not to cough.

'Of course not, but I think you should try being more brutal about it, take the hit, accept it will be tough for a while but one day you'll realize the Tube keeps going without you and you don't need the Tube.'

He was smiling with forced brightness and sat down next to her, gently crunching a strand of her hair in his hand.

'Sound like a plan?' he said.

It sounded terrible but the alternative was also horrible. She did not want the relationship to flounder. Even if it caused her physical pain, she would remain above ground for the day. But it did not work out that way. Ryan noticed she was on edge, that she did not eat much of their brunch, that she had to ask him to repeat most of what he said.

He sat back and folded his arms in the same place where he and Naomi had plotted out their love lives over a year ago.

'It's like being with someone who constantly needs a cigarette,' he said. 'Desperately needs one.'

'I suppose it is like an addiction,' she said, trying to smile, but she was close to tears now. She was sure she could hear the rumble of the trains. They were not taunting, they were reminding her, pleading with her.

He shrugged.

'Aren't you supposed to put up with a week of the shakes or something and then be OK?'

Without warning, she was cross. Her eyes flashed. His nonchalance was an act; he did not want her to know that he was really worried, but even so, his lack of understanding, even now, was insulting.

'You know it's not like that,' she said. 'I need to go there, there's a reason as well as a compulsion.'

'But there isn't a reason any more,' he said, keeping his voice level. 'We saw where she was killed, we met her sister, we saw the baby. There is nothing else to be sorted.'

'Well, apparently, there is.'

'What? Tell me what it is or at least try to work it out. You must have some idea.'

Her eyes softened. This was not an unreasonable question yet she rarely asked it of herself.

'I'm waiting. That's all I know. I feel there will come a time when I will be… released.'

A police car sped past causing a cyclist to wobble into the kerb. He unleashed a tirade of expletives and then appeared to stare at Sylvie's barely eaten pancake as if it was possessed. As he cycled off Ryan chuckled but he did not know why.

'Waiting,' he said. 'Come on, then, let's wait together.' And they walked hand in hand to Ealing Broadway, the nearest station to the café.

They sat in silence until they reached East Acton.

'Does it work when I'm with you?' he asked. 'Is it a meditative thing, do you need to be alone?'

She thought for a few minutes.

'I'd rather be alone because there's no need for you to suffer too but otherwise it sort of feels the same,' she said.

He squeezed her hand. He could not bring himself to say out loud that he would wait until her waiting was over, but he wanted her to know he was not about to abandon her. He remembered now that before he ever spoke to her she seemed separate to the other commuters and this was the reason why. She was endlessly waiting rather than travelling.

They reached Marble Arch. A woman, rather beautiful, in a burnt-orange sari, entered their carriage.

'Are you waiting to see Jaya again?' he asked, feeling as if he had stepped into the film set of a ghost story. He did not tell her that behind the sari had been Ellen, staring at him sardonically.

It was her turn to squeeze his hand.

'I've wondered that too,' she said, 'but no, I don't think so. I wish I could sound more rational or even knowledgeable. I'm sorry.'

They travelled on, all the way to Stratford.

'Now, this is a messy station,' Sylvie said as she led them up some stairs whereupon they turned left and escaped the throng who were making their way towards the huge shopping mall. They sat at the front of the Docklands train and Ryan felt he was five years old and at the funfair on a ride he thought was thrilling but was in fact tame. He also felt a bit of a fraud, having already accompanied Sylvie on this very train – only she had not known she was being accompanied and he had never told her and he now believed it was too late to ever tell her. He had tried to, once, but she had been happy to think the weirdness of him ended with him checking which book she was reading in the stops before South Kensington, and maybe that was oddness enough for any relationship. He sighed as the sun streamed in and it made a pleasant change from being underground. If he was doomed to wander the Tube network, he thought, he would spend far more time above ground than below.

She rose to her feet at Canary Wharf and he was almost seduced by her serenity. She did not rush or dash and to anyone watching them she would have been voted the most sane and calm and certain person on the line that day. A quarter-smile played on her lips. She was in charge and, chillingly, he thought, she was content because she was not fighting the compulsion. They would keep on trundling until at least 5 p.m. and nothing would happen to stop the waiting.

'Oh,' he said. 'Why do you keep a sort of office-hours vigil on the trains?'

'Because it was an office-hours day when it happened,' she said without needing to ponder the question.

They stretched their legs again at London Bridge and switched to the Northern line but, instead of taking the next train, she sat down on the northbound platform.

'We'll wait a while,' she said.

'Ah, yes, of course,' he said.

There was silence between them and after two more trains had been and gone she asked him what he meant by 'of course'.

Ryan did not grasp the mistake he had made.

'Well, you sat for ages at Warren Street so I guess you do something like this every day.'

This made no sense to her. She never talked through her day with him and she almost snorted at the thought of what that would sound like. 'And then I changed at Embankment and took the Bakerloo line to Maida Vale and spent about an hour and a half there and then and then and then…' but yes, she *had* lingered at Warren Street, maybe more than once. She stole a look at his face. It was not guilt-ridden, not embarrassed. He was bored. All the same, she could sense that pushing the issue of Warren Street might lead to her knowing something she would rather not know, so she let it go.

'This is significant, isn't it?' he said in a puzzled voice. 'I mean, this really is waiting. You must have some sort of sense of what *for*?'

He wondered if he sounded nagging. Pounding her with questions that were obvious and unlikely to be helpful.

'Sorry,' he said. He paused and decided to take away the pressure he was piling upon her.

'I've struggled more than I have let on,' he said. 'When I was small, I wanted to save my brother, I wanted to wear a cape and swoop down and carry him away before he was crushed but I never told Mam because her eyes would wobble whenever I mentioned him. And then Ellen. Ellen, she died in a split second too, so I felt I was bad luck, and I want to make it right somehow.'

She held his hand, grateful that he was vulnerable or at least understood vulnerability.

'Listen, you go home,' she said. 'I have a book with me. Please.'

She sat, elegantly, not slouched, and watched him head towards the exit. She half smiled as she pictured him as Superman, swooping down to save his sibling.

And in that moment she knew.

Ryan's words had somehow pierced the fog. There was no sound of angels singing, no blinding light. It was enlightenment of a mundane kind, like realizing you're not that fond of Earl Grey tea after all or discovering you stored your suitcase under the bed and not in the high cupboard. Of course, she thought, it makes perfect sense, but it brought her no comfort. Quite the opposite. It spelled out to her that she could be trapped for years. Forever. To tell Ryan would be to quash his dreams. She would have to keep it secret.

She chewed at a ragged fingernail. Another train came and went. Sylvie let the trains rock her brain into some semblance of order. She wanted, very badly, to devise a way to reach the end of what had become a kind of commute into purgatory. 'Knowledge,' she whispered to herself, 'is power. I know now what needs to be done.'

Gradually she formulated a plan. Her love–hate routine needed to be modified. All those intersections. They were unnecessary. She rolled her shoulders. They were useful, of course, and gave her some exercise. She was particularly fond of changing at Embankment on the Bakerloo line in order to reach the Circle line. That was a bizarre little route of short staircases and corners and what always felt like backtracking. Up and down and all around – but to what end? The corridors were not platforms. It was the platforms that mattered. The platforms mattered even more than the trains. And her books. They would have to go. What was she thinking, burying her head in a novel all day? She needed to get busy. She needed to get a life.

*

Instead of fiction, Sylvie burrowed into statistics. It was not quite as random an act of fate as she had supposed that she witnessed a death where she did. King's Cross St Pancras Tube station had experienced the most suicide attempts of all the network's stations in recent years. She sighed at all the hours she had spent on the platforms at Oxford Circus or Moorgate. She should have stayed behind at where it had, for her, all started. On the other hand, King's Cross was only marginally leading the way in death tolls. Mile End, Victoria and Camden Town were close behind, close enough not to be rejected out of hand. One conclusion she believed she could make was to dump her travels on the Bakerloo and Jubilee lines as these recorded the fewest attempts.

She turned away from the computer screen and wondered if there was a reason for this. Sylvie liked the Bakerloo and Jubilee lines but she doubted they were so pleasant as to change a desperate individual's mind when it came to the desire to end their own life. Still, a fact was a fact. No more changing lines because of a hunch. She would need to be more scientific. The dangerous lines were the Northern, Central and Piccadilly. She would stick to those in future until she found what she was looking for. In some respects, she was being truer to herself. She was a planner and it had been strange to engage in such unplanned days underground. Now she could add a semblance of order to her compulsion. She could take a smidgen of control.

Ryan noticed a change in her. She began to dress differently for her version of a commute. She wore jeans or linen trousers and a short jumper or short jacket. Gone was the large handbag, replaced by a small leather satchel she wore with the strap across her body. She bought herself a pair of navy suede trainers that she wore every day and declared to be comfy and with a good grip. Sylvie no longer looked like someone on her way to an office job. She was a student or a courier.

He was hesitant to ask what had sparked the change. Ryan was becoming increasingly convinced that all he had done in an effort to help Sylvie was inadvertently do the opposite. It was as if he had discovered a wild and beautiful flower that thrived on weed killer. He decided to give it all of two weeks and then pluck up the courage to find out what she was up to. But on the ninth day he found her curled up on the sofa, paler than normal, staring into the middle distance.

He gently sidled next to her and ran his finger along her forehead.

'Want to talk about it?' he said.

She lowered her chin and swallowed hard.

'Yes, but later. Give me a few minutes.' She looked up at him and smiled. 'Or hours.'

He jumped up with deliberate good humour and left the room, as Sylvie clung ever tighter to her knees, trying to decide if she was near the end of her quest or would have to start all over again.

Men, she knew, were more likely to jump, so she had been particularly interested in a man in a smart suit but creased tie who sat down almost opposite her and stared vacantly, if morosely, in front of him. He held no case, no paper, nothing, and he did not pay attention to where the Northern line train was stopping. He simply stared. Sylvie felt her veins fill with adrenalin. She kept tabs on the man by watching his knees and his feet. At last, at Camden Town, he stood. She stood too. He left the carriage but walked back towards the tunnel they had just travelled through and then sat on a bench. She decided to be bold and sat next to him. Two more trains entered and her nearly red hair blew across her face. He stood. She stood. She expected the worst, which would have been the best, for her, but he followed the signs for the way out. She followed him until the point he placed his hand on the card reader and entered the ticket hall and at that moment she turned around and headed back to the bench, her heart thumping.

He might come back, she thought. Or someone else might appear. Someone did. It was a woman with close-cropped brown hair dressed in dungarees worn over a fluffy purple jumper. She was all smiley and emanated a sickly sort of jolliness. She sat next to Sylvie and after a few moments turned to her and spoke.

'Do you need someone to talk to?' she said.

Ryan was nodding but he did not understand, not really.

'Who was she?' he asked.

Sylvie sighed.

'She was me, only a trained and better version of me.'

Ryan was silent, not wanting to be slow on the uptake, but this still did not make sense to him.

Sylvie rolled her tongue loudly and clapped her hands together before taking his hands in hers.

'Right. This is ridiculous. I'm talking in riddles. Sorry. I'll sum it up, honestly, no frills. Ready?'

He nodded, befuddled by the change in mood.

'I decided that what I needed – to end this ridiculous trap I was in – was to save someone. I had what I think is called an epiphany.'

She paused.

'Epiphany, yes, that's it. I realized that I have to physically save someone, pull them back from the brink the way I didn't pull Jaya back. I did some research, so I could concentrate my search in the right places, and there was a man today – a man who looked desperate, or at least depressed – and he sat down at Camden Town, a station that is statistically likely to be the site of a suicide. I thought he might try, you know, but he didn't, he left the station. So I sat where he had sat and this woman decided that *I* was a suicide risk. Me. And so what do I do now? I can't even be left alone to try to save someone. And I know that would have worked. I just know it.'

Ryan did not say anything. He was waiting for her to share more but for Sylvie that was the end of the story.

He opened his mouth and then closed it again and found himself shamefully wishing that the bloke sat next to Sylvie had tried to jump. He pictured her pulling at his arm or rugby tackling him to the ground. It was hard not to also picture it going wrong and the man shrugging her off and inadvertently pulling her under with him.

'Well,' she said at last. 'What are you thinking?'

'I'm definitely thinking,' he said with an embarrassed laugh. 'I'm thinking it's great you know what you need and... I'm thinking,' he paused.

'Yes?'

'And I'm thinking you should get a job on the Underground so you have a reason to watch people and save them.'

Sylvie exhaled. Would that be enough? she wondered.

'I could try that,' she said and Ryan had to ask her to repeat it because he had been so sure she would agree to no such thing.

Chapter 23

Ryan had a hunch that Stocky Stan from King's Cross would help. Stan tapped his nose, said he was owed a few favours and he could get the paperwork together and in the meantime allow Sylvie to shadow him in his office, which would let her to watch the platforms via his screens and watch the ebb and flow of the ticket hall.

Ryan had a hunch that Stan would not be unsettled by the reason behind this rather peculiar request and, sure enough, as he related all that had happened – how she was stuck on the Tube until she found redemption – Stan simply nodded along as if he heard such tales most working days. For Stan, the Underground was everything, so it hardly surprised him that it could so dominate a young woman's life; and he knew it was a place of light and shade, that it haunted as well as helped its passengers and workforce.

'Sometimes we get people handing leaflets out about the Samaritans or depression and we – in the office – we get talks about spotting those at risk. It's a blight on the system, actually. Drivers can be signed off for months – years if they get unlucky, get to be the one who sees it at its worst, so to speak. I knew a bloke who had two of them in the space of a year and he never came back. Heard he became a postie, eyes down, no drama.

'Never occurred to me they might need this redemption thing, makes sense though. An eye for an eye, a life for a life, so to speak. You leave it to me,' and here Stan laughed stockily, 'although actually, when you think about it, what we're hoping for is for someone to try to kill themselves and that's not right, not really.'

Ryan held his breath, wondering if Stan was about to change his mind.

'But they might as well try it while your girl is there to save them than when there's no one watching.'

'Exactly right,' Ryan said, relieved, although he too was very aware of the perverse nature of what they were all hoping would happen.

The problem was that nothing did happen. Sylvie sat and watched and sometimes roamed but all she saw were commuters, tourists, backpacking students and school outings, long lines of children led and followed by anxious-looking teachers and volunteer parents, counting heads, issuing commands to stay in line, to stay away from the platform edge, to hold hands, to sit down quietly when they entered the carriage.

She saw but did not notice Isak, now twenty-one years old, with his white-blond floppy hair and pale grey short stubble, who was on his way to Oxford Circus to buy swimming trunks. Isak loved and hated the big Nike and Topshop stores that greeted him when he emerged from the station. He loved that there was somewhere for him to shop right on the doorstep of the Central line, that there was always a new style, a new colour of swimwear or sports shorts waiting for him, but he hated the bustle, the cool dudes who stroked the black suede on the latest trainers, the staff who did not take kindly to his swimwear queries, and the resident DJs who would not look him in the eye.

Isak was tall and thin and ethereal and looked cooler than any of the suede fondlers but was intimidated by them all the same. He paid with cash because the card was a connection and Isak could, if he closed his eyes, see the infra-red pathways that led from his card to the finance department, to the bank, to his mother's savings account, to his stepfather's platinum card, to his stepfather's company where someone small and wizened would hear a ping and look at a screen and tut and say, 'Isak's been buying swimwear again.'

He gave the cashier – who wore her hair in delicate dreadlocks and smiled at him kindly, he thought, without suspicion – two twenty-pound notes and neatly folded his purchase of bright turquoise trunks into his smooth black nylon rucksack. Isak returned to the Underground and travelled as far as St Paul's. He would not visit the cathedral today, the man on the desk would need to search his bag and would see his swimming trunks and glance at him, maybe even make the joke he had heard too often before. 'No pool in here, sonny.'

Instead, Isak wandered Paternoster Square, which was busy but not crowded and where the air felt pure and the statues were clean – but someone had left a plastic tub with the remains of cold fusilli pasta, tuna and sweetcorn on one of the pristine benches and he flinched in disapproval. Two boys on skateboards encircled him and so he left the square and headed across the road towards the Millennium Bridge.

This was a moment that never failed to make his heart sing. He had watched *Lord of the Rings* and *Game of Thrones* many times and this bridge was part of those mystical worlds, the way it led into the mouth of the giant Tate Modern from the majesty of St Paul's. He would often stand in the middle of the Turbine Hall and pretend he was a prince and the scurrying tourists and slow art lovers were his people, his subjects.

He walked around the back of the Tate and through a small circular garden to an apartment block which required him to place an electronic fob on a pad to gain entry. He could take the lift but chose to climb the two storeys via the cream, matt marble stairs to the floor that belonged to his parents. His mother, also tall, also slim, also white blonde, was mixing together a horseradish crème fraîche to accompany the gravadlax all their guests seemed to expect to be served when they came to dinner. Ulla had never been drawn to the kitchen until she met Andrew, who had allowed her to reinvent herself, to make her nationality a personality trait rather than a dull fact.

The vogue among Andrew's set was for homemade food in a homely spot in their grand homes. Ulla suspected they all cheated to a degree although the Blakes had recently greeted them red-cheeked, aproned and glistening with Aga heat. Andrew did not join in the cooking but mixed a well-received gin and tonic and his wines were never without a narrative. They had met on a flight to Stockholm after Ulla had been upgraded to business class and told him she was so often rescued from economy that she had to assume she resembled someone famous.

He was glad she was not famous but had to admit she had the aura of an actress or a model or a Royal. She saw a rugged, well-dressed man, who was hedge-fund rich but not arrogant like some Englishmen with money she had dated. They agreed to meet at her favourite café in Gamla Stam early the next morning, before his meeting, and neither expected the other to turn up but when she did he knew that this was what he needed, someone who spoke English perfectly but lacked nuance, lacked the proprietorial curiosity of his previous, Surrey-born girlfriend who had always wanted to know what he *really* meant, where he *really* went, what he *really* wanted.

Isak did not like gravadlax. He did not much like eating and claimed he was supertaster, which meant he could eat the boring stuff at a fancy restaurant and not be chided for his lack of sophistication. He did, though, like a huge steaming bowl of spaghetti bolognese after a long swim. Andrew would be home soon and they could go to the basement and swim together after Andrew had said 'Cool trunks' as if it was perfectly normal to wear a new pair each time.

The pool, at 6 p.m. on a Friday, was always quiet. Isak had hated public baths as a child but this was one of his favourite places. He did not mind if Ulla joined them but it was better when it was just him and Andrew, who would compliment him on his muscle tone, his elegant breaststroke style, his powerful front crawl. They would race and it was always close and he did not mind if Andrew sometimes won but preferred it when he could shout, 'Beat you!'

'I fancy a long-distance slog today,' Andrew said. 'Thirty lengths. Been a tense sort of week. Fancy keeping pace with me?'

It had been a tense sort of week for Isak too, full of cognitive behavioural therapy – or rather, full of another stab at another programme of it as if they were all different versions when to Isak they all seemed the same. Lots of nodding, lots of pauses, lots of looking at the ceiling at the tiny camera in the corner that might be sending images to his stepfather's offices where the small and wizened man would tut and say, 'He's lying again. He needs more pills.'

Chapter 24

Narnia, Ed had said, and for the first few months it had felt magical. It had certainly felt almost pastoral but Naomi had begun to tire of sitting for so long on the District line to reach the land of limited fun.

'Would you say you love your house?' she asked him.

'Why?' he said.

'Oh, you know why, I'm not sure about…' She spread her arms. 'All this. It's a bit quiet for me.'

Ed did not react straightaway. He sat very still, staring into the middle distance.

'Where would you like to be?' he said, finally, evenly.

'More central. I like noise and lots of choice of bars and pubs and restaurants and big parks and grandeur on your doorstep, architecture, big architecture, and I never go to art galleries but I like the idea I could wake up one Sunday and just pop to one in fifteen minutes.'

'And can you afford that sort of life?'

'I coped OK living with Ryan. Ealing wasn't perfect but it was closer to everything than we are here, and maybe together we could live closer still. I mean, if you fancied that. Do you fancy that? I honestly can't decide if you arc here accidentally or deliberately.'

'It's been a long sort of accident if that's what it was,' he said.

'You're the one who said you thought it would take a few months to renovate. I got the impression this isn't what you always wanted, that's all.'

'I really don't think we'd get this sort of space in the centre of town,' he said, 'but if you want to go looking, there's no harm in that.'

Naomi could not quite work out Ed's tone. She was unnerved and was not sure why. She mulled it over and decided he was being controlling. He had no intention of moving anywhere and would veto any flat she found on the grounds it was too small for such tall lovers. He was content to let her waste her time.

'Would we survive if I lived in a tiny room near Gloucester Road and you lived here?' she said a few days later.

'For a while, maybe,' he said.

She met Ryan for a drink the next evening.

'Paul's gone so are you renting out his room again?' she asked. 'Just while I find somewhere else. It might take a while, given my budget.'

'Hmm,' Ryan said, 'he actually smelled really nice, so you've got to keep up his high standards.'

Naomi kicked at his shin and wished, for the first time, that he was taller. She knew that most men would have frowned, have worried about what their girlfriend might say, and, after all, she would be gatecrashing love's young dream. A second woman in the house – one who had known Ryan before he met Sylvie – was not an ideal recipe should Sylvie be the insecure or possessive type.

'Hey, look, ask Sylvie first. She might not like the idea.'

'OK,' Ryan said, almost bored. It would be easier just to have Naomi back, paying some rent, but if she needed him to ask Sylvie, then so be it.

Andrew was wearing the same red Speedos he wore the week before, and the week before that, but Isak did not think for one minute that he wore them to spite him, to make the point that swimwear could be worn and washed and worn again. Isak, his therapist had decided, adored Andrew more than anyone on this earth. They swam in unison as, under the spotlights, the quivering, mildly chlorinated water cast moving patterns on the walls and Isak imagined they were swimming in the Turbine Hall, in a work of modern art closed to the public. Turn and breathe, turn and breathe… until Isak was on his own, turning on his own, breathing on his own.

He stopped and let his feet drop and swivelled to face the other end of the pool where Andrew was making strange, horrible, but muted, gasping, gurgling sounds and slipping under the water only to bob back up then disappear again. Isak was cross. They had only completed sixteen lengths and his body was itching to finish Andrew's promised thirty but then he remembered that Andrew would never trick him, never tease him, that he must be ill, and so he dived under and slowly dragged him to the shallow end where he could more easily haul him out and he tried to—

He tried but Andrew's eyes were open and not blinking and Isak screamed the scream of a boy, much younger, at his first horror film until the brazenly wobbly Peta Parrish, who lived on the floor below Ulla, arrived with her extra-large fluffy white towels but no phone and tried to pull Andrew out of the water, but Isak would not help her so she was forced back to her apartment to call for an ambulance, knowing there was no point to one coming at all and now she had to weigh up whether to get dressed before knocking on the Swedish lady's door or to arrive in her swimsuit. She grabbed her dressing gown and called the lift and Ulla found herself face to face with a damp and barefoot Ms Parrish, who, having had no time to rehearse what she needed to say, stood in the hallway opening and half closing her mouth as if about to release a monstrous sneeze.

Amid all the anguish, the flapping of dead flesh on the side of the pool, the calm concentration of the paramedics, there sat, fixed quietly on the wall behind them, a landline, smooth and black and so stylish none of the residents had ever noticed it was there.

Isak was disoriented by the sudden gap in his life and needed his mother to fill the void, to be loud and loyal and enthusiastic, to open a designer bag and bring out, wrapped in glossy tissue paper, a new swimsuit for her and new trunks for him so they could swim together, but Ulla was quiet and sad and displayed no enthusiasm for the pool whatsoever. She had no close friends in London that were not connected to Andrew. She had found women kept a distance and had assumed it was because she was a foreigner but it was in fact because she was too blonde, too stunning, too *naturally* stunning.

The wives and partners of Andrew's colleagues and friends, however, were all of a similar age and all very attractive and all capable of absorbing another beauty into their cabal but few of them were terribly practical when it came to a sudden death and it was the men who rallied to help with the administration of Andrew's demise. The more they helped, the more distantly their wives behaved towards Ulla as she became more of a threat to their equilibrium. No one would ever leave rugged, rich Andrew but he had left them and now Ulla was a damsel in distress, a white-blonde, slender Swedish widow who might pluck away one of their husbands the way a sparrowhawk might prettily soar then swoop and dive, its claws ready to pin its prey to the ground without mercy. They imagined a glint in Ulla's eyes that was no such thing. It was desperation not for a man to replace Andrew but to have him come back to her.

She tried to hug her son but he refused and drummed his fingers relentlessly on the table, on the side of the sofa.

'Come and swim with me, Mamma,' he said and Ulla groaned in pain and left the room. She had not exactly forgotten about his clinic close to Cambridge, his routine, it was just that routine did not matter any more. It was Andrew who had found the therapists, paid their fees, paid for the four-night stays in simple luxury, paid for the medication, and who had always been there come Friday evening to swim with Isak, to provide him with fatherly protection. All she had done was sometimes drive him to the gate of the facility on Monday mornings and now she doubted she possessed the energy even to navigate her way out of the small underground car park.

They would have to return to Stockholm. It was unbearable here. Not one of the women who had eaten her meatballs and her gravadlax had pressed the buzzer to check if she needed food or a hug or a chat. Thcy all stayed away hoping she would soon be in a far away country.

Grace still baked. The starlings and sparrows were grateful. Every morning there was a sprinkling of barely stale golden-yellow sponge or deep brown demerara ginger cake on the small lawn. A squirrel appeared, a new arrival, who became a regular.

'We'll host rats next,' Hana said as she stood at the kitchen window, scrolling through her phone messages. 'Oh,' she said, unable to prevent her hand from shaking.

Did you see the email about the hike around Jersey? I'd like to go but only if you are too.

She read it three times.

'Oh,' she said each time.

'What is it?' Grace said. 'Shall I try baking drop scones? Might make a nice change.'

'It's a message from Ed,' Hana said, 'a message that is making me more angry by the second.'

'May I?' Grace said, trying hard to sound only moderately interested. Just in case. Just in case it was the wrong thing to be fascinated. Just in case it was the wrong thing not to be interested.

'My, my, no wonder you are angry. Is this the first time he's been in contact since…?'

'Since I threw my coat in the bin? Yes, the first time. I'm so angry.'

'I'll put the kettle on,' Grace said as her daughter left the room.

Hana was physically trembling. She was angry, she was certainly angry, but mainly with herself because her cheeks were flushed and her breasts tingled. She was angry at how happy she was feeling, how like a teenager, but then she looked over her shoulder at her mother swirling hot water around the inside of her favourite teapot and thought, I'd rather this trembling than that.

She scoured her trashed emails but could find nothing about Jersey so sent an email to Poppy, the hippy who probably hardly ever used her phone but was the only other member of the hiking gang she had swapped details with. Sure enough, it took two days for Poppy to forward the itinerary of the proposed ferry from Poole to St Helier in mid-September when the school holidays were over and hotels and fares were cheaper.

Before she replied to Ed, she booked her place. He could find out, if he wanted to, that she had only reserved a spot after she had heard from him. She was not sure she cared. She convinced herself, almost, that she would be happy to travel to the Channel Islands with or without him.

Yup, I'm booked on that one

she typed. She waited a few seconds before pressing send but then panicked that he might be at that very minute on his phone and would be able to see the signs, those little grey dots, of her indecision, of her desperation.

He replied almost immediately.

Then so am I.

And that was that. There would be nothing else, no more contact until mid-September. She knew that, he knew that, and, weirdly, Hana decided it was extremely classy of him. Classy of them both, in fact. She lay face down on her bed as if fourteen again and held her pillow with both hands in the tightest grip she could muster. When Poppy emailed to say how lovely it would be to have a buddy her age on the hike, Hana could hardly suppress her annoyance. No, Poppy, she thought, we will hardly have time to speak to each other, but later she was forced to concede that Poppy was a handy backstop should Ed be playing an unkind game.

Poppy was, it seemed, waiting for her as she arrived at the departures lounge. The rain pelted against the windows but it was rain that had long since cleared Jersey and the weekend ahead would be breezy, sunny and warm.

'It's the cream teas that get me every time,' Poppy was saying and Hana nodded as earnestly as if Poppy was explaining how she had found a cure for diabetes. Perhaps the cure was to avoid scones and jam. She nodded because she could hear Ed, his deep, carefree laughter in response to something the organizer had said. She nodded to seem unneedy. Hana remembered she was already booked onto this trip before Ed contacted her.

'I came as a child because you didn't need a passport,' Poppy was saying, 'and they speak English and it was a sort of fake foreign holiday and I remember how embarrassed I was when

I got back to school and we hadn't been abroad at all. Just pretended to be. But the cream teas were magnificent. Better than Devon. I hope they're still the same.'

An image appeared in Hana's head of Poppy's long, straggly hair blowing across her plate and whipping clotted cream across her nose and she struggled not to giggle. Instead she spluttered and Ed rubbed the palm of his hand between her shoulders.

'Getting overexcited, ladies?' he said.

Poppy glowered because she remembered now how Ed had monopolized Hana the last time they walked together and she could tell it was about to happen again.

'I thought we were a pair for this one,' she whispered sullenly and Hana puffed out her cheeks before giving Poppy a hug.

'It's so good to see you again,' she said in a noncommittal sort of way as Ed tugged at her arm and pulled her to the quietest corner.

'How can we dump the broad in the long skirt?' he said, in a Bronx accent, his eyes twinkling.

Hana thought she might simmer if he tried to pretend nothing had happened, that he had not made her throw her coat in a bin, but now, now she was here – about to board a boat to the land of cream teas, twinkling seas, castles and lighthouses – she thought it might be for the best, after all, if they just forgot all about the icy cold of Regent's Park and a tall girl called Naomi.

Chapter 25

Isak was not stupid. He had travelled from Cambridge to King's Cross to Oxford Street to St Paul's so many times that he could, of course, reverse the journey without help. But they were not expecting him. It was a Thursday afternoon and he stood in reception, his long back stooped with the tiredness of a grief he did not understand.

They tried to phone Ulla but she did not answer and Isak's most recent counsellor was in Prague in expectation of a marriage proposal. They decided that Isak could stay the night and speak to Christie, a new recruit, about his stepfather's death. The idea was to give Isak the chance to vent his pain and fears, to calm him down while they worked out if his mother would continue to pay for the same routine.

Christie was keen. Christie was enthusiastic. Christie told Isak about all the ways Andrew could live on in Isak's heart, in his dreams, that he would see him in a rainbow or a sunset, hear his voice in a crowd and that one day that would be a source of comfort. Some people, Christie said, choose to wear their grief like they would wear their favourite T-shirt. It was all about acceptance, of learning how to live this new life, one in which you would be sad but slowly less sad. Christie was interrupted by a blackbird flying into the window with an unsettling thump. Christie was keen, Christie was enthusiastic and told Isak that the bird was like him, stunned and in pain, but it would dust itself down and fly away and soon be able to enjoy the skies and trees and the breadcrumbs thrown by the children in the park.

'Andrew said not to feed birds bread,' Isak said, frowning.

Christie beamed.

'There, you see, Andrew is with you now because you remember all his advice, all his kindnesses. He is not truly gone if he is loved by you and remembered by you. Would you like to talk about what you loved most about him?'

Isak launched into a long exposition that lacked punctuation and revolved mainly around hot showers in new swimwear followed by bowls of spaghetti. It left Christie feeling uncomfortable and with a sense that he had been unprepared for the session, that elements of Isak's backstory were missing from his file. On the other hand, Isak was in better shape than when he had arrived and Christie made sure he was there to bid him farewell after Isak had eaten his usual Friday lunch of a baked potato, plenty of salt, no butter, sour cream and chives, washed down with iced sparkling water, a vase on the table containing a single yellow dahlia.

The clinic staff felt good about themselves. Morally good and also good about their medical choices. Instead of billing Andrew, they would simply bill Ulla and soon enough Isak would be back to his old routine. He left the reception area, straight-backed, waving his forefinger in time to the Vivaldi that was usually on in the background, the 'Four

Seasons' having been deemed the only piece of music none among the staff and none among the patients disliked. It went down very well indeed with the people who paid the bills. Sometimes they switched to Handel but it never quite fitted the vibe correctly. At Christmas they played, with success, 'Carols from King's' and at Easter there was the peculiar tradition of 'Peter and the Wolf'. But mostly it was Vivaldi.

'Autumn,' Isak said and Christie nodded.

A taxi, as usual, took him to the station. The driver, as usual, was sullen. There were never any tips on this run. It was just loads of distracted fares whether it be worried relatives or patients without social graces. Sometimes, they acted as if the driver was a member of the clinical staff, another stage in bloody self-discovery. As they overtook the students on their battered, flat-tyred bicycles and pulled into the station, Isak was on autopilot. He sat on the train bound for King's Cross, humming a little to the 'Autumn' in his head, and then went towards the Victoria line where he alighted at Oxford Circus, only to stand stock-still on the platform, the commuters exhaling in exasperation into his face, or rather his neck, for he was taller than most of them.

He had no need to buy new swimming trunks; he had no one to swim with any more and he had no cash with him anyway. All he had was St Paul's and his bridge, the thought of which cheered him a little, but then it would be back to the flat and his mother would be weepy or clingy or distant and cold and he liked none of these versions. He liked the Ulla who was serene and elegantly dressed and who squeezed his shoulders when she placed the bowl of spaghetti bolognese in front of him, his white hair still damp, his eyes mildly bloodshot, his

Speedos in his bathroom bin. He liked the Ulla who let him lie on his bed watching the CGI cold mountains of Winterfell, the blood on the snow, the sex between beautiful young men.

He was sad and suddenly very lonely. He did not want to cry – not in front of all these serious commuters – but neither did he want to leave the comfort of strangers, and he did like the Tube and its enveloping warmth so long as it was not too busy. He followed the signs for the Bakerloo line and was swept into a carriage heading for Elephant and Castle. That sounded funny, he thought, but when he arrived he shuddered at the thought of a street he did not know and headed back towards Waterloo. He would keep travelling. He would try the Northern line next, even though he was tired now.

Christie had said he would feel bad but that he was a bird, he could take a deep breath and fly. He had even been on a train that a bird, a pigeon, had caught too. It had pecked calmly at the floor where someone had dropped a Burger King carton and its cargo of half-eaten onion rings. He had wondered how the pigeon would know where to get off, if it would be lost to its family, but Andrew had later explained that pigeons were very good at working out where trains had taken them. Maybe that was why he was catching all these trains, he was turning into not a pigeon but a raven – a clever raven like the ones used to send scrolls from King's Landing and Gulltown. It was just as Christie had predicted, he would not always be sad and lost, he would fly to Andrew. He could hear Christie urging him on. 'Go for it. Isak, you can pick yourself up, see Andrew again, fly to him' – and there it was, a small gap in the platform's footfall, so he could run, run to the edge and let the rush of the air lift his bedraggled wings.

Chapter 26

She did not wear a high-vis vest but was in a smart trouser suit. She was shadowing a pair of British Transport Police officers. Their afternoon had been not too dissimilar to the days she had spent on her long vigil. They alighted and they disembarked. They climbed escalators and descended them. They had a word with a couple of lads in the tunnel heading to the Jubilee line at Waterloo who were trying to run the wrong way along the travelator. They walked slowly as if the air underground was precious and special and needed to be savoured by connoisseurs. Sylvie listened and watched attentively. The pace suited her. The job might just be one she was prepared to train for.

'Will you be back tomorrow?' Michaela asked her. 'Not too bored?'

'No, not at all, I'm really grateful to you allowing me to tag along.'

Michaela pointed subtly to Clem, her partner.

'Nice to have a new face, a pretty one,' she said, 'one that smiles.'

Clem threw them both a sneering glance but Sylvie guessed

he was a good bloke, really, if maybe not keen on being outnumbered by women.

The next day they supped the coffee that Sylvie had brought them on a tray from Starbucks, in the control room at Waterloo. She shyly offered them muffins. Clem refused but Michaela was enjoying being spoiled by a woman with such pretty hair she was in danger of developing a crush on her. The women brushed the crumbs from their laps and then all three went promenading.

It was not promenading, Sylvie knew that, but the way they sauntered, so casually, looking left and right as if taking in some breathtaking scenery, amused her. They told her you become atuned to the way people behave, able to tell if they are in a hurry for work or in a hurry for a date.

'How can you possibly tell the difference?' she asked.

'Lipstick and perfume,' Clem said sourly but then he brightened when he realized that Sylvie was genuinely interested.

'It's difficult to explain,' he said. 'There are obvious pointers, like the time of day, what they are wearing – but people who are late, socially, won't run too fast in case they perspire, they sort of shuffle quickly rather than run. But we don't care really about that, we care about those who sweat when not running, who turn a corner when they see us coming towards them and then of course—'

He was interrupted by a message in his ear.

'Left here and then down, now,' he said. 'Northern southbound.'

They all three ran with purpose and then halted suddenly.

'We're looking for...' Clem said and then he stopped talking and coughed and Michaela nodded. Sylvie felt their bodies tense. Ahead of them on the platform – which was expecting a Northern line train to Morden – a young man was stomping and thumping his head. As the wind of the approaching train picked up the man turned his head maniacally and began to run towards the lights in the tunnel.

'He's a jumper,' Clem said and he turned to speak to Michaela and his shadow but Sylvie had already skipped ahead of him like an athletic ballerina. She did not need confirmation from Clem that this was a jumper, she had waited so long to see one again that she had, without knowing it, become an expert herself and she darted purposefully between the heaving congregation of passengers, glad of her new trainers with their firm grip. As the man, a boy really, raised his long arms – the way a large bird might lift its wings in preparation for a tough lift-off from choppy water – she sprang forward and gripped, then pulled on his small black rucksack, which caused him to trip and fall onto the platform just as the train pulled in. He curled immediately into a ball and breathed heavily, desperately.

Clem spoke into his walkie talkie. Several passengers gasped, one screamed, the rest either did not notice or deliberately avoided the scene, while fervently hoping that the incident did not mean the train would be held up. A further two officials arrived and the man was half carried towards the surface, his striking white-blond hair bobbing merrily as if the whole escapade had been a joke, as funny as a pigeon in a carriage.

Clem closed the door as the young man was seen by a doctor and turned to Sylvie to tell her that a shadow was not meant to intervene.

‘Not AT ALL,’ he said, his face reddened with an anger born partly of the knowledge that had not this dainty creature acted as swiftly as she had, the boy might have jumped before Clem or Michaela could have reached him.

Michaela, knowing Sylvie’s story because she had quizzed Stocky Stan about her, tapped Clem’s shoulder firmly and then took her to one side.

‘Well done,’ she said, searching Sylvie’s face for a reaction.

‘Thank you,’ Sylvie said and Michaela would later describe her expression as gently and tiredly triumphant.

Ryan’s heart sank. Sylvie had sent him a text asking him to meet her for a drink at the cocktail bar overlooking the station concourse they had frequented back when he had no idea of the depth of her attachment to the Underground. She was already there, the same drinks, two Appletinis, on the small table in front of her.

Perhaps she was leaving him, giving in. He steadied himself for her to say she was moving in with her parents and would be commuting from Reading, traversing the Tube before heading back to Berkshire every evening. He had tried, he told himself, tried more than most boyfriends would have tried.

And now he tried to smile.

‘Hello, and, er – cheers,’ he said, talking a gulp of a sit-com drink.

‘It’s over,’ she said.

‘I tried,’ he said, mechanically.

‘That’s why it’s over,’ she laughed and he frowned. Sylvie had never laughed like this before and for some reason an image of Tinkerbell – from the animated version of *Peter Pan* he had watched as a child – popped into his head. Sylvie's laughter was like a happy wind chime.

'What do you mean?' he said, taking another gulp.

'I mean, Mr Kennedy, that I saved a boy today and I absolutely do not want to travel on another train ever again. Except to get home, later, obviously.' She began laughing again and then forced herself to pull a serious face.

'It's over. Thanks to you, it's over.'

Ryan wanted to know all the details and to know nothing at all. He was worried she might find a loophole and become downcast and lose the Tinkerbell laughter and start commuting again.

'Are you sure – how can you be sure?' he said. 'I mean, this is wonderful news, but are you sure?'

She kissed him playfully.

'Don't blame you for the cynicism,' she said, 'but you'll see.'

Ryan felt slightly overwhelmed. He had fallen for a pale and serious mysterious girl with nearly red hair who had become a dilemma of a girlfriend, someone with whom he might not have a future, who had been stuck as if in a fairy-tale labyrinth waiting for a wicked stepmother to release her from a spell. Even before the spell was broken she had become the woman he suspected would bring him to life, to a way of living and loving that was not wrapped in the absence of Ellen. And now, he was just a bloke, any sort of ordinary bloke, who most people would say was punching above his weight with a woman who was gorgeous and carefree and capable of anything.

He knew that for certain. He could tell Sylvie would be

energetic, busy, successful. She would make up for lost time if the compulsion was really at an end. Would he spoil the moment by putting it to the test?

'I'll bunk off on Monday,' he said, 'and we'll celebrate properly by taking the bus into town and walking everywhere and being tourists.'

'I'd like that,' she said.

Paul accepted he was not media savvy and that he would work on a script in collaboration with people who were familiar with how such TV shows evolved and yet he was beginning to lose his enthusiasm for the whole project.

'Oh, come on,' he said to his half-naked producer, 'I'm a parody. How do you keep a straight face?'

The tipping point for his exasperation had come as Lloyd, a short, lean editor with round, blue-rimmed spectacles too big for his, face had tapped at the pages in front of him.

'Diseases, yes, I can see, quite obviously, they are an important issue but we're not making medical drama here. This is science done well but with fun. The nation needs cheering up not dragged down by—' he looked down, 'Gaucher's disease or, or Usher syndrome.'

Lloyd looked up, beaming.

'Bit of a turn-off, aren't they? I mean, if you inherit a disease there's nothing you can do about it. We'd not even be educating. We can't say drink less cola and ward off sickle cells, can we?'

Paul stared at him sneeringly.

'You're being a touch medieval there, Lloyd,' he said. 'The right diet can help sufferers of sickle cell disease enormously.'

'Yes, yes,' Lloyd said as if he knew that all along, 'but I think you are missing the main point here, which is that twins are funny, triplets are fascinating, and finding out your daughter isn't yours on her twelfth birthday is full of drama and pathos.'

'Isn't that all in the latest episode of *Silent Witness*?' Paul said.

'Exactly,' Lloyd retorted, 'we see this vehicle as the unfolding drama of our genes.'

Paul took a deep breath and looked across at his producer, who made a pushing gesture with her hands to ward off the imminent flounce.

'I think,' she said, 'this would be a good time for us all to retreat, think again, refresh the script.'

Lloyd swiftly gathered his notes and leaped from the room in keeping with his carefully nurtured persona of a man too busy for niceties.

As the door glided to a close behind him, Paul stood and turned to the room.

'Episode one,' he said, 'should definitely cover the DNA behind small-man syndrome,' and Lloyd's willowy deputy snorted with forbidden laughter.

Just as Riya had wanted to thank Sylvie, Ulla wanted to thank her too. They met in the booth at Waterloo.

'You'll recognize me because I look like my son,' she had told Sylvia via email, and so Sylvie sat down, without checking she was in the right place, in front of a woman in her late thirties wearing no make-up, her eyes swollen but, still, quite possibly, the most distinctive-looking person she had met in the flesh.

'You have no idea how much I owe you,' she said with a slight Scandinavian accent. 'It was my fault he was so confused but now I have the chance to get him the help he needs. He's hard to like sometimes but I love him very much. He's my only child.'

Sylvie did not feel abashed or awkward. Saving Isak had lifted her so much that she bobbed everywhere she walked. She was a helium girl, cloud-walking, happy and full of bonhomie. She and Ulla sat for an hour and a half, bearing their souls, being more honest than they had ever been with anyone. They each shed a tear over the other's story, they clasped each other's hand over the table, they ordered the first wine Ulla had touched since the day Andrew died.

'I have no friends here,' Ulla said. 'I am toxic, it would seem, now that I have no partner, and so I think it for the best that I return to Stockholm. My father is there, and an aunt, and I can perhaps make new friends.'

'It's not my place to say, having just met you, but from what you have told me, wouldn't Isak be better with some of his old routine? A new clinic, obviously, but if you could find a swim partner, a father figure, then maybe…'

'They are not easy to find, these father figures who can handle boys with Isak's problems,' Ulla said, 'and I can't go near the pool. I need to leave but yes, I'll try to find him a routine he likes.'

Sylvie ran her index finger along the rim of her glass. She wanted to say, 'I'll be your friend, stay in London,' but she had to stop now; this mission to make things right – it was over. Ulla would do what she felt was best for her small family. Sylvie needed to be unambitious, unremarkable.

‘I should have gone for therapy,’ she told Ulla. ‘I can see that now. I was a bit weird. You might not have liked me had we met six months ago.’

‘Who knows?’ Ulla said. ‘But I like you very much now and I’d like us to keep in touch if you’d like that too.’

Sylvie nodded enthusiastically.

‘And the baby you saved, do you keep in touch with her family?’

‘Not after that meeting I mentioned but, you know what, I’d like to write to her auntie, who was kind to me when she needn’t have been.’

‘I think you should,’ Ulla said, sounding much older and wiser than Sylvie, who was still in a state akin to euphoria and while talking with Ulla had veered from wanting to cry to needing to smile.

‘I’ll come to visit you in Sweden,’ she said and Ulla raised her eyebrows.

‘If you do, you’ll be like no Englishwoman I have known,’ she said.

Chapter 27

Grace sat in Grandpa's chair. There was, for a few seconds, complete silence. No voices in the street, no radio, no TV, no traffic. Nothing but the sound of her own breath, which she decided did not count as a sound as without it she would be dead and unable to notice the silence in the first place.

She had had the house to herself for two days and seen no one, spoken to no one. She told herself this was a real treat but she was not convinced. Of course, the bathroom was always clean now and smelled lovely and the washing load was so reduced that she could go three days without having to touch the compact Hotpoint in the corner of the kitchen, but she did wonder: what was the point of being here? What was her purpose?

Hana would come home rejuvenated and move out, she was sure of it. Ryan's furrowed brow would be replaced by a smooth-lined devotion to his pretty girlfriend and she would see far less of her children. One day she would bake for her grandchildren instead of for Grandpa but that could take years. She had never sat alone and brought out the photos and she was not about to start now so she sprang to her feet, found a cardigan, and left the house, a woman on a mission.

*

Hana and the ramblers were on a break from the coastal path and had headed inland for a cream tea. Poppy was salivating as they walked into the walled garden with its fat black-and-white cat, ceramic pots of pink geraniums and tiny laminated menus detailing how the café made all the scones in its cottage kitchen and would be served warm unless advised otherwise.

'Who wouldn't want a scone that was warm?' Poppy said, convinced her tongue had swollen in excited anticipation of an afternoon tea par excellence.

An elderly couple in matching thin fleeces and matching silvery hair were already deep into their second round of scones and stared at Ed as if he could well be carrying a gun.

'Don't you get tired of that?' Hana asked him. 'I mean, the minute we leave London, people look at you as if you might be out to rape their daughters.'

Ed winked at her, stood up and approached the couple.

'Are you local, or on holiday like us?' he asked in a friendly voice.

The pair gawped and then the husband said they were visiting from Yorkshire.

'First time?'

'It's our – what is it, Archie? – our thirty-fourth year and this place has been going that long too.'

'No way,' Ed said, sitting at their table. 'You are quite the bonus discovery. Tell me, what's the very best spot – the most beautiful – the place you simply have to see every time, other than this café, of course.'

The pair smiled, flattered.

'We love St Brelade,' the wife said, 'it's very pretty with

excellent restaurants overlooking the sea and a church. I mean, how often do you see a church on a beach and—'

The husband interrupted her.

'It's bloody expensive is what it is, but we keep on going back. S'pose you'd call it irresistible.'

Ed laughed good-naturedly.

'I'd like to see it,' he said and stood up again and shook their hands.

'Lovely to meet you and thanks for the tip,' he said. Hana could hear the wife whisper too loudly and too incredulously what a nice man that was.

'Bravo,' Poppy said after the couple had walked to their hire car, 'but you shouldn't have to do things like that.'

'If good men do nothing and all that jazz,' he laughed and, for the one and only time on the trip, Hana, Poppy and Ed felt like a gang, all for one and one for all.

Hana stood on deck as they pulled out of the harbour on the Monday morning. Who on earth am I? she wondered. Not once had she raised the topic of their break-up, not once had she uttered Naomi's name. She knew there were two sides to this. She was either being incredibly mature or a lovestruck patsy, sending Ed the signal that he could leave her again and again and she would be there, waiting, until as silvery as the lady in the geranium café.

She gripped the deck rail tightly. There would be a time to let him know he could not do a repeat show – she would know the time when it came but, for now, she was, astonishingly happy and free of jealousy. She had won, after all. It had not been Naomi's nose from which he had licked some errant clotted cream. It had been her nose. Her little nose, positioned well below his, but that was fine. She could buy big heels for big occasions. She could grow, but Naomi could not shrink.

Grace was not there when she reached home. Hana sniffed. Something was wrong, or at least different, and then she realized the house smelled clean and anonymous. There was no lingering aroma from a freshly baked fruit loaf or coffee sponge. Hana placed her laptop in the bathroom, lit a candle scented with rosewood and treated herself to a long soak listening to Fleetwood Mac. She and Ed had played album ping-pong and *Rumours* was the only one they had both owned as well as downloaded. She placed some bubbles on the end of her nose and giggled. She told herself she was quite pathetic but she really did not care. She had won, hadn't she, and she was closer to death than birth and living in a world that had a Doomsday Clock, so did it really matter if she had once thrown her coat into a bin?

As she wrapped herself in the fluffy dressing gown she could tell her mother had washed for her while she was away, Ed sent her a message.

Bring an overnight bag to my house,

he said,

bring it now

and Hana, being the new Hana, packed for three nights and did not spare a thought for how ghastly her commute to work would be for the next few days.

When she returned on the Thursday evening, Grace was,

again, not home. Hana sniffed the air once more. No cakes but something was different, an earthiness, and something else, Grandpa's chair had vanished. The key sounded.

'Hello, Hana, are you here?' called out Grace. 'Come and meet Jarvis.'

Hana turned to see her mother with a gold-and-white speckle-faced cocker spaniel. Grace decided to cut to the chase.

'He needs me,' she said, 'and I need to be needed. So here he is, two years old and in need of a home, he is.'

Hana felt her eyes sting, which startled her as she was not overly fond of dogs, but she quickly realized she was in the middle of a life shift. She and her mother would be living apart more often; she might move out permanently and Grace had sensed it, her dear mother, a mother who refused to hold photographs of her beloved Tom, a mother who strode on in her mission to nurture.

'I love you so much, Mam,' Hana said, giving way to tears and, for the first time in a very long time, Grace let tears fall as well. 'Does he come with the name Jarvis, then?'

'Yes, Jarvis Cocker Spaniel. I like it? Don't you like it?'

'I like it, Mam, I like it. But the big question is, do you think Jarvis is as homophobic as Grandpa was?'

Grace laughed, her eyes still sparkling from the surprise of crying.

'I don't know yet for sure, but he's better toilet-trained, most definitely.'

*

Paul was in too deep, so said his producer, but her loyalty to Lloyd over him meant he noticed that she had a small old scar on her left cheek and elbows that were too pointy and her accent could become an Essex drawl when she had drunk too many vodkas.

'We are not in too deep, are we?' he said and regretted how callous that sounded because she blinked rapidly and wobbled on her four-inch heels.

It left him alone in a high-ceilinged flat with a balcony and the sound effect of tennis balls being hit sometimes elegantly, sometimes poundingly, but rarely badly. He decided he had let the seduction of the world of television interfere with his common sense. There could be a quite brilliant series made about genetics and he was not about to be part of a stupid one. He pulled out the script and looked at all the information – allied to wit – that Lloyd had placed a black line through. It was not quite a redacted text, the sort seen in films about conspiracy theories involving politicians, presidents and national security. He could still read what it was that Lloyd was seeking to bin. He attached the script to an email to all involved.

> Please see the amendments I accept and the original points I, as the expert and the presenter, feel strongly should remain.

Paul rejected every amendment made by Lloyd bar one.

> Excellent point,

he typed next to Lloyd's rejection of the word 'phenylalanine'.

> We should replace with the phrase 'this particular amino acid'. We could be accused of dumbing down, especially as phenylalanine can cause brain damage, a reasonably serious side effect, I would argue, but sometimes, perhaps, the flow to a script for a TV show should take precedent.

Paul pressed send without re-reading his sarcasm. He had nothing to lose. He would happily be ditched if the alternative was to let the idiotic Lloyd have control of a project that could yet be worthwhile. He had no insight, no notion that to be so unapologetically defiant would create a stir. Lloyd interpreted the missive as a climbdown. He adjusted his blue-rimmed spectacles and absorbed only the words *the flow to a script for a TV show should take precedent.*

To his astonishment, in spite of the climbdown, he was removed from *Blue Genes* (working title only) three days later and Paul was taken to lunch by an executive with seductive, intelligent brown eyes and a hard-to-pronounce Sri Lankan name.

'Don't worry about the whole twelve-syllable thing, just call me Gani,' she said. 'You know, I let schoolfriends call me Annie to avoid attention but then had a lightbulb moment aged, oh, about six, and realized I was burying my ethnicity. Born in Paddington, but even so, I refuse to be an Annie.'

'Maybe tomorrow, tomorrow?' Paul said, hoping he would not have to explain his joke, and Gani smiled.

'Maybe that's why,' she said 'I loathe musical theatre.'

'That's a shame,' Paul said, 'I was hoping we were here to discuss turning *Blue Genes* into a musical. "Jean Genie", "Forever in Blue Jeans", "Baby's Got Her Blue Jeans On". I could go on but am sensing crossed wires.'

Gani pursed her lips.

'I will now have David Bowie's voice in my head for the rest of the day.'

'Not Neil Diamond? That indicates an advanced filter system for your subconscious.'

'There, you see, this is why I am here. I just don't think Lloyd thought you were very funny in spite of wanting to make the whole shebang a sort of *Strictly Come Genoming* or something.'

Paul shrugged.

'Lloyd and I, we didn't see eye to eye on anything at all. Are you, effectively, my new Lloyd?'

Paul assumed, later, he must have imagined it, but he thought he saw Gani uncross and re-cross her legs as she leaned in to whisper: 'Sits like a man, but smiles like a reptile.'

Paul coughed.

'Sums up Lloyd for me,' he said, uncertainly, and Gani chuckled.

'We are going to have fun "DNA Paul", we are going to have such fun.'

Chapter 28

'Oh, Ryan,' Hana said with deliberate exasperation, 'you've been here ten minutes and not even noticed.'

'What, what?' Ryan said. 'Have you cut your hair?'

'The house, stupid. Look around you.'

Ryan swivelled in his chair.

'Ah, that,' he said, pointing to a freshly re-upholstered armchair, Grandpa's chair, but now a deep red velvet.

'And?'

'And, and, ah, the curtains, they've gone and we didn't have those blinds hiding behind them, did we?'

'No, we most certainly did not,' Grace said. 'They're calling them plantation blinds. It's like living in the Deep South.'

'Um, sort of,' Ryan said, 'but shouldn't Jarvis be a raccoon or a prairie dog or something in that case?'

Hana glared warningly at her brother.

'Mam, it all looks really great, a nice change,' he said.

'Well, I'm pleased with it,' Grace said.

'Except,' Ryan said, as Grace stiffened, 'I don't see why you can't bake when you know I'm popping round. I love your cakes.'

'That's because we're going out for cake,' his mother said.

'We never go out for cake,' Ryan said.

'I'm changing it up,' Grace said defiantly and both her children spluttered with laughter.

She linked their arms as they walked to the new café she had noticed on her now frequent walks with Jarvis, whose leash was being held by Hana. Inevitably the cakes were comparatively dry but perhaps that was the point, thought Ryan, perhaps his mother was in need of compliments and attention.

'Still, the tea's nice,' Grace said as the sun lit up her face to reveal a complexion remarkably low on wrinkles given the life she had lived.

'You're really rather pretty, Mam,' Ryan said.

'For an old woman, maybe,' she said.

'No, really, you are,' Hana said.

There was a pause.

'As you're both here…' Hana said and both Ryan and Grace placed their mugs carefully and expectantly on the white pine table. 'I'm, er, back with Ed, as you know, and I'm moving in with him. Soon. Not tomorrow, but soon.'

Ryan nodded as if he had been expecting this all along but he was in fact taken aback and wondered if he was fated to always be the last to know about any sort of gossip at all.

'Hey, he's a nice bloke, is Ed,' he said, 'sounds a good plan to me.'

Grace thought, for a second, she might start shaking. The room had suddenly become chilly as the sun disappeared behind a slow-moving thick grey cloud and the joy of being out to tea with her beloved offspring curdled into a meaningless gesture. She had wished for nothing more than for both of them to find happiness, to find love, and now that they were close, on the brink, she was full of trepidation, selfishness. Grace sat there, in her new 'Dogs Welcome' café, and wondered at her own character. I am, she concluded, too needy. This, I have to be curbing and quickly.

'You OK, Mam?' Hana said, blinking with alarm that she might have delivered the news too abruptly.

Grace took her hand.

'I'll not sit here and lie to you, my darling,' Grace said. 'I am an old woman who doesn't know how lucky she is to have children as wonderful as you two and I'll miss you but they could pay me a million pounds and I wouldn't ask you to stay here. I'll just need a few days to adjust, that's all it is.'

She gazed out of the window at a lonely world.

'I knew anyway, didn't I just?' she said. 'It's why I have Jarvis.'

Neither Hana nor Ryan knew what to say. They wanted to point out that a far-from-old Grace was free, now Grandpa had gone, to do as she pleased when she pleased, but they were silently computing that most of what their mother might wish to do would entail one of them doing it with her. Grace had many acquaintances but no close friends. She was a mother bunny for whom the outside world was full of pain and so she had burrowed deep into family life.

Hana had, many years ago, been in a field rampaging with rabbits and she had lain flat on her stomach to peer down a warren, hoping to see a Beatrix Potter world, to spy miniature beds and a tiny stove upon which was a pot of steaming carrot soup. She did not see these things but had tried so hard to and then dreamed so intently of them that if she was to be hooked up to a lie detector even now and asked if she had seen a rabbit in a pink-striped pinafore holding a rolling pin and answered that she had, then the detector would reveal that she was telling the truth. In the years after seeing her little girl peering down the rabbit hole, Grace had told her bedtime stories full of the fun had by the rabbit family as they hid from hungry foxes and cruel cats. At the time Hana had not spotted any parallels but the rabbit family she fell asleep imagining huddled by a little stove was, really, her family – a family under threat from the memories of a dead father and a little boy who would never grow up, a family who were different from other families because they had known tragedy and would rather not be asked questions that required sanitized answers.

Grace did not want to say she had two children when she had three; Hana did not want to say she had one little brother when she had two; and Ryan did not want to say his father had passed away when he was child when in fact his father had chosen to be crushed by a truck, leaving behind some, but not all, of his children. Heart attack was the assumption, closely followed by cancer. Then came the notion that it might have been a terrible accident, a car crash or a fall from a ladder. Electrocution perhaps or drowning while on a family holiday on the Algarve. They had never been abroad as a family, not even before Ryan was born, and he recalled how cross he had become – after a friend's mother had suggested the Algarve as a location for the tragedy – that he would never go on holiday with his father, never know if he would have taught him how to surf, raced him across the sand, placed him on his shoulders while they queued for an ice cream. Now, sat in the gleaming new café, he realized how carefully Grace had constructed their childhoods to compensate for the lack of a father; that maybe Grandpa was there so much until he was there all the time as a deliberate ploy to give the home a father figure, the smell of masculinity, a gruff voice, a cantankerous sense of humour leading, eventually, to the gruff adoration of Tiffany from the shopping channel.

For the first time, Ryan was forced to contemplate the ways in which his character had been forged by Grace. He had assumed he was on the quiet side and in search of ethereal perfection in his love life because of Ellen but he had not known Ellen well enough or long enough for her to carve his soul. He had known the dead Ellen far longer and far better than he had known the living one.

Grace, though, had always been there, the brother and father he could not remember had always been there too, but Grace was warm and tactile and fussed and flapped and smiled and laughed, and Hana had been standing in the shadows, somehow appearing when he could not make head nor tail of the poem by John Keats that his English teacher loved so much that she would blank, actually blank, any student who dared question its beauty or, in the case of Ryan, its accessibility.

'Thou hast thy music too,' Ryan had said, despairingly, adding, 'But no one speaks like that any more,' and Hana had suggested he do what she had done with the same poem and the same teacher, which was to read it a hundred times until the words became his words, his language, and he could feel the sumptuousness of them, until he could whisper, five years later, the phrase 'the soft-dying day' and it would bring tears to his eyes, blurring his vision so that the girl alighting from the bus or the girl serving him in the bakery or the girl facing him on the escalator was, for a few seconds at least, his Ellen.

He held up his finger.

'Autumn,' he said and Hana shook her head.

'"To Autumn", "Toooo Autumn", dearest brother.'

'Well, that was his biggest mistake,' Ryan said. 'He should have kept it simple. "Autumn". Much better.'

The three of them looked outside at the yellowing leaves and the soft sun which had just that moment reappeared. Hana pictured a Christmas tree in Ed's high-ceilinged living room; Ryan pictured Sylvie, waiting for him in Cotton Lane; Grace pictured Jarvis running through mud, chasing a stick she had managed to throw an impressive distance.

'Let's go home via Gladstone Park,' Grace said. 'Bet you haven't been for ages, either of you – and it's nice and clear now, so we'll be able to see the City skyline from the hill.'

It was true, neither of them had been there for some years, having used up all the magic it had to offer in their childhood, but they were happy to go now, to see for themselves how their mother would be spending her days now they were empty of the need to bake, to wash, to worry.

They took it in turn to throw sticks for Jarvis and all three of them were surprised at how natural it felt, as if they had always had a dog. A boy, aged about five, started running after him and tripped. He was closest to Grace when he did so. She put her hands under his arms and lifted him to his feet as his father jogged towards them.

'Sorry, sorry,' the man said. 'He runs after dogs all the bloody time.'

Grace was speechless. She had become pale.

'My son used to do that too,' she said but the man had hoisted the boy onto his shoulders and was striding off towards the playground.

Grace turned to Ryan and Hana.

'I'd like us to go home and look at some family photos,' she said. 'I think there's one of our Tom and a puppy in a park.'

The siblings looked at each other, eyebrows raised, but smiling. Leaning against the nearest tree was a young woman who stared at Ryan and then slowly slid against the bark until she was sat among the dead leaves, her legs outstretched. It was Ellen's way of telling him he ought to bring out photos of her.

He leaned in towards his sister.

'I don't have a single photograph of Ellen,' he said.

'I do,' she said and the three of them walked home in slight trepidation, but also warm anticipation, of the reminiscences that lay ahead.

Sylvie was with Theo at the shop when Ryan reached Cotton Lane. It was Naomi who was waiting for him.

'Just like the old days,' she said. 'Remember when you didn't know Sylvie's name and I lusted after Cappi?'

Ryan snorted.

'That was, actually, very recently on the reminiscence scale,' he said. 'Er, did you know my sister was back with Ed? Didn't you date him for a bit? I wasn't sure how serious it was with you two.'

Naomi did not know that Ed was back with Hana. In fact, Naomi was not entirely certain that it was over between her and Ed. She had wondered if they were at a juncture – that he might come to realize that he liked her more than his bucolic high-rise cottage, that a few weeks or months apart might be something they one day chuckled about as they peered through their living-room window at the black cabs, red buses, neon theatre lights and late-night bistros. Not for one second had she wondered if Ed would need time to realize he liked Hana more than he liked her. Hana had been collateral damage but someone they had treated with respect. Naomi wondered what Hana had done to reclaim him, this mesmeric man who was much too tall for her.

'I have to pop out,' she told Ryan and she grabbed her jacket and tried not to slam the front door, particularly as Jenny had told her she had a recognizable way of leaving Number 4 and Naomi had found that slightly creepy – that it was a bit sad that Jenny would even notice and sadder still that she felt the need to tell her about it. But she ended up slamming the door anyway. 'Theo and Jenny sitting in a tree,' she muttered to herself, 'Ryan and Sylvie, all kissy and cosy, Ed and Hana laughing at me.'

Naomi had nowhere to go so she strode with exaggerated purpose to the Tube station, sat on the first train to arrive and simmered, but not without boredom, which allowed her to calm down. The commute between Plaistow and South Kensington had been deadly and almost every time she travelled it wondered at those poor people who were coming in from Hornchurch or Dagenham, much further back along the District line. It took her just under ten minutes to reach

Hammersmith, where she alighted, determined to use the news about Ed as a catalyst for her to find her urban nirvana. She mooched through the streets, some dirty, some tree-lined and pretty, stopping at the windows of letting agents and gradually realizing she could afford neither a river view nor a bin-lined alley vista.

This was topsy-turvy pricing, she grumbled. There must have been a time when to live amid the fumes and bustle and noise would have been the cheap option but no, Ealing was more affordable, Plaistow was more affordable. She would have to quit academia and find work that paid enough for the life she craved. The thought of heading back to love-nest lane was unappealing and so she hopped on the nearest Tube – now Shepherd's Bush – travelled along the Central line to Tottenham Court Road and then walked to Chinatown where she treated herself to a sat-all-alone lemon chicken with egg fried rice while she watched the tourists scurry past her window or stop to survey the menu. As she waited for the bill from the scowling waiter she saw a silk scarf slide from the neck of a distracted woman and land on the pavement. Naomi waited for someone to pick it up for her but no one did and the woman failed to notice she was missing her scarf. Naomi tutted, ran out onto the street, scooped up the scarf and raced to catch the woman who, in her long cream knitted cardigan coat, was distinctive even now at the far end of Gerrard Street.

The woman turned as Naomi tapped her shoulder, saw the scarf and frowned.

'You dropped it back there,' Naomi said. 'And it looks too nice a scarf to leave it to be trodden underfoot.'

She did not wait for thanks but ran back to the restaurant in case the scowling waiter thought she'd run off without paying, which indeed he had assumed her to have done – but he assumed most customers were out to rip him off in some way so was not particularly upset. Naomi settled her bill and returned to the street to be faced by a woman in cream knitwear and a scarf patterned with a cityscape, its orange-lit windows shining out against a blue-grey sky.

'Hello, again,' the woman said. 'Let me buy you a cocktail.'

Naomi felt this invitation to be faintly ludicrous but, even so, a better option than the claustrophobia she had now decided Cotton Lane had become. The woman, tall and elegant, strode purposefully across Shaftesbury Avenue and led Naomi into Kettner's, which was busy but there were two bar stools empty and the woman glided towards the grey leather chairs as if she had reserved them weeks ago. She wriggled free of her cream coat but kept on her scarf.

'What do you think? Two champagne martinis?' she said, confusing Naomi with her air of them having met before – been long-time colleagues – for the woman was at least fifteen years older than her, maybe more.

'Why not?' Naomi said and she noted how the slender, handsome barman responded immediately when the woman lifted her hand towards him.

'You don't have a bag,' the woman said. 'I have to say I find that rather liberating as I have never left any house without one.'

Naomi smiled and opened her phone wallet, which contained, as well as her phone, her credit card, her house key and a few notes and coins and, then, as if she were a table magician, she tapped her faded satin bomber jacket and revealed an inside zip pocket which held a tissue and a small tube of lip salve.

'You should try it sometime,' she said as the woman threw back her head and emitted a peal of expensive laughter.

'I'd like to, really I would,' she said as though Naomi had asked her to come skydiving over the Namib Desert. 'In the meantime, I'm Donna.'

She held out her hand, which Naomi noted was smooth and elegant with fingernails painted a pale shade of pistachio, which she suspected was either trendy or about to become trendy.

The barman placed their cocktails in front of them without a flourish to let them know that these were not two women for whom a Sunday-evening cocktail was anything other than passé.

'Let us toast a rare example of public-spirited kindness,' Donna said. 'You wouldn't have known, but this scarf is…' She paused and ran a pistachio-lit finger along the edge of the cityscape. 'It is valuable. Emotionally valuable. Designed by my dear friend, boyfriend, lover, whatever. Designed by him for me – and look.'

Donna removed the scarf and told Naomi to hold out her hands. She laid the scarf over her new friend's outstretched arms and pointed to a black-framed window at which stood a woman with sleek golden-brown hair just like Donna's.

'That's me,' she said, 'and I feature in no other scarf. So. So, this is why we are having cocktails. Thank you.'

Naomi raised her glass.

'No, thank *you*,' she said. 'I was in full-on-avoidance mode, on the possible verge of self-loathing, and so this is really lovely in an unexpected and crazy sort of way and a middle-of-London sort of way, which is what I want so much I threw away my own lover for it.'

The two women looked at each other, both wearing a half-smile as though in the middle of a John le Carré plot.

'Am I to surmise you do not need to dash off anywhere right now?' Donna asked.

'You deduce accurately,' Naomi said.

'Me neither,' Donna said. As she ordered a second round of champagne martinis, Naomi mentally tapped her stomach, glad she had lined it for what promised to be a booze-laden evening. Donna led her through a heaving Soho to an art deco labyrinth about to serve a dose of cabaret. She ordered a bottle of house champagne and some olives and sat back as if in her own sports car. Naomi decided to relax and enjoy the ride – even though she still knew next to nothing about her host; but it was possibly on the verge of trendy not to ask her anything personal and vice versa. It would emerge naturally, in an uptown manner. This was sophisticated and urban and every bit as seductive as the downtown Hammersmith version, much better than Ealing and in a different universe to Plaistow.

Just after 11 p.m. Donna led Naomi back into Soho and to a patisserie that was still open. It held just two small tables and they sat down to eat crème anglaise donuts accompanied by the most flavoursome filter coffee the younger woman had ever tasted. On the adjacent table sat two plump pink-cheeked middle-aged men – clearly in love – for whom the late-night gorging of pastries seamed a regular habit. Naomi wondered if she and Donna made a match or looked incongruous. Or perhaps intriguing.

‘Are we intriguing?’ she asked Donna sleepily but they were so close to the other couple that it was unavoidably a question for them too.

‘You are *so* intriguing,’ the less plump one said.

‘In what way?’ Donna asked lightly and they took turns to explain.

‘In every way.’

‘Attractive, stylish, tall.’

‘A small age gap.’

‘Monied and less monied.’

‘Maybe gay, probably not.’

‘But devoted.’

Both women giggled.

‘We only met this afternoon,’ Donna said.

The men pouted as if they had been deliberately tricked, wiped their mouths on their napkins and left. Donna laughed her expensive laugh.

‘Take out your phone,’ she said. ‘Now, put in my number and don’t send me a message until tomorrow evening. You’ll know what I mean by that but you won’t know before tomorrow evening. Now, I’m putting you in an Uber.’

The car arrived ninety seconds later and Naomi waited for a hug or a peck on the cheek but none came and suddenly she was heading back towards Ealing. She had Donna’s number and Donna had her address and that was that.

Cotton Lane was in darkness. The Mizwa family was asleep, as were Theo and Jenny, as were Ryan and Sylvie. This time Naomi was quiet with the door even though her head was beginning to feel clogged and her arteries felt parched. The ceiling spun as she lay down so she fell asleep sat bolt upright, bolstered by every pillow and cushion she could find, and in the morning she sat on the floor by the fridge drinking glass upon glass of chilled water until she remembered that in spite of being as drunk – if not more than usual – after a night of booze, she had neither babbled nor stood and swayed while with Donna. She was convinced she had not embarrassed herself at all for she could remember every moment, beginning with the sight of the scarf slipping elegantly from around the neck of a tall and fascinating woman in a long cream cardigan coat.

It was 7 p.m. That was tomorrow evening, wasn't it? Or perhaps in Donna's world it was late afternoon. Naomi had begun a new strand of research and was supposed to be preparing a briefing on her plans for the upcoming year but instead she spent the day doodling and dozing and dreaming of living elsewhere. It was now 7.15 p.m. What had Donna meant anyway about knowing about the evening deadline? Naomi had not a clue so she decided it must be too early and she climbed the stairs to the living room to find Ryan and Sylvie curled up and watching what sounded suspiciously like *Breaking Bad*.

'But, Ryan, you're a chemist,' Naomi said. 'You must have seen this already?'

'Nope,' he said. 'I never wanted to be hooked into a box set before, but now it seems I am ready,' at which point Sylvie chuckled conspiratorially.

'And I was waiting to date a chemist before I watched it,' she said and Naomi rolled her eyes and pottered in the fridge, thinking that something was going on with those two.

Something had changed, they were both so darned relaxed in each other's company. It was cloying. It was cloying but it was not without ripples of concern. For several weeks Sylvie had wondered why Paul now behaved as if it was she who had saved Ryan rather than the other way around. She knew Ryan's girlfriend at university had died but that had happened fifteen years ago and she assumed it was not something he wanted to talk about but there could be a sadness to Ryan, as if he was rehearsing in his head the lines from a tragic play.

It was now 7.45 p.m. and Naomi had rid herself of her headache and felt no guilt about how little work she had done that day. Instead she wanted to walk out of the front door and onto a street teaming with life, with noise, with jazz, with martinis, with adventure. She smiled. It was clearly the right time to send Donna a message.

Let's do it again,

she typed,

from your new, slightly besotted, certainly intrigued, friend, Naomi.

She deliberately did not add a kiss. That would be too much. That would be cloying and she was trying to escape cloying rather than run into its arms. She returned to her room, partly because she knew she would be incapable of not uttering spoilers as Walter White cooked yet another batch of blue meth and partly because she wanted to be alone when Donna replied, no doubt with something cryptic or at least hypnotic.

Donna did not reply.

Naomi spent the next day feeling jittery and it almost amused her that even in the first flush of flirtation with Ed and, before him, the also, tall Cappi and, before him, the less-tall-but-captivating Hamish, she had not been so attached to her phone and its to indicate a new-message-ping. Three days passed and Naomi began to wonder if her initial text had been unsuitable in some way, that perhaps she had misjudged the mood, or misunderstood what Donna had been expecting.

'You'll know what I mean,' Donna had said but now Naomi was convinced she knew nothing of wit or drama or suspense and then it was Sunday again and a full week had passed with no word from the cream-cardiganed woman. Just as she'd let her scarf fall to the floor, maybe she had left her phone in a bar or in the back of a cab, but there was no way for Naomi to find out for sure beyond sending a pathetic message asking if Donna was alive and well. She vowed to shrug it off, to try to simply be thankful for the brief adventure, the brief encounter, but every time her phone pinged her fingers would throb and over that she had no control at all.

'What are the sad things you think about?' Sylvie asked him when their *Breaking Bad* session was over.

'I try not to think about sad things at all,' Ryan said lightly.

'But you do,' she said softly. 'They wrap you in a mist and you become distracted. Sometimes you look at a car or a tree or out of the window as if you have just seen—'

He finished her sentence. 'A ghost?'

'Well, not a ghost, but a reminder, a memory, a prodding, something like that.'

'OK,' he said.

She changed the subject but a few hours later, as she ironed a skirt, he loitered miserably.

'I'm really happy,' he said. 'But I didn't realize you could tell I'm interrupted by less happy thoughts.'

'I don't mind,' she said, 'except that, maybe you should tell me, in case I can help.'

'That wouldn't be fair on you,' he said.

She lightly stamped her foot.

'Really? I want to help. I need to help. It wouldn't be fair *not* to let me try.'

She led him to the edge of the bed. They sat down and he wrapped a strand of her candyfloss hair around his index finger.

'Grandpa said she was a reminder of happiness, but why do I need a reminder when I am happy? It was a nice thing for him to say but now I'm convinced – well, almost convinced – that I'm making *her* unhappy or cross or something.'

Sylvie wanted to nod encouragingly but was not certain what it was he was talking about.

'I feel stupid asking, but who is she and what does she do?'

Ryan shrugged. He was both embarrassed and bored.

'She visits me. Ellen, I mean. You know, my girlfriend at uni. I see her sometimes, usually when I'm very happy. I don't think of her and then see her. I see her when I haven't even thought about her. I'm not summoning her out of guilt, she just randomly appears.'

‘And what… does she speak to you?’

‘No, she looks… sort of disapproving at how I’m living my life and then she vanishes.’

Sylvie said nothing. She tried to imagine all the ways someone in her position would respond and how they would all be selfish; all themes on ‘do you still love her?’, which were stupid because Ellen had died.

Ryan mistook her silence for cynicism.

‘Do you think I’m joking?’

She held his hand in hers and shook her head.

‘Can I think about it rather than say something tactless?’

That night she could not sleep. She had decided to believe him, not in the sense of believing he believed it but that she would take his word for it that it was Ellen who decided when to show up and that she was not controlled by Ryan’s subconscious.

She realized, slowly, that Paul – and maybe everyone who knew Ryan well – had assumed that now he had found a new, serious relationship, he would be free of the haunting by Ellen and that he must feel so isolated if she was still popping up out of nowhere. She realized too that she owed it to Ryan to break the spell, just as he had broken hers.

Chapter 29

'There's a Riya Mannan here to see you,' one of Jonny Smalling's underlings said. He frowned. He remembered the name but was reluctant to return to a case that was, for his department, concluded. Still, she was here, in the building, so, using the stairs, never the lift, he lightly tapped his way down to the reception area.

She was leaning on a buggy in which was, he supposed, the child who had almost died at King's Cross. The toddler was sporting a pink dress with a lace trim over pink tights. She wore a pink heart-shaped hairclip in her dainty black hair. Riya, though, was dressed like a tomboy in frayed jeans and a faded green rugby shirt, her sleeves rolled up. She smiled at him and it was impossible for him to not smile back.

She held out her hand, which surprised him as so few people connected to his cases ever did. He was so often the enemy or a failure or an interfering git, or the people he dealt with were too ill-educated to feel any obligation of politeness. He had learned to accept a 'Yo!' as a handshake of sorts.

Jonny shook the small, wiry hand.

'How are you, Riya?' he said.

'I'm OK, thanks,' she said. 'It's my work-experience week next month and I wondered if I could come in here cos I might want to be a social worker.'

'We, ah, well, that might be tricky, Riya, we don't really offer that, given the privacy element, and it can be distressing too, especially for someone under eighteen.'

'Then how am I supposed to find out if I really want to do it or not?'

'Very valid point,' Jonny said.

'And I'm nearly eighteen anyway so I can sit in your office and watch and then do more active stuff after Christmas. When I'm eighteen.'

'Right,' Jonny said. 'So you are studying for A levels now, I take it?'

'Course,' she said. 'Psychology, sociology and maths.'

'Sounds good,' he said. 'And have you looked at universities?'

Riya rocked the buggy although there was no need as pretty-in-pink Nisha was serenely taking in her new surroundings.

'Edinburgh's the best but that's too far from her,' she said, pointing at the toddler, 'so I'll go to Bournemouth or Portsmouth. They're on the sea,' she added in case Jonny might not realize that.

'Sounds to me like you are fairly sure you want to study social work regardless of being here,' he said gently.

Riya frowned. 'But it's important I've got something to say at an interview,' she said. In a flash Jonny saw how she was behind the curve, on her own, that maybe she overheard other students at an Open Day talking about their passion for the course and just maybe it was asking too much of such a young woman that she explain how it came to pass that her sister committed suicide and that that was how she had come into contact with the world of the social worker.

'Leave it with me,' he said.

'So that means what? I can come here for a week?'

Jonny smiled. He had been having a tiresome morning and yet he knew, deep down, having Riya looking over his shoulder for a week would, rather than add to his misery, bring something pleasingly different to his job.

In a rare moment of indulgent bonhomie he sent an email to Ryan Kennedy informing him that he had just found out that Riya was planning to become a social worker.

> It's another, small, way in which your friend Sylvie has made a difference and I thought you might like to tell her that in case she is still coming to terms with what she witnessed that day.

Ryan, though, hesitated to pass on the news. It was over, wasn't it? He and Sylvie did not speak now of Isak, the boy who tried to jump, nor of Jaya, the girl who did. Much to his relief, Sylvie had informed him she did not want to work for the British Transport Police or take up a career on the Underground. He had pointed out to her a new breed of Trespass and Welfare Officer at Clapham Junction one day, assuming she might be drawn to such a role, especially as their primary job appeared to be to check that passengers were happy. No, she said. It was over.

His heart had run cold when Sylvie described the meeting

with Ulla at Waterloo. Why Waterloo, why that booth? He had been distant with her for a few hours, annoyed at what seemed to him to be a childlike approach to serious matters, but as Sylvie was still splashing in the entrails of euphoria she did not notice and her happiness was too contagious for him to remain moodily wary for long.

There was another reason he hesitated. It was buried and he was not consciously aware of it, but it was there. News of Riya getting on with her life thanks to Sylvie might well prompt Sylvie to turn to Ryan and remind him that he had been the one to track down the young woman, he had been the one to inspire Riya, he had been the one to save Sylvie. Such reminiscences might prompt Sylvie to wonder why Ryan was at Waterloo that day. They might prompt Sylvie to wonder why a man who read so little fiction could recall the works of Mrs Henry Wood, a reasonably obscure novelist who died in 1887. They might prompt Sylvie to wonder how he knew before she told him about how she would spend a few hours on the platform of one Underground station almost every day.

There were practical reasons too, for hesitating. Sylvie needed to earn money, get back into the world of work beyond Vinyl Vibes. Even though Theo wanted her there and involved every day, he paid her very little. On the other hand, she could easily claim to be the manager or whatever title she chose to have depending on the next job she applied for.

Sylvie, though, was not thinking about returning underground and neither was she much concerned with the novels read by Ryan and the small discrepancies in what he knew about her and ought not to have known. She was thinking about Ellen.

‘You know,’ she said later that day, ‘I won’t be able to take much holiday in the first six months of whatever job I get so why don’t we go to Florida at Christmas? My parents will pay for my flight and the apartment and we can stay for a few days and see my nephew and wow everyone with our cute English accents and then go off on our own for a bit.’

Ryan wanted to object but there was nothing objectionable about what she had just said. He could not scoff at her sense of duty to family, of wanting to see her new nephew. He could not object to the price, he could not even claim his mother needed him given how often he visited her compared to the rare trips to Reading made by Sylvie, but, then again, if Grace was to be alone on Christmas Day, then they could not possibly leave.

‘Sure, I’m up for that,’ he said, ‘but I think Hana is away with Ed and that would leave Mum sharing a turkey crown with Jarvis for Christmas lunch.’

‘Not a problem,’ Sylvie replied. ‘We can fly on Boxing Day or the twenty-seventh. My parents are there for three weeks, for goodness’ sake.’

And then, very casually, she asked Ryan for a favour.

‘The next time you see Ellen, would you tell me straightaway. Please.’

Paul guffawed.

‘Sounds horrendous, mate,’ he said. ‘I’ll be filming on location in the Middle East. Congenital deafness. Fascinating. No prospective in-laws, just the very lovely Gani.’

‘I’ll not be getting arrested for having a drink or taking an aspirin,' Ryan retorted but he was glum all the same. What little experience he had of Sylvie's family did not bode well. He had found them rude and self-centred and in the only way a man in his mid-thirties can have a tantrum, he had a tantrum, telling Sylvie he was popping over to see Grace after work without suggesting she join him.

There was no one home, though. The dog-walking community of Gladstone Park had enveloped Grace and Jarvis, and Ryan's mother was in the pub along with three other live-alone dog owners including Ron, a gangly, slightly stooped former local bank manager who had, thought Grace, the eyes of someone hoping to be amused but rarely getting the joke. He was just offering to buy her another drink when Grace – although enjoying the evening – experienced a tug at her heart and declined. Neither Ryan nor Hana had indicated they would be visiting her today but, as she would tell Ryan as she found him about to walk away, back to the station, she just had a feeling one of her children would be at the house.

They went, without Jarvis, for their first-ever curry together and Ryan was able to talk, also perhaps for the first time, without thinking first whether what he was saying could be upsetting. She was not so fragile, this sixty-five-year-old woman who had lost a child and a husband, and she had shed some of her anxiety over his future. He even considered telling her about Sylvie wanting to meet Ellen, but as he had never told Grace that he sometimes saw his dead girlfriend, it all seemed too complicated, so instead, he simply smiled fondly at his mother.

'You seem very happy, son,' she said as she broke in half a poppadom.

'Hmm,' he said, 'well, that's strange, given I'm a bit miffed at having been railroaded into a trip to see Sylvie's Florida family this Christmas.'

'As long as you don't have to go by the actual railroad,' she said, chuckling at her joke. 'But that is what I mean. Only a happy person can be unhappy about a holiday in Florida.'

'Maybe you could come with us,' Ryan said absently, and Grace wondered, later, as she lay in bed, Jarvis at her feet, whether they might have been the most beautiful and heart-warming words ever uttered by her younger son. She fell asleep, Jarvis snuffling and snoring, a distant fox barking, with more contentment than she had felt in a very long time.

Hana had been bold and carefree. She had suppressed the desire to ask questions she knew most men would hate to be asked.

Did you leave me for Naomi? Did she dump you or you did you dump her? Did I win or did I come second?

She had no idea because she did not ask but as she carried the last box into his tall, quaint home, she was overcome by the nausea of jealousy. This, she thought, is a mistake, this is not who I am.

'Hey, what's up?' Ed said.

'Last-minute nerves, I think,' she said, unable to prevent her voice from quivering in what must be, she thought, a most unattractive fashion.

He took hold of her hand, led her out of the front door and then scooped her up into his arms and carried her over the threshold.

‘I’ve never done that for anyone before,’ he said. ‘I have a history but so have you. We start now – in love, I hope – and just enjoy life, yes?’

‘What happens when one of us can’t hike any more?’ she said, unable to digest what he had just said.

‘Then we will walk, then we will walk slowly, and then we will let people drive us around or push us to the bathroom. Or you will push me or I shall push you. That’s called growing old together.’

‘Oh,’ Hana said. ‘Or we can defy the aging process and have a baby together.’

‘Now you are making me get cold feet,’ he said, but tenderly, and she wondered who she was and who he was and whether it mattered if she admitted to ignorance about both of them. In that moment she decided Ed could very well hurt her again but as he had already given her more happiness than the sloth she had married – and if he was highly unlikely to be capable of hurting her the way the sloth had hurt her – then she was prepared to be strict with her jealousy, fight it if necessary, and start living dangerously.

Donna never did return the message. The wording of it haunted Naomi and she was convinced she had failed a test by not realizing sooner that she was taking one. She inwardly groaned at having indicated she might be besotted because no one wants to be friends with someone who is besotted. And to say she was intrigued, that might have been a little unkind or at least unthinking given how generous Donna had been over their enchanted evening. Naomi could not help it, she would compose different messages that were more intellectual, more grateful, more amusing and send none of them. She began to believe herself condemned to discover enigmatic people of similar height only to be dumped by them. She began to doubt her ability to be sufficiently interesting until, having decided she would have to buy Sylvie a Christmas gift – given she never scowled when Naomi shared the living room or asked to be part of her and Ryan's supper – she stopped off at the Oliver Bonas store on Ealing Broadway.

Naomi detested shopping and hoped that just by being prepared to spend £30 in a relatively classy shop would result in her finding, without really looking, an acceptable present. Her eye was caught by some silk scarves, which caused her to quietly gasp. The scarves were blue-grey and orange with small black squares which revealed themselves on closer inspection to be windows in a cityscape.

Naomi pulled one off the rail and laid it out on a shelf of silver-threaded white woollen scarves. There – in one of the black-framed windows – was a woman with long sleek golden-brown hair. Naomi pulled a second scarf off the rail and laid that one out as well. There she was again, the woman with golden-brown hair.

She stood, motionless, wondering if she was supposed to laugh or cry. Or perhaps she had found the perfect message now.

Dearest Donna, I hate to break it to you, but you are in the window on lots of scarves, love, Naomi (not my real name).

She looked at the price. It was £30. She bought it for Sylvie.

After mulling it over for two days, Naomi decided there was a chance, albeit a small chance, that Donna had fallen for a con man who pretended to have designed a one-off scarf for her and a slightly bigger chance that her lover had intended the design to be unique only to sell it to whoever bought patterns for scarves. It was far more likely that Naomi had been spun a yarn but, just in case, she did not send the message. There was no need to hurt the woman, who had, after all, spent around £150 that evening and not accepted a penny from her new friend. Naomi would have to learn to file that Sunday as a surreal and wonderful time with a mystery attached that she would probably never solve.

Chapter 30

Sometimes Ryan and Sylvie walked to the station together. She preferred temping, not least because it meant she could find time for some blitz marketing for Vinyl Vibes. Her sacking had been a footnote while trapped underground but, now she was back at work, she found it difficult to trust whoever was in charge. And she was recovered, fully recovered, but sad from time to time, still wondering what must have been going through Jaya's head when they looked into each other's eyes that day. Sylvie might have understood a little of what Jaya felt, for the teenager had been living a life on autopilot, functioning, but only in the way a prisoner functions.

Jaya knew she needed to get out of bed, change a nappy, feed a baby, ask her husband if he wanted anything… only she didn't have a husband. Ghosted. She had been ghosted. She knew she was supposed to adore the baby but sometimes she saw just a bundle of blankets and no one feels anything towards a bundle of blankets. The numbness was terrifying. She was sure she used to laugh with her sisters, tease them even, but she could not remember what that felt like. Her body was, to her, a lump of dough, her brain was a soggy lump of dough that had just the one brainwave. As she could not drive, Jaya thought the best way for the baby to sleep was to take it on the train. And it worked. The baby became warm and sluggish and so did Jaya. The only problem was she had to return home at some point and the thought of it filled her with bitter boredom and acute fear.

She tried to be useful and would sometimes find herself staring at a tub of ghee not knowing why it was there, why she had opened its plastic lid, and somewhere in the background the baby would wail as if on TV. It was not real to her, this life. Mondays were just like Thursdays which were just like Sundays. It was a monotony that frightened her.

She opened her eyes. The train was pulling into King's Cross. She had no idea where King's Cross was. She had never been before and had never intended to visit it but she left the carriage, worried she had strayed too far from home. She wondered if she should she follow the exit signs but they were very complicated and featured with words like 'international' and that sounded far too far away from Harlesden. She cursed that she had woken up. Sleep was best. She would like to sleep forever. She pondered this idea. No more pain, no more anguish. She could step in front of a train and have done with all of it. The notion brought her some peace, some relief, but she was slightly feverish again today and wandered the tunnels, looking for a sign that would tell her the right place to fall asleep. She used to be superstitious and was reluctant to do anything significant without a sign. Not that her falling asleep forever was significant. She was but a speck of dust in the universe, a speck of dust that was hurting.

There was a poster advertising a theatre production of *Death and the Maiden*. She stood in front of it, entranced. This was surely a sign. It was, she thought, pretty unambiguous. She at last moved away from the poster to the end of the platform, away from the other passengers, concerned they would smell both her worthlessness and her intentions. They might not be able to see her but she must surely stink. She could not remember the last time she'd bathed. She remembered bubble baths. She had liked them once but now they were too much effort. It was too much effort to answer when her mother said, 'Shall I run you a bath?'

The baby made a snuffling noise and Jaya gazed down at her, perplexed. Should the baby go with her? She considered placing it on the platform but it all seemed too complicated. Someone might step on it as they left the train or accidently kick it onto the track. Or someone would notice her placing the baby on the ground and run over and stop her jumping. She had to be with her baby, that must be the right way. She rubbed at her temples, she was hot, and so tired. If they jumped together would it end the way she wanted it to? Her body might offer the baby some protection and Jaya might be gone but the baby could lose a leg or an eye and that would be so unfair. Her head hurt now, a pounding headache of stress and worthlessness. Sleep was the answer. Death and the Maiden. She closed her eyes, took a deep breath and upon opening her eyes saw an angel walking towards her. She had seen her before, on a birthday card perhaps, her long, wavy, nearly red hair rippling in the Underground's breeze. She sighed in relief. The angel had come if not for her, then for the maiden's child.

*

They could not sit together so chose to stand. Sylvie was working at a fashion chain's head office near Oxford Street, covering not for maternity leave but a stroke. No one was very friendly but that suited her just fine. Ryan, on a whim, rubbed her nose with his nose, knowing she would blush but also smile. Behind her, leaning on the driver's door, a girl in a cable-knit sweater pouted at him in mock disapproval.

He exhaled; he frowned.

'What?' she said.

'She's here,' he said. 'Behind you.'

Sylvie had hoped they would be in Cotton Lane or in the park when it happened, not on a crowded train but she had made a vow to herself and so she turned around. She breathed in deeply. She felt the nerves of every actor on first night, of every public speaker. She bit her lip and swallowed slowly.

'He loves you, Ellen,' she said. 'If you were really here, you would be together. I know that I can only love him because you are gone. I'm truly sorry for Ryan and for you that you are gone but I want you to know I will try to make him happy, not the way you would have made him happy, but another way. I'm older, he's older. He saved me and I want to save him from the losing of you.'

The train had eased to a halt between stations and Sylvie's voice was the only sound to be heard above the low churning hum of the engine. Someone clapped; a few commuters strained to see who the slight, pale-faced woman was addressing. An amused voice shouted, 'You tell her, girl!'

Ryan held his breath. Ellen bent down and did not stand up again. She was replaced by a schoolgirl wearing a white plastic raincoat.

*

They enjoyed Florida more than either of them expected to and Sylvie found her parents to have softened, as if they now appreciated the subtlety of their daughter's many attributes when contrasted with the brash dazzle of Franklyn's new social network. Ryan smiled more than he ever had, amused and amazed by his girlfriend's brave speech on a crowded train, but mostly convinced that it had worked. His grandfather had not been wrong. Ellen wanted him to find happiness and Sylvie had convinced her that he had done so while accepting he would have found it with her.

They returned to another January of light sleet and biting winds and, most days, they commuted in together when possible, but some weeks Sylvie had to start off much earlier than Ryan and on such days she liked to scan the carriage, not looking for someone who needed saving but for someone who might be her and someone who might be Ryan. On this day there was a young woman with bold pink lipstick who was reading a book entitled *Marxism and Patriarchy.* Sylvie smiled and wondered if anyone else had noticed at her smooth bare legs and sleek hair, and then gulped and turned away upon recalling what book she was engrossed in. Ryan always blushed when she brought up Mrs Henry Wood but he might have been deterred from pursuing her at all if she had been reading something so evidently feminist.

She alighted at Green Park, not noticing that in the seat opposite to Ms Marxist Lipstick was another young woman, pulling nervously at her fingers, trying to find the right words, failing and then grimacing self-deprecatingly as the sleek-legged one left the carriage without either of them speaking at all.

Acknowledgements

I would like to thank the HQ Stories family and, in particular, Katie Seaman, my wonderful editor. Thank you, also, Jon Appleton, my diligent copyeditor, and I am so pleased that the famously meticulous Sarah Coward could be involved.

I am grateful to Clio Cornish for being so supportive at the very start and for the wit and wisdom of Oli Munson, my agent at AM Heath.